RIDING F...

There ...
Counts ...
for anyt...

Now ...
would ...
five mil...

I kick ...
south d...
between...
stomped-out brush bunny.

Below us, Counts and Grimes heard him go, and held up to follow the sound. Next minute, the brush along the ridge thinned. They had me spotted. They wheeled their horses, digging them hard to cut me off where the ridge spurred down onto the flats.

They missed me there by a hundred yards, for two reasons. Little Hawk had headed them by a dozen jumps before they saw him; the going along the top of the ridge was downhill and not so rocky as that at its base.

On the flats we lined out. The run for the $25,000 Fort Goodwin Handicap was on.

Other *Leisure* books by Will Henry:

FRONTIER FURY
MEDICINE ROAD
BLIND CAÑON
THE SCOUT
WINTER SHADOWS
THE LEGEND OF THE MOUNTAIN
GHOST WOLF OF THUNDER MOUNTAIN
TUMBLEWEEDS
FROM WHERE THE SUN NOW STANDS
THE GATES OF THE MOUNTAINS
CUSTER
ALIAS BUTCH CASSIDY
THE HUNTING OF TOM HORN
ONE MORE RIVER TO CROSS
YELLOWSTONE KELLY
RED BLIZZARD
THE LAST WARPATH
WHO RIDES WITH WYATT
CHIRICAHUA
JOURNEY TO SHILOH
MACKENNA'S GOLD
THE CROSSING
THE BEAR PAW HORSES
SAN JUAN HILL
DEATH OF A LEGEND

The Blue Mustang

Will Henry

LEISURE BOOKS NEW YORK CITY

A LEISURE BOOK®

March 2009

Published by special arrangement with Golden West Literary Agency.

Dorchester Publishing Co., Inc.
200 Madison Avenue
New York, NY 10016

ISBN 10: 0-8439-6148-1
ISBN 13: 978-0-8439-6148-5
E-ISBN: 1-4285-0644-6

The name "Leisure Books" and the stylized "L" with design are trademarks of Dorchester Publishing Co., Inc.

Printed in the United States of America.

10 9 8 7 6 5 4 3 2 1

Visit us on the web at www.dorchesterpub.com.

Dedicated to the memory of a gallant and long vanished breed, the pureblooded Spanish mustang.

And to the proposition, in fiction, that the beloved Texas legend of the five-dollar saddle and the fifteen-dollar horse will not die with the wonderful old men who created it in fact.

The Blue Mustang

Chapter One

I was seventeen that spring, coming eighteen in July. And there never was a north of Texas ranch boy more glad to be alive than I that early May morning of '74. It was all I could do to wait for daylight. The minute it came sneaking in around the edges of the old cowhide hung across the open doorway of the lean-to, I was off and running.

Outside, no matter I was so raring to go, I just had to hold up and look around a spell. That was how beautiful our old place was in the springtime.

Here was a boy who had never been farther away from home than Fort Worth, an easy day's jog, east. An uncurried ranch kid who in something less than an hour was due to be setting out on the biggest ride of his life. Yet that old homeplace on the Brazos was so breathtakingly lovely, so quiet and blessed peaceful, he just had to stand and have a head-shaking look at it.

Over east, the sun was no more than a sleepy pink nod, still yawning and stretching somewhere past the Sabine Basin. On out west, looking over the ridgepole of the big house, there wasn't a thing but two hundred fifty miles of buffalo grass between us and the New Mexico line. Down south there was nothing save the five o'clock rustle of the dawn breeze wandering through the chaparral and mesquite trying to make up its drowsy mind whether to ease on down another four hundred miles to Matamoras and the Gulf, or fool around another forty-eight hours up there in Palo Pinto County. But north! Oh, there was something all right! It was just about the prettiest sight, I reckon, there ever was in the prairie world.

Did you ever see the upper run of a high plains river in early May? Way up high in its course where the water runs bright and clean and sundance shallow over the bottom sand? And where it hasn't yet got all muddied up with squatter's silt, nor been ditched and channeled and spread out to die irrigating some bottomland Mexican's forty acres of pinto beans and tortilla corn?

It's just plain beautiful.

All tall cottonwoods and fat willows and reedbird rushes and the border meadow grass growing up high and graceful enough to brush a pony's underside or stand wither-high to a yearling heifer.

Well, that's the way the Brazos was where it curled around our lower pasture and looped back to run and laugh and play lazy in the morning sun just beyond our workstock corrals and the cool shade of the six big cottonwoods that landmarked our place for half a day's ride coming in from any direction.

But a boy of seventeen, even one only sixty days shy of eighteen, can stand still for just so much beauty. After that, providing he was as full of sap and springtime as I was, he's got to cut and run. Especially when he's set, the minute breakfast's done, to saddle up and ride with his two big brothers clean down to Mason County to pick up a 1600-head trailherd of Llano River longhorns.

What brought me down out of those rosy daybreak clouds was the rattle and bang of Doak fumbling around in the cook-shack to get the coffee on and the sidemeat sliced for frying.

At the same time I heard Brack and our old daddy stomping into their boots in the main house. I had to grin. Dad, as usual, was wheezing and coughing and carrying on like a mossyback herdbull that had spent a damp night on low ground and wasn't yet quite sure whether he was going to get his feet under him or not. Or whether, once he had, he was going to live long enough to walk to water.

But I wasn't really worried about the old gentleman.

He'd lived a long time. Long enough to carve that beautiful upper Brazos spread of ours out of the brisket of Comanche country with nothing but an old Sharps buffalo gun and more guts than you could hang on a forty-mile linefence. He sure wasn't going to break down now that he was right on the edge of closing the biggest deal any old-time cattleman could hope to work up in one lifetime. No, Dad wasn't cut out to die in bed. Nor in getting out of bed either. He was all he-coon and two Texas yards tall, and no three boys could ever have been prouder of their tough old daddy than Brack and Doak and me were of ours.

When I'd finished scrubbing my teeth with a forefinger full of the wood ash and salt we'd been taught to use since we could stand up and stick a thumb in our mouths—Dad always said he wouldn't give a Union nickel for any horse that didn't have a clean mouth—I went in to help Doak.

We all had our jobs. Doak was cook, being the middle boy and made to learn because he was the younger when Mother died. Brack was the oldest and from that had been the first taught on cattle. So he looked after the range stock, with Doak naturally siding him when he wasn't rustling grub or riding into Mineral Wells for supplies. Me, I was the horse wrangler. There were two reasons for that. First place, the wrangler was the lowest form of cowranch life. Second place, I had a way with horses. "A light hand and a thick head," Dad called it. So I got to ride herd on our *remuda* from the time I was tall enough to climb on a thirteen-hand mustang with the help of an eight-hand rain barrel.

Doak didn't even look around when I came in.

He knew it was me from the "sneaky" way I walked. "Like a damn Comanche," he used to say. But he always grinned and mussed up my hair when he said it and I knew that when it came to me he was pretty partial to Comanches.

Of course I wasn't any Indian, nor any part of one. Doak just said that to rile me. Our family was one of the few in that part of Texas that didn't have at least some strain of what Brack called "red bronco blood" running in it. Most did. For in those early days the Caddo and Kwahadi squaws were a lot handier than white women and a sight easier to sign on, not having any more morals than a wet dog wanting to get into a warm tent. I reckon most likely half the famous families in Texas got started on a Comanche blanket, but ours wasn't one of them. Dad was right straight out of Red Dirt Georgia stock and Mother was pure Blue Ridge Virginia. I don't say all this to run down the Indians nor yet to be waving the Confederate flag. It's just that I was little and dark and on the scraggly side, not big and handsome and light colored like Brack and Doak. I really did look like a scrub breed alongside of them and so felt all the time called on to fight back when anybody said "Injun" looking my way.

"Hello, Button," Doak grinned, keeping right on cutting the fatback. "How many slices you good for this mornin'? You ain't rightly big enough to be fed with the men but as long as I left the gate open and you got in, we'll overlook it this once."

That was another thing. That cussed "Button." So I didn't answer him right away.

I had a name as good as either him or Brack but they never used it on me. In the old Bible Dad hadn't looked at since he'd closed it alongside Mother's bed seventeen years ago, it said "Walker Austin Starbuck, July 7, 1856." To my way of thinking "Walk" Starbuck was every bit as ringy a Texas name as Brack or Doak.

Yet, even there, I knew they had me topped. Walk just didn't have the class and snap to it that Brack and Doak did. Still I never let on that it didn't.

"Better fry me about a dozen," I came back at him. "I don't set in the back of the buckboard to nobody when it comes to hanging on the feedbag."

That was true, anyway. I could eat half my weight in buckwheats the weakest morning I ever crawled out of my bunk. They knew that and somehow always kind of admired me for it. Maybe it was because of the way Dad looked at it. "First thing I do with a new hand," he'd say, "is watch him eat. If he ain't a good doer, he don't stay on my ranch long enough to loosen his cinch."

Doak grinned again and said, "Well you sure don't, Button, that's the skyblue gospel. Never yet saw the hand could win a chuck wagon go-round with you." He glanced past me, out the door, his blue eyes crinkling at the edges in that crispy, crow's-foot way that warmed you through like a woodfire on a frosty morning. "Set down and dive in. Yonder comes the Old Bull of the Brazos, along with brother Brack. You don't get your share now, you're apt to weigh in short come sad-dlin' time."

While we all four ate, I let Brack and Doak and Dad do the talking. That was just some more of the way things were run on our ranch. Up to the time you were old enough to vote for president you just sat back and listened.

Usually that took some doing, but not that morning. I was so excited about the big ride and so set on not missing a word of what they were saying about it that I only ate six griddle cakes, which wasn't the half of what I was ordinarily good for.

Dad did most of the talking, and even though he had pawed up the same ground a dozen times in the past ten days we all stood back and gave him respectful room to toss its dust over his shoulder. It settled out about this way.

Deep back in the past winter, when the terrible cowmarket panic of '73 was still on and when it had gone ninety days down our way without a drop of rain or a single snow flurry to offset the driest summer and fall since the big die-up of '68, Dad had got one of his sometime cow hunches.

. It was the kind that had kept him in the cattle business right on through the war and the ruinous $3-a-head days that followed it—that disastrous stretch of Texas time that busted half the big beef outfits south of Red River and all the little ones except his and maybe four or five others in the whole state. It was the kind of a hunch, the dry-grinned way he put it, "that made a steer keep tryin'." He knew it wasn't going to do him any good but damned if he wasn't going to rear up and ride it for all it was worth, anyway.

He'd had a notion, along about the middle of February, that '74 was going to be one of the best grass years in a granddaddy coon's age. He'd right away gone down to his bank in Dallas and mortgaged our place four feet over the fence posts. Then he'd saddled up Old Samson, his pet personal pony that was shaggy as a sheepdog and never been clipped because he said it would sap his strength, and rode off south with $1000 of the mortgage money in one saddlebag and six pounds of dried beef and red beans in the other.

He was back in a week, grinning like a catfish gumming a chunk of raw liver with no hook in it.

And that was the first we found out what he'd been up to.

All he had done—with our range sprouting nothing but sand drifts and our own stock staying alive by picking mesquite beans and chewing the prickly pear cactus me and Brack and Doak spent the winter burning the spines off of—was sashay down into Mason County and contract 1600 head of four-year-old steers for May delivery at $15 a head.

We thought he'd slipped his bit for sure. We'd heard they'd had upwards of 400,000 head of Texas cattle jamming the yards up along the railroads in Kansas that past summer, with the eastern buyers turning down choice grassfat stuff at $13 and $14 a head. Now here was Dad contracting for range-run scrubs at $15! It was plumb crazy.

We spent the next thirty days moping around the place like three draggletailed fryers down with the croup and hoping to die by sunset.

I was the worst.

I was so bad hit by the thought of losing the ranch that I went off feed and began dropping weight. Every day I rode out to say good-bye to another of my secret places along the Brazos; the ones I looked at like they were real people and old friends and not just spots of land. Places like the upper sandbar bend where I had my summer swimming hole. And like the cottonwood grove over on "Little Sam" Island where they said Houston had camped with his Comanche bride for their honeymoon, and where I snuck off to read the books Mother had left me. That was maybe the best place of all, that little island. For you see I had to be careful about those books. I was the only one who had been to school and could read. So I didn't dast let Brack nor Doak catch me at it for fear it would make them feel funny or get onto me about showing off my book learning.

But I never did get done saying good-bye to my secret spots. Before I got down to the last one— the old south bank bluff at the ranchhouse bend, where I used to daydream something scandalous while keeping count of how many minnow chubs my pet family of kingfishers were spearing out of the cattail shallows and how many times an hour my mother reedbirds flew in and out to feed our babies—it began to cloud up off southeast.

Within an hour it had come on to set in as gentle and sweet a rain as ever pocked the prairie dust with that wonderful spring shower smell every ranch boy can remember long past when he's forgotten everything else in his whole happy life.

And it kept right on coming. Up from the Gulf and the warm rain country down around Matamoras. Not hard nor sudden enough to be a gully washer, cutting away more grass than it grew. But regular and easy, with always two or three days of sunny clouddrift in between to settle it deep and grateful into the thirsty ground. It was just as though God himself was turning it off and on the careful, cautious way he would to water his own back pasture.

By May 1 the whole range, from Red River to the Rio Grande, was so green it hurt your eyes to look at it. The cattle were tallowing up better than a pound a day and the only thing that was filling

out faster than our steers was the Missouri and
Kansas trail markets. From early April, when
grass-fed stuff was limping along at $16 a head,
with the big packers laying off and their commis-
sion men scarce and scary as shot-at coyotes, to
that first week in May, the market climbed $13 a
head. And that was pasture delivery down south,
not up there trackside at Abilene or Ellsworth on
the Kansas Pacific, or Newton on the Santa Fe.

All it meant was that inside of thirty days Dad
had made close to $20,000 on his Mason County
contract. And without doing a blessed thing to
earn it save to set on the ranchhouse *galería* listening to the grass grow.

Also, it meant, as he and Brack and Doak now
tailed off their talk, that within the next ten minutes us three Starbuck boys were going to saddle
up and head on down to Mason City with a
$25,000 letter of credit on the Stockman's National
Bank in Dallas in our hip pockets. The same to be
handed over to a man named Ransom Buchanan
for contract delivery of the herd he had figured
he'd been smart enough to stick Dad with back in
the bone dry middle of February.

But like they used to say down in that Palo
Pinto country of ours, "the pony ain't bin saddled
that won't stumble if you leave off watchin' his
feet." We were, all of us, Brack and Doak and me,
so all-fired worked up about Dad's big kill on the
market rise that none of us were keeping our eyes
on the ground in front of our horses the way we'd
ought to have been.

Within those ten minutes of mine that I was so
sure were due to see us cinched up and hitting out

for Mason City on a high laughing lope, we had run our little mustangs into a set of prairie dog holes that broke our hearts and brought us down harder than any real fall off a leg-snapped pony ever could have managed.

Chapter Two

Outside the cookshack Dad had just handed Brack the downpayment receipt and our copy of the Buchanan delivery contract when Doak, who had just come out, squinted off east and nodded quickly. "Yonder comes trouble or I cain't read a dustboil no more."

All of us looked down the river, not arguing any. Doak had the best eyes for far seeing in the county, and could outlook an antelope when the light was right. Which it was. Brack just nodded back and grunted, "Likely you're right. Who do you make it out to be?"

We could all of us see that it was a rider on a dun or light bay horse and in a six-foot, four-inch hurry. But it was only Doak who could cut his saddle sign. "It's old Sec," he said. "There ain't nobody else sets a full gallop thet clean and straight."

Secondido Gonzales was our first neighbor down the Brazos. He was a *mesteñero*, a Mex mustang hunter, who broke horses for us in the off season and was a particular friend of mine. He had taught me all I knew about horses, wild or tame, and I looked up to him more like a favorite uncle than like a Mexican. But I never was much of a one to worry what color a man was so long as we had the same way of seeing things. Which me and old Sec sure did.

"That's Mozo he's riding," I said.

"It is," agreed Doak.

It was a pretty bobtailed exchange, even for us Starbucks, but it said a lot in six words.

Mozo was the old man's top running horse, a genuine *criollo*, one of the last of the pure Spanish horses. Sec had bought him off the Escadero Ranch six hundred miles down in Coahuila State, giving three hundred American dollars for him as a green-broke yearling. He could walk down the toughest mustang that ever lived inside of two weeks or run him to death in twenty miles, whichever way he wanted it. And what made all that important to us standing there in front of the cookshack was that old Sec would never saddle him short of having something mighty serious on his mind.

He did, all right. We found that out when he slid him up to us the next minute. He stepped down off of him while he was still moving, graceful about it as a twenty-year-old Comanche buck, though if he was a day under seventy I'd buy the drinks till next spring.

"*Patrón.*" He bowed to Dad. "*Amigos.*" He nodded to Brack and Doak. Then, like always, with that little extra eye twinkle for me. "*Caballero—*"

It was a tolerable small joke and mostly Mexican at that. But he enjoyed it and so did I.

To the *Mejicano* born and brought up on one of the old Spanish haciendas down in Chihuahua or Coahuila, there were only two kinds of men. The *peón*, the peasant on foot, and the *caballero*, the

king on horseback. So it was the highest compli-
ment old Sec could hand anybody to call them
caballero. And even though he always put that little
question mark of a grin back of it when he used it
on me, I knew he partly meant it for serious all the
same.

"*Qué pasa, Tio?*" I asked him. I called him Uncle,
like that. He took to it the same way I did to him
calling me *caballero.* "What's happened?" I came at
him again in English.

"*Estamos en un aprieto apuro, chico,*" he answered
gravely. "We are in trouble, little one." Once the
formal greetings were over with, Mexican style,
his pet name for me was that "little one." But now,
before he could go on past it, Brack broke in in
that acid slow way of his.

"Anytime you and the kid are done patting one
another on the backside, Gonzales, we'd admire
to hear what's brung you up the river in such a
hell of a hurry."

"*Dispense me Usted, Señor Brack.*" The little
mesteñero put just a touch of stiffback Spanish
courtesy into it. He was afraid of Brack, like most
of the Mexes and a good cut of the whites in our
part of the country. He never did get cozy with
him, or even Doak, the way he did with me. "It is
that cursed *entero negro* again. He has come once
more for the *yeguas.*"

"*Pues bien?*" put in Doak quietly.

Sec was a little more sure of Doak than of Brack,
and answered him just as quiet. "*Pues, amigo,* this
time he got them. And the *kehilan* before them."

Brack snarled, Doak shot his jaw, Dad broke

forward and hooked at it with that sideways shake of his head that he used when he was stung bad, and that was so much like the way a Spanish bull will throw his horns into the *muleta* after he's been stuck deep with the *banderillas*. "Ye mean to say thet black scrub has killed my blood studhoss and run off my mares!"

The old *mesteñero* only nodded. He had already said it once and for a Mexican he was a rare quiet one.

Entero negro was black stallion in anybody's Spanish. In this case it meant the raunchy mustang stud that had been after our choice *manada* of brood mares all winter. *Kehilan* wasn't Spanish to begin with but the original dons had borrowed it from the Arabs so far back over in the old country that it had become standard Mexican for "pure-bred all through" by our time. Applied to any horse it meant a thoroughbred in English and right now it stood for Dad's prize Kentucky stud he'd imported all the way from the Lexington sales last spring to grade up our best band of range mares.

You could see now, the way he sagged in the shoulders as he turned to Doak, that the old gentleman was hit where it hurt bad and where he couldn't handle it right off.

"Doaker boy," he said huskily, "what we goin' to do?"

Doak was the levelheaded one. He was two years younger than Brack, but sounder nerved and went a steadier gait. "Well, Dad, there's only one thing to do. Button'll have to go along with Sec to git them mares back. They're most of them siding

Lexington's first colts and carrying his second. I'll be damned if any broomtail stud is going to get away with them, no matter it means breakin' Button's heart."

"That's for sure," growled Brack. "You ain't goin' to get no more colts like them, now your stud's kilt."

"No," said Doak soberly. "And what's more we cain't hold up to help Sec and Button round them up. That Buchanan contract's dated May seven. We don't git down there and take delivery by then, we're out the best part of $20,000 profit and likely the ranch to boot."

"Yeah," breathed Brack, that bad light which made most men give him plenty of room at the bar getting into his pale eyes. "Ordinarily there wouldn't be no trouble over bein' a day or two late. But I've heard Buchanan is a pure bad one."

"He is, Brack. I know that." Dad said it real slow, like he meant he really *did* know it. "It's why I'm sending you down there instead of goin' myself."

We all knew what he was getting at, saying that to Brack. To listen to Brack put the bad brand on anybody else was kind of unfunny humorous. He was my big brother and couldn't do any wrong for me, but he was a mean one all the same. A real mean one. You couldn't walk around that if you wore out six pairs of Sonora boots trying.

"Well, we all got some use in the world, Dad." Brack grinned it, but that wasn't any sign he thought it was funny or figured anybody to laugh about it.

"Button—" He came around on me, freezing the grin on the way. "What for you standin' there? You heard Doak. Git your hoss."

There was no use to argue it. Not with Brack.

I was going with old Sec after those mares and they were going on to Mason City without me. If Sec and me were lucky and got within rifle range of the mustang stud by noon, we'd be back with the mares by nightfall. By that time Brack and Doak would be sixty miles down the road.

"All right," I muttered, keeping my head down so's he wouldn't see I was setting my jaw stubborn. My bent for bunkhouse arguing had a way of curling up pretty quick when Brack got that funny look in his eyes. Once, and just once, long past, it hadn't. I'd talked back to him and I could still remember him standing over me rubbing his fist and saying it ugly and soft. "Button, don't you never try putting off on me again. You hear me, boy?"

I heard him then and I heard him now.

I went for the pole corral back of my lean-to where I kept the little steeldust mare that was my best pony. Dad limped along with me, favoring his game leg like he did before the sun got full up to warm it through. Sec followed along behind us, leading Mozo. Brack and Doak had cut out their horses the night before, haltering them in the hay shed so's not to have to be fooling around roping them in the morning. Before I'd got the bars down to let my mare out, they were shouldering up their cinches.

And before I'd got my hull on and tied down, they were just jogging dots topping the last grass swell, south.

A boy coming eighteen down Texas way was mighty close to man grown. Anyway he was supposed to be. But watching my two big brothers ride out of sight that morning was more than I could get to go down past the lump in my throat. There was salt water in my eyes and it wasn't from sand nor windsquint.

I knew I dassn't blink or it would go to spilling over and Dad would see it. So I stood there staring off south, keeping my back as much as possible to him and Sec and making out like I was mainly concerned with seeing that Brack and Doak got over that last rise all right.

By the time they had, my eyes had dried up enough to turn around.

Sec was already mounted up and waiting. Dad was letting on like he was looking over Sec's Mozo horse and hadn't been watching me at all. But when I legged up and swung the little steeldust around to come up to them, he peered at me kind of odd and then squinted off at some spotty clouds over across the river.

"For a spell there," he grumbled in that old man's sort of a soft growling way he talked, "I thought sure it was comin' on to sprinkle." He looked back at me and put his big hand, all knuckle-popped and broken from forty years of flanking calves, on my nearside knee. "But I reckon she's all blowed over now."

"I reckon she is, Dad." I grinned down at him. "Step back lively, or you'll git stomped on!"

He was still standing there, still peering after us, when Sec and me put our horses around the last bend and sent them into a trailgait lope down the south bank of the Brazos.

I never saw him that way again.

Chapter Three

We got onto the wild stud's track about nine o'clock, running it for the next three hours without a break. By noon we'd been in the saddle six hours, not seeing a solitary thing but horse tracks, with here and there some warm sign. But old Sec didn't seem worried. Every so often he would get down and look at the fresh droppings. He would toe one of them over, and then step on it lightly to see how it hung together. With that, he'd look up at me and say, "*Pues, chico, qué dice?*"

Well, that was asking me what I said, so I would peer down and see the way that dropping was still good and moist and I'd tell him, "Well, I'd say he's still taking it easy and don't yet know we're after him. *Es verdad?*"

The old man would grin, "*Sí, muy bueno,*" and get back up and we'd go on.

It made him kind of proud, I reckon, to see that what he had taught me stuck with me. In this case I showed him that I remembered that when a horse knows he is being run he gets nervous. Then he squinches up inside, pretty quick starting to leave drier sign. That was mighty simple stuff but he was

like the schoolteacher down at Mineral Wells
when she would ask one of us ranch kids to spell
"house" or "barn." She'd know very well that we
knew how and could most likely go right on and
give her tougher ones like "sassafras" or "Con-
stantinople." But she just all the same wanted to
hear us do it with her own ears, so's she'd know
the county school board was getting their money's
worth. And that was the way Sec was with me. He
didn't mind having spent ten years learning me a
quarter of what he knew about horses, just so long
as he could be reasonable sure some little of it had
sunk in.

Just short of noon he cut away from the trail
and headed left to top out on a rocky ridge.

I thought maybe he was getting too old when he
did that. The mustang stud would see us, sure, if
we showed ourselves high up against the sky like
that. It turned out this was exactly what he wanted
him to do. But that wasn't clear to me just yet, and
I grumped and carried on about it something dis-
graceful.

We sat up there on the skyline at least twenty
minutes, and though I never took my eyes off the
broken-up country ahead I didn't see a thing. But
Sec just smiled and said, "It is not for us to see
him, *niño*. It is for him to see us." I still thought he
was slipping, but said no more.

After a bit we went on and pretty quick he
smiled, "*Ahora, chico*. Now you will see. In two
miles, *así no más*, the droppings will start to dry."

He was right of course. We had gone about a
mile and a half, just getting into the rocks ahead,

when I spotted some of the stud's sign and piled off to have a kick at it. It crumbled and fell apart like it was a day old.

Sec only nodded. "He was not turning, *chico*. So we let him see us. Now he will go on around in the big circle. Remember?"

I just nodded too. But not easy and good-natured like him. "Yeah, and what in heck'll we do then? All join hands and promenade home?"

I said it plenty salty and not too overjoyed about it. But the old man only smiled again and grunted. "You'll see, *niño*," and swung Mozo around and head him right back the way we'd come.

That is, he did until we were back behind the rocky rise where we had set up against the big empty sky and let that sneaky wild stud look us over. Then we cut hard right and lit out on a long canter, due west. The ground hadn't yet dried out from the April rains. A full stampede wouldn't have raised enough dust to shake the birdlice out of a Barred Rock pullet. Added to that, we were behind that cussed rise clean back to within five miles of the Brazos. We couldn't have seen the stud and our mares if they'd been following us the whole blessed way close enough to spit on with the wind in our favor. But along about the time I was ready to strangle Sec, for free, we began to get into the Palo Pinto outcrop country and I finally caught up to the old rascal's foxy drift.

"*Las tinajas?*" I scowled.

"*Sí, por supuesto,*" he shrugged, lifting his shoulders in that warm quiet little way nobody but a Mexican can manage.

A *tinaja* is a rock pool that holds rainwater for a spell. A mustang would go twenty miles to drink out of one, where he could get to river or slough water in maybe half that. Which just went to show what good sense those little broomtails had. That groundwater in our part of the *llano* was so hard you could sharpen a knife on it. And so full of alkali it would do to scald a hog with, without adding any lye.

Well, along about then my disposition was getting as tender as the open end of my chaps. No matter what you read in books, the rider has not yet been born who can set a horse that's making eight miles an hour, for six, seven hours on end, without getting shook to pieces. A man just can't take it that far and that fast without he builds himself up a set of blue ribbon saddleboils.

So I was plenty stiff and sore and plenty riled with old Sec for taking me on what looked like an awful long way around to get a drink of soft water.

But I hadn't had time to more than ease down off of Little Blue and start thinking up my best Spanish cusswords when Sec gave me a warning "Pssst!"

"*Allí*," he whispered, bobbing his head toward a little arroyo that cut down from the level of the prairie to the *tinajas*. The next minute we were both grabbing our horses' noses and backing them into some handy rocks, all the cover there was available. The rest went quick and easy and I never did get to use those four-bit Mexican insults I'd been storing up for old Sec.

Out of the arroyo, head low and ears swinging

loose, to show he was tired and not looking for any trouble, came the little mustang stud. Behind him came our twenty head of choice coyote dun brood-mares and their light bay and line-back buckskin babies. The wind was our way. The broomtail stallion wasn't thinking about anything but the rain-water in those rock tanks. He never heard us nor saw us.

Sec let him get his head down and go to drinking, so he would be holding still. Then he shot him just over the right eye where that little hollow is and where there's nothing between the bullet and the brain but a little thin skin and rubbery skullbone.

He didn't make a sound going down. The mares paid him scarcely any heed. Horses are dumb like that, pretty near as bad as buffalo. A couple of them ambled up to sniff him and two or three of the colts skittered around and danced off a ways when they got the smell of the blood. But that was all. We had the bunch of them lined out for the Brazos and the homeplace inside of five minutes. We cut in across the back pasture just ahead of sundown. The hazy red and gold light was still warming the ridgepole of the big house when we shoved the last of them into the workstock corral and headed on around the cookshack to wash up for supper.

While we were getting the alkali dust out of our ears I didn't bother any about how unnatural still it was around the house. I knew Dad liked to set a spell this time of evening out under the old 'dobe arches that strung across the *galería* out front, just dozing and looking far off out west watching the sun ease down out there beyond the Rio Pecos.

When I was little I used to set with him those times. He would see all sorts of wonderful things in the sunset clouds. If there was enough of them and they were wild-colored and broken up enough, he would get to telling of the old days down in south Texas when he and Mother had their first little spread on the Nueces, and when the Comanches were still raiding free-style and for deadly sure.

His favorite yarn was the one about how, as a young bucko before he met Mother, he had been with the boys in the Alamo. This one had always gone bigger with Brack and Doak than with me. I'd been to school and learned a few dates. Enough, anyway, to know Dad hadn't even left Georgia till two years after Santy Ana had got his for the massacre at Goliad. I never said anything though. It would have spoiled it for both of us.

Well, after Sec and me had used up a couple of ollas of well water, we stood back a minute to un-kink our leg muscles and stretch the ache out of our kidneys. Then we moved on through the house to wake Dad up and let him know he had his precious mares back. And not alone back, but every one of them safe and none of them with the mustang stud long enough for him to settle them with any fuzztail colts.

We didn't get three steps into the main big room leading across to the *galería* before I held up so sudden old Sec bumped into me from behind. The twilight dark made it hard to see in there, which was maybe just as well. The place looked like it had been funneled through a Kansas twister. The Indian rugs and soft-tanned buffalo robes had been pulled up and piled back against the walls. The old leather Morris chair, that was Dad's favorite for setting by the fireplace when the blue northers were blowing down from the Arkansas, had been ripped and slashed to ribbons with a knife. Every stick of other furniture, including Mother's mahogany china closet, had been pulled over or kicked upside down. Dad's big rolltop desk, which he always kept locked even from us, was smashed open and cleaned out emptier than a gutted calf.

Sec was out onto the *galería* first. By the time I was over my dumbstruck look at the main room and had followed him out, he already had his hat off and was crossing himself.

It didn't hit me right off. Sec just kept standing there alongside the old cane-bottom rocker looking down at Dad. And Dad was just setting there like he always did, for all the world as though he had dozed off watching the sunset and was sound asleep and dreaming of the old days.

Only all of a sudden I knew he wasn't.

His left arm didn't hang right, the way it dangled straight down outside the arm of the chair. His other hand had ahold of the end curve of the right chair arm too stiff and queer and awkward looking. And his game leg was bent back at the knee in a way he hadn't been able to bend it in twenty years.

If he was asleep, he was going to be asleep a long time. If he was dreaming, it was a dream that was never going to end.

I hoped mightily that it was a good dream and that he was seeing a sunset the most beautiful and wild and lovely clouded that ever a brave old man stared into. For he was not going to see another one.

Dad was dead.

Chapter Four

We carried him in the house and laid him on his bed in the big room that had been his and Mother's. Sec helped me dress him in his old Confederate cavalry coat—he had enlisted with Price's Texas volunteers when he was over sixty years old—and fixed him up to look the best we could. Then Sec left me in there with him and went out into the ranch yard, past the *galería*, to look for sign of what had happened.

I shouldn't have—Brack and Doak wouldn't have—but I cried like a little kid.

He was such a wonderful old man, gentle and good and rough and hard-tongued and tough and mother-soft all in the same afternoon, that, to me, losing him was more than I could manfully face up to. Seventeen, most eighteen, was pretty old for a boy to be breaking down the way I did in the dark of that musty old room. But things had been different between me and Dad than they'd been with him and Brack and Doak.

I had been a late baby, one of those that comes along when a couple haven't meant to have any more kids, nor don't really want any. There was more than ten years between me and the others.

Brack was thirty-one and Doak twenty-nine. It was Mother being so well along in years, and Brack and Doak not getting back from Mineral Wells with the doctor soon enough, that had taken her off when I was born.

That might have made a meaner man than Dad turn against me. But, instead, he had made things so for me that I never missed not having a mother, nor was let to know why it was I didn't. I just happened to hear that one day when Brack and Doak were talking and didn't know I was around. But Dad himself never let on. Raunchy and runted as I was, and never did get over being, he treated me like I was bigger and better looking than Brack and Doak put together. For my part, I took to him like an orphan range colt, and was fooled with and made over and rotten spoiled like one, too.

That was likely why I was crouched down there now by his and Mother's bed patting his big hand and sobbing and carrying on so blind and broken-hearted.

Brack and Doak would never have got down on their knees that way. They would have been on their feet, standing tall and tough—like him. And they would have been out there in the yard with old Sec using the last of the daylight to unravel what sign they could find of the killers who had come in and done this to him. But they had all petted and pampered me too long. I didn't have their kind of insides. I was still crying there in the dark, lost and scared and sick-lonesome, when I heard Sec come in to stand behind me.

"Chico—"

"Sí."

"Llevantese!"

It was soft-spoken, like everything a Mexican says, but it was a command. I had never had old Sec use that tone of voice on me and it straightened me out, somehow. I got up and went with him out onto the *galería.*

We set out there a long spell, not talking and just watching the night close in and the first fat white stars go to blooming low and big and far-beckoning way over across New Mexico. Later, I figured out that was Sec's way of giving me time to catch hold of myself and get to thinking about what he had found out there in the yard, and what I was going to do about it. But just right at the time I reckoned it was no more than his ignorant Mexican slowness and dumb, chest-crossing habit of accepting whatever God saw fit to parcel out— even to killing a gentle old man in cold blood and without giving him any more chance than you would a distemper-sick dog or leg-broke horse.

Naturally, and as usual, I was wrong.

After a bit he got out a couple of crooked black *cigarillos.* I had never smoked in my life and he knew it. Yet he handed me one and struck a match for it like I was a Mexican kid and had been on tobacco since I was weaned. I took it, too. And, for once, was bright enough to figure out something for myself. Even grief-galled and choked up as I was, I could understand and be grateful for, and some little scared by, what had brought him to offer me that *cigarillo.*

It was to let me know I had grown up, sudden and necessary. That we weren't any longer an old man and a boy playing at chasing mustangs and

funning away the long summer afternoons learning horse savvy out on the *llano.*

We were two men now.

And out there in the dark of that ranch-yard
dust lay a tangle of shod hoof and high-heeled
boot sign that had made me old enough to vote
and smoke a seegar in the thirty minutes since
sundown.

Chapter Five

"There were five of them," said Sec, when at last his *cigarillo* had burned down to where he was ready to talk. "I will tell you what I have learned of them from their tracks. The rest will be in God's hands. And in yours, *niño.*"

What he had learned, from only fifteen minutes of studying their sign before the twilight went, was more than a lot of men could have told you from being there and seeing it happen. But that was the way it would be with a *mesteñero* who could tell you from one good set of hoofprints everything about a horse except maybe his color and what kind of a mouth he had. And the way it would be with an *anciano* who could read in a man's boot-marks how old he was, what he weighed, whether he was right- or left-handed and, likely, which side of his mouth he spit his tobacco out of.

So I just sat and listened and soaked it up.

Four of them had stood back while one of them moved in to do the talking. That one had met Dad in the patio dust, just past the *galería*. He had hit him on the head with his gunbarrel, knocked him down, shot him twice through the stomach as he lay there helpless.

But first there had been an argument. The boot-marks of both of them had moved around in a very small space while they stood facing one another. Dad's not so much, the other man's a great deal. He was evidently a nervous man, probably a fast and a sharp talker. Not afraid—none of his prints stepped backward—but a restless, uncertain-tempered man; strung up and tense and too full of animal energy to stand still.

There was more Sec could say about him.

He was medium tall, or else undue long-legged, and not young. About middle age from the way he walked. Not slow like an old man, nor quick like a young one. But careful and sure, every step thought about and measured out in his mind. He was left-handed, by the way he led his stride with the nearside leg, and he was lame in that leg too. His bootsole was worn along the inside and the foot dragged and turned in at the heel.

As for the horses, they had come a long ways and were tired. They had all stood hipshot in the rear and spraddled in front. From the fact none of them had wandered from where their reins had been dropped, they were all trained cowhorses. By that, Sec said, you could figure their riders were first cowboys, and murderers only by being with the left-handed man. There was considerable more he told me, but even he couldn't say who they were or where they'd come from.

At least I didn't think he could and, actually, he couldn't. Yet he had found something that could. And did.

I hadn't seen him take it out of Dad's clenched

Will Henry

right hand but the minute he handed it over to me I knew where it had come from.

It was a page out of Dad's little yellow-paper tallybook, which he would no more think of walking around without than he would without his pants. That and the stub pencil he kept tied by a greasy string to the top button of his vest so's he wouldn't lose it out of his pocket bending over to bust a big calf down, or to slit and underbit an ear which was the way we marked our young stuff.

When Sec gave it to me, he scratched a match and held it for me to see by, but didn't say anything.

He didn't have to. The last entry in Dad's tallybook said it for him. In four shakily printed words.

Somehow he had dragged himself up onto the *galería* and into his old rocker after his killers had downed him and gone in and torn up the house and ridden off leaving him for dead. With his last strength he had hoisted himself into the chair, squared around to be looking into the sun like he had his whole life, fumbled out his tallybook and written down the roadbrand of the man who had come to kill him.

He couldn't have told us more if he'd had a Philadelphia lawyer there to take down a ten-page testament.

All that wilted piece of yellow paper said was, BILL OF SALE. Then a slurred scrawl, like he had tightened up to a bad pain, with after that just the one word more—BUCHANAN.

That was it

The man who had been there with his four hardcase hired hands was Ransom Buchanan, of

Mason City, Texas. And the reason he had come was to get back the bill of sale he had given Dad for those 1600 head of May-delivery steers.

In that last minute, staring down at the tally sheet and letting that hated name sear into my memory while Sec's match hissed and went out, there were only two thoughts left alone and wicked inside me. One was in my mind: they hadn't got that bill of sale, Brack and Doak had it with them. The other was in my heart: if it took me my whole life and if I had to trail him around the world to do it, I was going to track down Rance Buchanan and kill him.

Out past the corral cottonwoods there was a little headland topping the bluff that overhung the ranchhouse bend of the river. It was a rise of not more than fifty feet, but from it you could see off west up the Brazos clear out to where the prairie turned purple and hazed off into the Staked Plains over New Mexico way. Dad used to say that from up there, looking out across the last of the virgin *llano*, you were standing on one of the Lord's little footstools; put there a'purpose for a man to climb up on and see how little he was.

Brack saw it different. He would growl that it was dismal as the backside of the moon and flatter than an old maid's chest. Doak, he would just grin and shake his head and allow that it was nothing but miles and miles of miles and miles. For myself, I always liked best what old Sec said about it: that it ran free and wild and unbroken as a mustang stallion, from the Brazos, *"a la cola del mundo,"* to the tail end of the whole wide world.

But any way you saw it, that little headland bluff, with its tawny wind-waved crest of bunch and buffalo grass and its necklace of silver water and green cottonwood beads, was a restful, lovely jewel set in the sage-gray center of an aching, lonely land.

That was why Dad had put Mother to rest there seventeen years ago. And why Sec and me were up there now, laying him in beside her.

When it was done and the last spadeful of prairie turf tamped carefully back into place so that it would root and grow over and not look like a grave but only the same way God had made it to begin with, Sec said the words. After he had crossed himself, we turned away and went down the rise and Dad was alone with Mother and the stars and the soft rustle of the nightwind moving down the Brazos.

Back at the house it didn't take long.

I knew what I had to do, knew I had precious little time to get it done in.

Somewhere, sixty or seventy miles to the south, Brack and Doak were riding into a trap. And somehow, covering that dark and guessed-at distance between now and daylight, I had to find them and warn them before they boiled their breakfast coffee and rode on.

It was a fairly big order for a boy who had never aimed a gun in anger, nor been more than an easy day's ride from home in his short, sheltered life. I thought I knew that at the time, as I stood with old Sec in the ranch yard out past the *galería* listening to him tell me how to handle his Mozo horse, which he had insisted I take instead of my own Little Blue pony.

Actually I was a long, long way from knowing it.

I found that out a hundred miles and twenty-four hours later.

Chapter Six

I started south about eight o'clock, riding by the stars the way Sec had taught me when it was moon-dark and you were in a strange country.

Mozo had an outreaching singlefoot that was the easiest gait to set to ever built into an 800-pound Spanish pony. And one that put the miles behind so quick and painless you couldn't keep count of them. I held him on it for the best part of four hours, keeping track of the time with Dad's old German silver stemwinder, which I had taken off of him as he had always said he wanted me to have it.

I was careful to see that Mozo got a five-minute blow-out every hour, getting off of him and hand-walking him around so that he wouldn't cool out and go stiff on me. I knew Sec had never let another man use him. For him to let me take him was like borrowing a man's wife. So I handled him exactly as I was told, worrying about him nearly as much as about finding Brack and Doak. Sec had said that if I rode him to order, I could set Dad's watch by the fact he would make fifteen miles an hour. And that when four hours had gone, providing I had read the stars right, I could head for a high point and start looking for Sipe Springs—the place Brack and Doak would most likely be camped.

Accordingly, when my last-struck match showed me both hands of the old stemwinder pointing straight up, I hit for the nearest rise.

Sure enough. Down yonder there in the starlight, maybe a mile off east, was a dark blotch of willow and cottonwood. It stood out black and clean from the hazy gray of the open sage around it and any prairie boy could spot it for a big ground-seep, moondark or not.

I set out toward it feeling sinful proud of myself. To come sixty miles across land you'd never set eyes on, even in broad day, going only by the hang of the stars and the drainage direction of the little east-west creeks you forded every now and again, and then to top out within five minutes of the place you were aiming for, was pretty good.

The trouble was that "pretty good" wouldn't quite cut it.

When I got down to the springs, Brack and Doak weren't there. They had figured to camp there the first night out, as they weren't in any prime rush, having until May 7 to take delivery on the Buchanan cattle. Now all I could imagine was that they had made better time than they had allowed and had drifted on to the next stop. That would be the little town of Comanche, and would be brother Brack's doing.

Brack liked his whiskey and liked going to town to get it.

Doak was more like me. And like Dad. We all took a mighty far-off view of going to town for

any reason and would most generally do anything short of stealing cows or shooting a man in
the back to keep from having to do it.

But no matter. Brack and Doak weren't at Sipe
Springs. They hadn't held up there longer than
enough to water their horses and maybe to roll a
smoke. The next move was mine but I wasn't up to
making it.

I had been in the saddle since seven o'clock that
morning, with only the rest of digging Dad under
to spell me. I had ridden close to one hundred ten
miles, the last, best part of it at a pushing gait. I
didn't know just how much farther along Comanche was, either. But I did know one thing. If it
was any more than another five miles, I wasn't going to get there that night.

I got down off Mozo, so lame and stove-up in
my legs and the small of my back that it fairly near
killed me to walk him out before putting him on
picket and breaking out my blanket roll. I was so
tired I didn't eat. It was all I could do to stay
awake long enough to lug my saddle over and
dump it at the head of my blankets. I didn't even
remember laying down and covering up.

I must have done it, though.

For the next thing I knew the redwings were
noising it up something scandalous in the bull-
rushes around the spring, and the sun was slanting in under my hat brim strong enough to start a
fire through a magnifying glass.

I saddled up and lit out for Comanche, eating a
little cold beef and tortillas on the way. I began to
feel better right away. If Comanche wasn't too far
and if Brack had taken on his usual load the night

before, I would hit town before Doak got him up and straightened out fit to ride.

Comanche was a town that was born asleep and never woke up.

When I cantered down the mainstem about six o'clock, there was only two horses keeping the street from being empty as a busted bottle. Those two were cowhorses and were saddled and standing outside the town's one fleabit beanery, and they were Brack's light bay and Doak's line-back dun.

I swung Mozo for the hitching rail but never got to get down off him. The boys came out just as I was throwing my off-leg over the cantle. I dropped it back into the stirrup, knowing that when I'd said my piece we wouldn't be long for Comanche.

And we weren't.

Brack saw me first, but Doak saw me best.

"Mornin', Button." Brack was always one to try and let on like nothing ever snuck up on him. He didn't like to be surprised and I never knew him to admit that he was. "You enjoy your ride?"

With that, his voice went heavy and rough to match his early morning looks. "Damn you, boy, what's the big idee? You still figure me and the Doaker cain't handle this detail without you stickin' in your two-bits' worth?"

I didn't dast say anything. Not to him. Many's the Sunday morning I'd seen him ride in from Mineral Wells looking just like he did now, his whiskers two days old and that bad whiskey sneer working overtime. So I sat his stare out, looking hopefully past him to Doak.

Dad always said there was three kinds of men.

Doers, thinkers and daydreamers. And he always figured he had got a full set of three in Brack and Doak and me.

Doak was the one in the middle.

He took a long look at me and Mozo, adding up in his mind that it came out a bad total to see me and old Sec's prize running horse standing in the middle of Comanche's main street at six o'clock in the morning. He jerked a headbob at Brack and said, "Lay off, Brack," and moved out to come up to my onside stirrup. "What's the matter, kid? What's happened?" he asked softly.

They took it standing rock-still. Brack's face didn't move so much as a jaw muscle or an eye-corner twitch. Neither did Doak's. But you could see the difference in their eyes. Brack's just got paler and uglier. Doak's turned dark and deep, so full of dumb brute hurt it made you want to cry to look at him.

But nobody was going to cry that morning in Comanche's main street.

They let me finish without a word. Only when I had got shut of the last of it—how old Sec had promised to round up a bunch of his *mesteñero* friends and follow down to Mason City to help us out with the herd or with any trouble we might run into taking delivery on it—did one of them break. Then it was Brack and he kept it short.

"Well, let's go," was what he said.

I thought he meant let's go on to Mason City. But Doak knew him better.

"Hold on, Brack." He didn't move to follow Brack up onto his pony. "What you got in mind?"

"Rance Buchanan. What's yours?"

"It won't wash, Brack." He said it real slow. "We got a herd to pick up. Remember? You'll see Buchanan soon enough. He'll be at the ranch when we git there."

"Well, you're halfways right, anyhow," grinned Brack.

"What you mean?"

"I'll see him soon enough."

"But—?"

"He won't be at the ranch when we git there."

"You dead set on thet?"

"I am."

"You reckon you kin cut his trail 'twixt here and Mason?"

"I do."

I started to say something but Doak said, "Shut up, kid," and moved for his pony. He stepped up on him, swung him away from the rail and said, "All right, Brack, let's go."

I had looked for him to take a more long-headed view, not siding at all with Brack on goose-chasing after Buchanan. And I guess Brack had too.

"Now *you* hold on," he growled. "I had in mind *me* cuttin' Buchanan's trail. You and Button jest head on down and git them cattle. I'll be along."

Doak shook his head. We were, by then, walking our horses down the street heading out of town, south. There still wasn't anybody around but Doak talked quick and low, as though he was afraid somebody would show up to hear him before he got done. "No, we'll stick. You got it in your hard head to go after Buchanan, ain't nobody goin' to turn you aside. I reckon we all know thet. It sure ain't the smart way to play it, but you never took no prizes for bein' bright."

"What's thet supposed to mean?" Brack scowled and kicked his horse into a lope. We shook out our reins and came up to him.

"Button says Sec figured there was four of them with Buchanan," Doak told him.

"So?"

"Three to five's a fight, Brack."

"And?"

"Five to one's a funeral."

Brack just grinned. "Without flowers and no slow music," he agreed.

There wasn't any more talk after that until we were out of sight of town. Then Brack swung west and Doak, who had been riding with me, eased up to side him. They argued for a mile or better, while I stayed behind where they both wanted me. Pretty quick Doak dropped back and I got my first earful of Brack's real drift.

He had it all figured. At least he did for the hardcase way he figured things.

First off, Buchanan didn't know any of us. Dad had gone down alone to make his deal and as far as we knew, Buchanan had no idea there was three of us Starbuck boys. Or any Starbuck boys at all. Brack was counting on Dad's close mouth with strangers having kept that little piece of information in the family.

Doak thought that for that part of it, at least, you could go along with Brack's thinking. I agreed you could, for I knew us Starbucks.

You hear a lot about how neighborly people

were out in that frontier country. Maybe it was that way back in the old days before the Rangers took the starch out of the Comanches, but in our day it just wasn't so. We had neighbors, likely good folks, too, close as forty miles down the Brazos that we had never howdied nor shook with. That north and middlewest of Texas country was too full of men who wanted to be left alone. The aloner, the better. That was true for a good fifteen years after the War and it wasn't any truer of any of them than of us Starbucks. For one thing, Brack had been in some kind of big trouble down around San Antone after our folks had come up into the Palo Pinto country. For another, both Mother and Dad were pinewoods, hill-bred, folk. And it was natural, from that, that we were a pretty close and clanny bunch. It made it easy, too, for Doak and me to buy Brack's hunch that Dad had kept his mouth shut about us.

But if that first part of his idea did make sense, the rest of it was ringy as a she-bear with sore nipples nursing three cubs.

He meant, providing he could head Buchanan's crew before they got back to Mason City, to get the drop on them at some good spot along the trail. Then, with me and Doak covering them, he would cut Buchanan out and take him the same way he had took Dad. He would first tell him who we were, then beat the life halfway out of him with his bare hands. When he was down and done and bellied-up, helpless, he would shoot him through the stomach and leave him lay to suffer and bleed out and drag himself around in the dirt like he had done with Dad.

It was a crazy, wild scheme, as full of holes as a woodpeckered telegraph pole. Still, the way Doak saw it, him and me had no other choice. If we didn't side Brack, he would brace them alone. The best we could do was hope he was wrong in calculating they would take the old Paint Rock stage road, home, instead of following the new road which ran due south out of Comanche by way of San Saba and Lampasas. That was the one we'd been on and just cut away from, and the one Brack reckoned they would want to steer clear of "just in case."

We made forty miles in six hours, hitting the Red Fork of the Coleman River a little before twelve. We noon-halted in a cottonwood swale, ate some cold beef and let the horses graze for two hours.

Brack stretched out on a shady spit of bank sand and slept like a baby full of goat's milk and molasses. Me and Doak talked. We couldn't either of us sleep. Doak, especially, was nervous.

I hadn't ever seen him that way and it got me to bridling right bad. He wouldn't talk anymore about where we were heading or what, additional, Brack aimed to do when we got there. All he wanted to talk about was times past on the ranch and how happy we had all been through the years. He even got clear back to the day Mother had died and how she had called both him and Brack in and told them always to look after me and see that I was sent to school and brought up civilized and all the things done for me that she was sorry hadn't been done for them.

Well, it got powerful heavy before Brack finally woke up and said it was time to be moving along.

We slipped on our split-ear bridles, shouldered up our double-rigged cinches, crossed over the Red Fork and headed straight south.

We rode for another four hours but a lot slower, letting the horses take their own gait. This was that miserable shuffle-footed running walk that the Devil invented and gave those Spanish-blood mustangs a patent on. It would jar a man's liver loose in twenty minutes, shake it down to his tail-bone in thirty and have it banging against his spur-shanks somewhere short of forty. No matter, it was good for five miles an hour, uphill or down draw, pear scrub or open *llano*, and it brought us out on the North Fork of the San Saba and the old Paint Rock road at six o'clock.

Brack pulled his bay in on a little rise overlooking the stream, and the run of the road off to the northwest, up toward Paint Rock. Doak and me reined in alongside of him. Nobody said anything for the best part of a minute. The only sound was the grunting and wind-breaking of our horses as they let down and blew out after their long afternoon jog.

Finally Brack got down and dropped his reins. Doak did the same and the two of them walked off a ways, sat down on a sandstone outcrop overlooking the road, and passed the makings. They were still building their smokes when I came up to them.

Brack just glanced at me and went back to scowling along the Paint Rock road. But Doak smiled kind of tired like and said, "Set down, kid, we got a little waitin' to do." When he'd said it and I'd eased down beside him, he looked at me again.

It was a long look this time. Frowning and worried and inside hurtful, as though he wanted to say something in the worst way he couldn't find the words to fit whatever it was that was eating him. He gave it up with a slow headshake for me, and a pretty hard stare for Brack. After that he handed me over the makings, still not saying anything more. He did it in the same way Sec had given me the *cigarillo*, not watching what I did and letting on like I had been rolling my own with the grown men right along.

I managed to make a smoke that was limper and lumpier than a three-day-old *enchilada*, and to dry all the extra spit off of it and get it going with only four matches. Then I couldn't keep still any longer. I just had to blurt out what was bothering me. I knew it wasn't any use talking to Brack. He was busy downing the last of the two pints he had brought along from Comanche to tail-off on. Besides, him and me never was close in the same way me and Doak were.

"Doak—"

"It's what they call me, Button."

"You said we had some waitin' to do."

"Thet's right, boy."

"Well, doggone it, what for? I mean, why here? I don't see nothin'.."

He nodded slowly. "You ain't looked hard enough, little pardner. Try agin." He chucked his head to indicate the Paint Rock road. "Way yonder, there, where she curls between them twin buttes. Low down. Right on the skyline. You see it?"

I did, and nodded back to let him know I did.

Likely he thought I was being pretty tough for a green kid, taking it without saying anything. The truth was I couldn't have made a sound to save my life. My throat had pulled in so hard and tight it was all I could do to breathe, let alone talk.

There had been a hot wind all day and that part of McCulloch County we were in was sandy and thin-soiled. The rain-damp was fairly well sucked out of it and it was getting dry enough to raise a tolerable decent dust. Which was what it was doing, right then, way out there across the North Fork *llano* where Doak had nodded. And it wasn't any wind-dust, either. Whirlygusts and sand devils just didn't act that low, drifty way. *That was horse dust.* And it meant only one thing.

My belly pulled in and knotted up so bad I thought I was going to be sick. Brack hadn't been wrong. He hadn't missed his Paint Rock road calculation by more than twenty minutes.

That was Rance Buchanan coming yonder.

Chapter Seven

Below us, where the Paint Rock road angled in off the prairie to cross over the Fork, it ran down through a little barranca to get to the bottomland level of the stream. At its lower end the cut was about thirty feet deep and no more than fifteen feet wide. It made a nasty trap for coach traffic coming in from the northwest and was the main reason the Paint Rock route had been abandoned by the stagelines just after the War, when there had been more road agents than paying passengers in that part of Texas.

Brack had been there before. You could tell that. He had homed in on that crossing from forty miles out on the wide open *llano*, as certain of himself as he would have been to hit the old homeplace coming in from Mineral Wells or Fort Worth, off one of his high lonesomes. And once there he had acted as "at home" as though he was in the cottonwood corral out back of the cookshack.

Neither Doak nor me said anything. We just looked at one another and thought our own thoughts, as we got on our ponies and followed him down off the rise. But if Doak was thinking the same thing I was, he was thinking that when big brother had been there before he hadn't been holding any stage ticket nor paid any honest fare to get there.

If there was any doubts about that, Brack now laid them to rest by the way he read off the lay of the land around the crossing as he led us toward the mouth of the barranca.

"Now you two listen." He scowled. "Also take a good look around you while you're doin' it. And don't cut in on me." We both nodded and he went on. "I figure this to run smooth but there never was a heist planned that somethin' couldn't go wrong with. It's why they invented fast hosses and face masks, understand?"

We understood all right. Maybe a lot more than he thought. But we still didn't say anything.

"Now in case somethin' goes wrong with this one," he said, scowling harder, "here's how we ride it." He pointed up the Fork, where it bent around the south wall of the barranca and disappeared into a tangle of cottonwood and brushwillow that looked solid enough to stop a rifle slug. "Offhand, you'd likely say a runt *javelina* couldn't get through thet scrub, yonder, if he'd bin dipped in antelope tallow and turpentined under the tail. Now, wouldn't you?"

We both nodded again. *Javelinas* were the nasty little wild musk hogs that infested the rough country off southwest, occasionally working up as far north as the San Saba and the Coleman, where we were. I'd never seen any but had heard plenty about what hellers they were, "looking like a bundle of bristles with a butcher knife stuck through the middle," and so contrary they'd tackle a man on foot in a minute. They hung natural to heavy cover and were said to be able to squeeze through any knothole they could get their nose into. So when Brack said that upstream brush looked *javelina*-proof, he was the same as saying it couldn't be dented by anything less than a ten-penny spike.

But he no sooner got us to agreeing with him on the bad look of that bank-tangle ahead then he broke in on our nods with one of his crooked, hard grins.

"Well, boys, you'd be wronger than a nigger saint in Nashville," he rasped. "If you foller around thet south wall, stickin' close to the base, you'll hit a track thet tunnels it clean through. Comes out at another little crossin', about a quarter mile up the Fork." He held up for a minute, and quit grinning.

"It'll only take one hoss at a time and you got to plaster yourself down like a sweat-stuck saddle blanket, or you'll git scraped off quicker'n a scalded hawg. But it's a way out. See you remember it." Again the little pause, then the last of it, quick and sharp.

"Once across the Fork, it leads up into thet pile of *mal país* you see juttin' up, yonder. And once up on top of them rocks, two men and a bareface boy could stand off Santy Ana's army till next spring. Amen. End of sermon."

I had never heard Brack talk so much nor act so stirred up. But when I opened my mouth to brace him on a few details, Doak caught my eye and shook his head. I'd never gone against Doak that I didn't later learn I shouldn't have, so I shut up. But the next minute, when Brack got off his horse and went up the barranca a ways to get his ear to the ground and listen for Buchanan's bunch, he grabbed my arm and gave me a look I'll never forget.

"Button," he said real quiet, "I got a bad feelin' about this. I ain't had nothin' to set on me so heavy since the night Ma died. I want you should listen and do just what I tell you and don't argue it none. You hear?"

I heard. And I sure wasn't about to argue it any. I'd been doing some tall thinking since the first sick excitement of seeing that far-off horse dust from up above. I was beginning to wish I had hung back to come down with old Sec and his Mex *vaqueros*. Or maybe even have stayed clean behind and just watched the ranch. So I just bobbed my head like it seemed I'd been doing ever since him and Brack came out of that beanery back in Comanche.

When I did, Doak went ahead. He still kept it low and quiet, but he didn't fool me any. He was scared.

"Now when we back Brack's play, you stay to his left, up agin thet south wall. The minute anything goes wrong, the second any of them touches a trigger before Brack does, you cut and run along thet wall. And, Button, you see you do it with your spurs all the way in. For if you don't, by Gawd, I'll be so close behind you I'll run right up your tail!"

He tried to lighten it up with that crinkly grin of his, which was about as much like Brack's as a friendly hound's to a loafer wolf's. But it wasn't any use. "Doak," I said, "I'm scairt. I'm so scairt I cain't hardly move." It was a hell of a thing to admit, but I knew he would understand and wouldn't say anything to Brack about it.

"*You're* scairt, boy!"

He laughed soft and warm, making out to size it down by whacking me on the shoulder, offhand and careless.

"Man alive! What you think this stuff is I'm settin' in? Saddle sweat?"

It still wasn't any good. He was scared, all right, but not for himself. Doak was a quiet one and softhearted and sweet-natured as any man ever born. But he wasn't afraid of God or the Devil or anything that walked on two legs in their image. I was glad, for him, that Brack came legging it back out of the barranca just then. It kept him from hurting himself anymore on my account, and spared me the upset of having to watch him while he did.

Brack was moving fast now. He swung up on his pony and yanked his saddlegun. "Five minutes!" he snapped. "Mebbe three, four. Let's go!"

We all had Winchesters, mine a brand-new Model '73, engraved at the factory with my name and given me that past Christmas by Dad. I had never fired it at anything more inclined to backtalk than a southbound jackrabbit and the idea of pointing it at a grown man and having him take me serious seemed crazy. But I reached under my leg and hauled it out when I saw Doak go for his.

I darn near dropped it, too. It felt all of a sudden heavy as a cast iron crowbar and awkward as a five-foot Kentucky squirrel rifle. But I knew it weighed only seven pounds and was less than forty inches long from buttplate to barrel-crown. So I held onto it, somehow.

We moved up to where the cut narrowed down to fifteen feet. There we sat and waited. Brack was in the center of the old wagon tracks. Doak was to his right. I flanked him to his left.

A minute went by. Then another one. Finally, three. It was so still I could hear Dad's watch ticking away in my vest pocket.

Brack tensed, easing up in his stirrups.

He cocked his head forward, like a redtail hawk on a cottonwood snag hearing a fieldmouse rustle the buffalo grass. He twisted around, signaled to us, reached up along his horse's neck and clamped his fingers across the bridge of his nostrils. Doak and me did the same.

Then I heard it.

The powdery *clump-a-clump-clump* of shod horses walking in deep dust.

After that there was a crawly twenty seconds of roller-bar bits and cartwheel Sonora spurs jingling, stirrup leathers squeaking, tired ponies grunting and blowing out as they picked up the welcome smell of the Fork water. And a last, endless, held breath when their shadows ran out of the cut ahead of them, long and tall and twilight black in front of the backing set of the six o'clock sun.

Then Rance Buchanan rode out.

Chapter Eight

For a spell—long enough to spill a rice paper full of pouch tobacco—nobody moved or made a sound.

Buchanan sat his horse looking at Brack. The four men behind him eyed Doak and me. I could hear the watch ticking again.

"You Buchanan?" said Brack pleasantly.

The other man studied him instead of answering him. He looked him over a full five seconds, and still didn't answer him. Instead, he half turned his head and gave a little nod to the others. They started edging their ponies clear of him.

"Hold them hosses, boys." Brack didn't jump it at them. He just sort of "suggested" it, as though maybe it would be a good idea if they'd set still a minute. They agreed that it would, apparently. Their ponies stopped moving.

"We'll start over agin," said Brack to the man in front. "You Buchanan?"

The thin rider shook his head, and now he talked.

"Never heard of him. Name's Lockhart."

"Sego Lockhart?" There was a funny look on

Brack's face. When the other answered him, the look spread to me and Doak. Only on us it wasn't funny. It was plain sick.

"The same. Who might be askin'?"

"Brack Starbuck."

"Heard of you." His voice was high and raspy, reminding me of the way a piece of hard chalk will squeal on a blackboard, or a sharp file hit a rusty nail in crossgrained wood. "Could be you've heard of me."

"Could be," was all the admission Brack made to the fact we had our Winchesters pinned on a mighty chancy customer. Maybe the chanciest.

Sego Lockhart wasn't a man, he was a legend. At least he was in our time and part of the country. They said of him that when God had got all done making up professional gunmen, he'd poured out what was left of the mix into the middle of Mason County. What had set up from that last batch of badman mortar had been Sego Lockhart.

He looked at Brack now, nodding in that nervous, quick way of his that was so like old Sec had figured the man would act who had downed Dad. "You still want to talk about Buchanan, or'd you rather quit while you're ahead?" He frowned.

"Git down off thet hoss," said Brack.

"Oh? What you got in mind?"

Sego asked it fast and choppy, the way he put everything. But I was beginning to see that it wasn't being nervous, not shaky nervous, that made him talk like that. He was only strung up and edgy in the same way a hot-blood horse is. Again, I had to think about old Secondido Gonzales telling me, so close, how he would be; and from no more than a line of bootprints in the dust out past the *galería*.

"I got in mind," growled Brack, "seeing if you walk crooked. Git down."

"No thank you."

Brack's eyes blazed. "I said git down, mister!"

Sego only shook his head. "So I take a little stroll. Then what?"

The whiskey and the drawn-out way things were going were getting to Brack now. His voice got deep and ugly and I saw that his hands were shaking when he punched the Winchester toward Sego.

"Then," he gritted, "providing you go lame in your onside foot, I'm going to beat you within an inch of your lousy life."

"And?"

"Put two slow holes in your belly, just like you done to my dad back yonder."

For the third time in the past five minutes I heard the watch ticking.

Then the man who had put it there was bobbing his big head at Brack.

"That," said Sego Lockhart, "might take a bit of doin'."

I never saw him move. But I saw the stab of flame and the smokeburst that came out of his left hand. And I heard Brack's bay scream like a woman and go up in the air and spin and scrash over backwards.

That first shot of Sego's, missing Brack and hitting his horse in the throat, was the only thing that kept all three of us from being killed. Brack was the best horseman I ever saw. He knew he was going clean over. He was off his bay the minute he started up, had hit the ground clear of him and started levering his Winchester before he went on over, smashing the saddle to a pulp. But between the time he parted company with the bay, and hit the ground on his feet, Sego got off two more shots. One at Doak. One at me. Both mighty near misses.

Mine cut away half my saddlehorn, quartering on off into the bank so tight past my stomach I could feel the push of the air ahead of it punching me like a fist. I figured Doak's must have been just as close and much the same shot, for I heard him yell and saw him bat at his stomach as he spun his horse over to cover Brack.

After that there wasn't time to see much.

Brack had got behind his downed horse, which had caved in and dropped as though it'd been hit with a slaughterhouse hammer. He was levering his rifle into the swirl of pony dust over in the barranca's throat, past Doak, and screaming for him to get the hell out of the way so he could see what he was doing. Doak yelled back at him and jumped his horse in my direction.

Other than Sego's three shots, the Mason City bunch never got into action. Apparently they didn't mean to hang around, boxed like they were in the squeeze of the barranca. Whether or not Brack hit any of them—for some reason Doak wasn't firing—was hard to tell. But it didn't look to me like he had. None of them, including Sego, was in sight by the time Doak had slid his dun up to me and gasped, "Git out, Button! Git out!" and then wheeled back to make a Comanche pickup of Brack.

It didn't seem possible that five men had evaporated themselves and their ponies out of that barranca throat inside of ten seconds, yet they had.

For as Brack swung up behind Doak, they were beginning to fire back from beyond the narrows. They had evidently skinned out of there only far enough to get back of the bend of the barranca walls before piling off their horses and running back on foot. There was still a lot of dust hanging in the air, however, and the daylight was late and uncertain down there in the bottom of the cut. It was all that saved us. I could see the dirt fly all around Doak's dun gelding and hear the lead smacking into and whining off of the wall beyond me as him and Brack headed my way. But neither them, nor the gelding, took any hits. In less than a dozen jumps the three of us were safe around the south wall bend, me in the lead. In another two, three jumps Mozo had me into the willow scrub.

It was dark as starlight inside that brush tunnel. All I could see, looking back, was that Brack and Doak were coming with a rush, right on Mozo's tail. Even that was more like *feeling* them than actually seeing them. I could make out neither one of them for sure, but only a smudgy double blob of swaying shadow that I knew was them. Yet, where I couldn't see too good, I could hear chilling plain. And the sound that was coming from back there was more frightening to me than any gunfire or scream of mortal-hit horse.

It was Brack crying.

Cursing, yes; and snarling at me to "ride up! ride up!" like he was mad enough to kill me for something I'd done, or was doing. But back of the foul language and raging orders to "push on, damn you, Button! push on!" there was a choke and strangle never put into any man's voice by outright anger, alone. Brack was bawling. The sound of the tears was as wild and wet and heartbroke as a lost kid's. And it put a shiver into me that ran clear down into my boottops.

Five minutes later I found out why.

We crossed over that North Fork four hundred yards above the Paint Rock ford, scrambling up the cliff beyond and into the rocks above.

At the top of the trail there was a little boulder-rimmed meadow that stood up a hundred feet over any other high point around. It wasn't more than forty yards across and was a natural hole-up if God ever designed one with three desperate brothers in mind. I knew, at once, it was the place Brack was heading for and that he'd said two men and me could stand off Santy Ana's army from. I slid Mozo to a stop and got off him as Brack and Doak topped out behind me.

Brack wasn't crying anymore and in the stiff climb up, I'd had time to get over the first upset of hearing him do so down in the brush below. I had also had time to remember that I'd froze up back in the barranca, not getting off so much as one shot to help out. Thinking to make it up to them for not using it before, I now grabbed my Winchester and dodged back past them as they came over the rise.

I'd hoped to see Buchanan and his bunch down below, so that I could cut loose at them and show Brack and Doak I'd got over my yellow. But I was out of luck. From the edge of the stream, where it broke free of the brush, to the lip of the rimrock where I now crouched so brave there wasn't a sign of life in or on that narrow trail. There was nothing at all down there, save the slow settle of our climbing dust.

I was still peering down, still poking and tensing my rifle to let on like I was cut out of the same cloth as my brothers and hadn't *really* been scared sick down there in the barranca, but had been maybe just saving my shots for when they'd count, when Brack's voice touched me on the shoulder.

"It's all right, Button. Slack off, boy."

I'd never had him to talk soft and gentle to me before. I knew, as I came around, that something had gone bad wrong. But in the first minute of looking, I didn't see it.

Him and Doak were still setting Doak's dun, easy and natural as though Brack's horse had broke a leg in a dog hole and Doak had packed him home, double, to get a new pony.

Then Brack was getting down from behind Doak and there was nothing easy or natural about it anymore.

Brack had stopped the dun close behind me. The last dull red of the sun was tipping the rimrock and slanting off across the little meadow. Its angle struck just above the dun's withers. Below that was a shadowy twilight purple. Above it was the splash and stain of the dropping sun. In its warm, lazy glow and just before he slumped and Brack caught him, I got a look at Doak's face.

It was the same as Dad's had been.

Empty and calm-eyed and unafraid. And looking far off and quiet into its last lonely sunset.

Chapter Nine

Brack didn't give me any time to break down. He pulled Doak off the horse and actually *dragged* him over toward an extra heavy outbreak of rock along the east rim. I couldn't take that. I ran after him. "Damn you, Brack!" I choked. "He ain't to be drug like thet, you hear!" He stopped and I bent down to get Doak's feet, so's he'd at least be carried decent and not hauled along like a grain-sack.

I never got to touch him. Brack lashed out with his boot, catching me across the wrists as I reached. I pulled back, mouth twisting with the pain of where his spur had raked me. I hated him then. He couldn't have missed it either. It was burning in me too hot and ugly. But, deep down, I was still deathly afraid of him and that was what he was watching.

"Now, boy," he said between his teeth, "you git yonder and look to them hosses. We're going need 'em. When you got 'em tied, hump your tail back over here and give me a hand."

I did like I was told. It took me a little time to get around Doak's dun and gentle him down. He'd been spooked by the smell of the blood and by the rough way Brack had handled him up the slope. By the time I got him quiet, and him and Mozo reins-tied to a mesquite snag, then got over to where Brack was, he had already rolled Doak into a deep crack in the caprock and was shoving loose scrabble and tub-size slabs of broken sandstone down on top of him.

I looked down in the hole, seeing the way Doak was all twisted and crumpled up in the bottom of the crevice, and the way his poor body was jumping and sagging to the thud of those big rocks. Then all of a sudden I couldn't see him. There was a white glare in front of my eyes, like I was looking straight up into the noon-high sun. I went for Brack as though I meant to kill him with my bare hands.

But he had been watching me.

He whirled around, catching me under the jaw with a backhand slash of his forearm as I came in. I felt my back crash against the hardscrabble and knew he'd knocked me flat. The next minute he pulled me to my feet and pinned me against the rimrock with his left hand.

He must have hit me with his open hand a dozen times, having to hold me up to keep me from sagging to the ground after the first three or four. Then he spun me away from the rock, kneed me in the stomach and kicked me away from him. That was the last I remembered of that.

When I crawled back up onto my hands and knees I was spitting blood and brush twigs but except for my ears ringing my head was as clear as a blown-glass bubble. I knew I'd gone crazy on Brack and that he'd had to beat it out of me.

He was never like Doak, not in any way. He didn't take time, now, to tell me he was sorry he had needed to do it, the way Doak would have done. The minute I got my knees under me, he grabbed me by the back of my collar and hauled me to my feet.

"You all right now, boy? You hearing good?"

I nodded yes, and spit out some more rock gravel and a part of one of my jaw teeth.

"Well, then, you listen to me!" He shoved me ahead of him to where the rim overhung the trail we had just come up. "Now you take a good long look down there, damn you!" he snarled. "And while you're at it, you take a good hard listen, too!"

I did it and after a minute he asked, "You hear thet?"

I nodded that I did.

There was a slithery sound of the brush moving around down below. With it came some ugly grunting and choppy, nervous squealing, the scary likes of which I'd never heard.

"*Gawd A'mighty!*" I breathed, "what is it? Sounds like a pen of starvin' hawgs gittin' slopped. Or a sty full of brood-sows after one another's pigs."

"Them's *javelinas!*" rasped Brack. "We kicked up a whole big herd of them back near the main crossin'. Jest after we hit the brush. Must have been fifty, sixty head of them."

"Naw! Thet many?" For some reason the slobbery jaw-chopping from down there in the dark of the Fork brush was putting my neck hairs on end. "What's rilin' them so? They always carry on like thet when you stir them up?"

"No, by Gawd, they don't," said Brack. "Generally, they'll light out so quick and quiet you'd never know they was there in the first place. That is, unless."

The way he tailed it off didn't let any of my nape bristles lay down again. "Unless what?" I said, swallowing hard.

"Unless there's fresh blood around. Blood sets them crazy every time. They'll foller and tackle anything thet's bin hurt."

"What you gittin' at, Brack?"

"They're trailin' us, Button. We got to git out'n here fast."

"Naw!" I said again. I still hadn't got his meaning and it was all I could think to say. "Why for?" I went on. "Hell, they ain't no bigger'n a span'el dog. How they goin' to bother us?"

Brack swung around on me, his eyes going pale in the darkening twilight.

"I told you to look and listen, boy, not ask questions. Now you do it!"

He broke off, jerking his thumb down the rise.

"Them little pigs is killers, you hear? Once they've got the smell of warm blood in their snouts they'll go for anything that moves or breathes. It don't make no difference to them if it's a full-growed man or a fresh-dropped calf. Just so long as it's got a smell of blood to it and is afoot. Doak bled a lot, all the way through thet brush down there and up the slope to here. You foller me now, boy?"

"Yes sir!" I said sir to him lots of times, just like I did to Dad and Doak, though not for the same reasons. "Yes sir, I sure do!" I repeated, still having trouble getting it to go past my Adam's apple.

"Well, you'd better, Button," he said low and quick. "Lookit down yonder."

I glanced over the rim, peering hard into the darkness below.

My stomach crawled and I got pale.

I could see them moving out from the brush. They looked no bigger nor more dangerous than so many tumblebugs from up where we were. But they didn't sound like tumblebugs. And they didn't move like them.

They were coming fast. Shoving and fighting and squealing for the lead and the first chance to root their wrinkled snouts in the next bloodspot up the trail. You got the same sick feeling looking down at them, as you did when you spotted a raunchy yearling with a week-old hole full of screw-worm maggots where he'd got hurt and the heelflies had blown him rotten.

Brack's voice, soft and gentle for the second time I could remember, nudged me from behind.

"All right, Button. Let's git on with it. We cain't leave them git at old Doaker."

I was too choked up to answer back, but I shook my head that we couldn't, and ran to keep up with him as he legged it for the crevice. We rolled in another ten or fifteen big rocks, some of them needing both of us to tilt them over the edge. When we'd done with it, no wild pigs, nor nothing else short of Judgment Day was going to get at or to bother our brother Doak down in that hole.

But we'd squandered time we didn't have to spend.

We stood there a bad minute, looking down at him. Neither of us had the nerve to try any praying. Nor to say anything out loud, at all. At least I didn't dast try it. Finally, Brack just sort of knuckled his hat brim and nodded down in a low whisper. "So long, Doaker, we got to be goin' along," and turned away. He moved quick for the ponies, with me right behind him.

We hadn't covered half the way to them when Mozo threw up his head, whickered sharply, pinned his ears and swung his rump toward the head of the slope trail.

"Run for it!" yelled Brack. "He's winded the pigs!"

If there was one thing I could do, it was run.

I could run like a forkhorn buck. Or a pear-thicket steer. Or a coyote downwind of a dog-wolf.

I beat Brack to the horses by ten steps and was in time to pile on Mozo and grab Doak's big dun by the cheekstrap just as he reared and tore loose of the mesquite clump. That horse would have been long gone and far away, if I hadn't got ahold of him. He was near crazy with the pig fear and had he got loose I never would have headed him in time to swing back and pick Brack up.

As it was, the lead sow of the bunch got to Brack, anyway, ripping his calf open to the bone as he got his foot in the dun's stirrup. Her tushes hung up in his boottop and he dragged her six or eight jumps before he could kick her off. She fell under the dun's feet and he near went down, but Brack stayed with him and got him free of her, though he was running plumb crazy now.

"Give your hoss his head!" Brack yelled at me, fighting the dun to try and hold him in hand and let me and Mozo get ahead. "For Christ's sake let him out, Button! I cain't handle this crazy bastard. You got to lead him or he'll take me over the edge!"

"All right, hang on to him!" I yelled back. "He'll foller Mozo, crazy or not!"

I screwed myself down in the saddle and turned Sec's old mustang runner loose. He went by the dun like he was a settlement plowhorse and, looking back, I saw that it had worked and that the dun was lining out after us, not running blind anymore. The next minute Mozo was on his way down the south side of the rimrock drop-off. What followed was the worst sixty seconds I ever put in on top of a horse.

The south trail fell off a good hundred feet to the level of the *llano*, below. And it made that drop in less than a quarter of a mile. The pitch of it was so steep that old Mozo had to take a good half of it setting on his haunches like a black bear going down a rockslide. The rest of the trail quartered back and forth across the slope in a series of hairpin bends that would have given a goat a bad time in broad daylight. But that old Mozo horse got down it without a stumble and, what's more, picked such a good way of doing it that Doak's wild-eyed dun was able to stay upright behind him all the way.

Once down, we lit off southeast across the

prairie. We hadn't got more than a mile or so away when Brack said we'd have to hold up. His leg was bothering him pretty bad.

While I peeled off my undershirt and tore it into wrapping strips, he pulled his boot and poured the blood out of it. He did it like he'd no more than stepped into a deep spot wading a buffalo wallow and got it full of water. It made me quease up inside just to watch him do it, but all he said was, "Cain't take no chances catchin' cold with wet feet at my age."

While I bound up the gash as best I could, he lay back against the little cutbank we'd stopped in and built himself a smoke. When he'd got it going good, he took a deep lungful and started bringing me up to date on where we stood.

It was bumping into Sego Lockhart in Rance Buchanan's place, he said, that made the whole difference for us. It was what had got Doak killed and was apt to do the same for us if I was going to take all night wrapping up that little scratch on his leg. He never did let on how come it was so, but he went on to tell me that we could bank on Sego knowing that brush-tunnel trail and these hole-up rocks back yonder as well as he did. What that meant was that he would also know just how long it would take a good rider to get up and over that rimrock, providing he was on a top horse and in a big hurry to hit for Mason City.

This added up to us, Brack said. And it gave us maybe twenty more minutes before we could expect company to be coming in from the northwest.

The point of not waiting around to welcome

them was nothing personal but had only to do with a slight matter of money. Adding one thing to another—say like Dad's $1000 deposit to the amount the market had gone up the past forty days—it meant something like $25,000 to Rance Buchanan if nobody named Starbuck showed up in Mason City by midnight, May 7.

"We kin take the liberty of assumin'," Brack finished off, "thet where thet kind of money is involved Sego's boys are bein' paid purty fair wages and will want to do a good job for Mr. Buchanan. Comin' to Sego himself, he ain't a salary man. He'll be takin' percentages and you kin lay a freemartin heifer agin five proved brood cows thet his cut'll be higher than a mad cat's back."

It wasn't like Brack to look on the happy side of a bad shake. I could tell he was trying, overhard for him, to lighten things up for my benefit. To sort of back me up and get my mind off of Doak laying crumpled up back there under those rocks. It didn't come off. Not with Brack. He never did have the Doaker's sly way of seeing things and of making you laugh over a busted cinch or getting kicked in the belly by a bull calf.

No matter, I didn't let on. I just grinned, stiff faced, and held his stirrup for him to get his bum foot into and said, "Sure, I reckon you're right, Brack. How you want to ride her from here?"

He told me, and I climbed up on the Mozo horse and pointed him where Brack said we wanted to go.

I took the lead, naturally.

On a moonblack night like this one it took a *criollo*, a pure Spanish mustang like Mozo, to see prairie dog holes in the dark. And on the trail Brack and me were riding now, it wouldn't do to stumble. Not again, anyway. Not twice in front of the likes of Sego Lockhart. Brack, nor nobody else, had to tell me that.

With his kind, mistakes came one to a customer.

Chapter Ten

We didn't stumble. It was forty-five miles from the North Fork crossing of the San Saba, down to Mason on the main Llano. We rode it in seven hours, cutting in out of the sagebrush to jog down the mainstem about one o'clock in the morning.

Right off, I saw that this was some town.

Mason, or Mason City—it was called both ways—wasn't anything near like Mineral Wells or Salesville or Palo Pinto, the little burgs I was used to. They bedded down with the pullets and rolled out with the roosters. Not Mason.

Mason was the headquarters cowtown out that way. It was in the middle of a big grass country and was the main gathering point for trail herds making up to go north from that part of Texas. It was more than that, too, Brack told me, as we walked our horses down the street with him looking for a likely saloon.

In '74, the federal law, which was all that counted with the real hardcases, hadn't come much west of Austin City, nor north of San Antone. Only the Rangers got out into that Mason County country and they didn't get there more than once or twice a year and only then if they were running out a spe-

cial bad murder warrant, or had come to put down
some outbreak of Indian trouble—the Comanches
still kicking up an occasional scare even that late,
though nowheres near like they had in Dad's and
Mother's day.

As a result, Brack said, Mason County had become a sort of stopping-over place between their
last job and the Mexican line for half the high-line
riders in the outlaw business. There had even
been some talk, he told me, that the honest ranchers were aiming to run an "outlaw roundup" in
the county just the same as they would a big beef
gather. But of course that was just talk.

"Look at it this way, Button," Brack grunted,
pointing down the street to the blaze of oil lamps
and double-hung slat doors just starting to burn
bright and swing wide at 1 A.M. "Mason, she's a
sort of a cross between a straight cowtown like
Doan's Crossing up on Red River, and a out-and-
out rustler roost like Mobeetie up yonder past the
Injun Territory in the panhandle. Or, better yet,"
he added with a hard scowl, "put it this way. You
could ride till hell froze over and linger a spell on
the crust, without findin' a better town *not* to turn
your back on to nobody in."

I just kept looking at those bright lights. They
like to blinded me. Either way you wanted to put
it, so far as I was concerned, right then, Mason
was a wide open and a real tough, exciting town.

Pretty quick Brack saw a saloon that suited him.
We turned in in front of it and he got down. I
started to follow him but he gave me a wave to
stay mounted. I did, and he looked the place over
real careful, holding up for a full minute while he

watched it and the men coming and going in and out of it. Finally he gave me a nod.

"Take the hosses acrost to the livery, yonder." He pointed to a big barn across the street. "The hotel's thet crummy shack next to it. Git us a room, best they've got." He peeled a twenty off the roll of traveling money Dad had given Doak at the start. There must have been $200, which was the most in cash I'd ever seen in one chunk. He caught me looking at it and gave me one of his twisty grins.

"Dad figured it'd be Doaker handlin' the payroll. If he'd a'knowed I was goin' to wind up with it, we'd be sleepin' under the stars and eatin' saddlebag beans. Somehow, Button, your old man never trusted me with money."

I nodded back and should have let it go at that. But I was worried about all that money, and trying hard to sort of fill in for Doak, as to keeping count of it.

"Brack—!"

He had already started away when I bleated it out. He came back around with the grin long gone.

"Yeah?"

It bluffed me and I stalled, white-livered as usual.

"How'll I sign in at the hotel? Mebbe we'd ought to use a fictayshus name."

"A what?"

"Somebody else's name."

"The hell. You sign in jest the way it is in Ma's Bible. I *want* them to know there's Starbucks in town."

"Yes sir. There's only the one other thing—"

"Sure, Button." He spread his legs, slanting his heavy-stubbled jaw up at me and rubbing it real slow. "You jest name it now." Brack was thirsty. His nerves were frazzled raw by the long ride and the throb in his hurt leg. I knew how he would take it but I thought of Doak and Dad and our contract herd, and I had to say it.

"The drinkin'."

"Uh-huh, what about the drinkin'?" He said it awful quiet. Way too quiet. I folded again.

"Nothin'. I'll go put the hosses up."

Looking past him as I started to move the horses, I saw a couple of local cowhands had slowed down along the boardwalk to listen to us. Brack caught my look and swung around on them.

"Move it along. I want an audience I'll go on the stage and you kin pay to watch," he told them.

"Sure thing, stranger." The smaller one of them bobbed his head. "No hard feelin's."

"It's the only kind I got," said Brack. "Cut and drift."

The second man, a big stoop-shouldered cuss who didn't appear to stampede worth a damn, took a second look at him.

"You stayin' long, mister?" he asked slowly.

"Long as I need. Who wants to know?"

The big man moved out from under the boardwalk roof in front of the saloon. The little man followed him. When they stepped into the street the lamplight from the swinging doors cut across them, belt-high. I saw the wink of the pewter stars hung on their saggy vests and figured we were in for it. Way in. Past our hocks and halfway to our haunches.

Brack didn't like lawmen. He never had. It was something to do with the trouble he had been in as a boy. Whatever it was he had done, or'd had done to him, it had left him powerful down on peace officers.

"Name's Blackburn," the big man drawled. "Ewell Blackburn. Mason County Sheriff's office."

"What the hell you mean, *office?*" sneered Brack. "You're the sheriff, ain't you?"

"I reckon I am. Who are you?"

Brack moved into him. He did it deliberate, so that the lamplight would hit him square and give Sheriff Blackburn and his deputy a good look at him.

"Name's Brack Starbuck. Don't forgit it. And don't forgit the face thet goes with it."

"Not likely to," agreed the sheriff. "Rememberin' names and faces is the best part of what I git paid for. Starbuck, eh?" He scratched his chin. He looked Brack over, hat to bootheels. Then he shook his head. "Ain't no Starbucks down this way. Least, none I recollect right off."

"We ain't from down this way."

"Figures. Care to say what way you *are* from?"

"Love to!" snapped Brack. "We're the Mineral Wells Starbucks. Old Henry Starbuck's boys. See you spread it around."

The sheriff shifted his quid of Bulldog cut-plug, parked a stream of Burley juice between Mozo's forefeet, nodded at me.

"What's the kid's name?"

"Button," said Brack.

"Smart kid. Don't talk much."

"Not as much as some sheriffs."

"Uh-huh. Well, watch yourself, Starbuck." He looked at Brack thoughtfully for a minute, then said good night to him and started off. He held up and shot me a kind of a funny sideways nod and added, "Good night, Button," real pleasant. I answered, "Good night, sir," quick and polite and without thinking. I got another pleasant little nod from him and a real hard look from Brack for doing it.

When he'd walked on off, Brack whipped around on me, mean as sin. "You all done lickin' the sheriff's hand, yella belly?" he gritted out.

I didn't answer him. He was my brother but I had no use for Brack when he got within the sight and smell of where they sold whiskey. He knew it, too, and it only made him uglier.

"Now you git, damn you! and don't you bother comin' back. There ain't nothin' going' to happen to me, nor the money. You hear? Not nothin' you could help by standin' back suckin' your thumb and watchin' the bullets fly past!"

I heard all right. It was all he ever said about me not firing a shot back at the barranca when he was pinned down back of his pony and Doak shot through the belly and dying atop his. But I never forgot it.

"Yes sir," I mumbled, and got out of there.

Across the street, the livery stable man was setting out in front of his place on an old busted-down buggy seat puffing a corncob pipe and counting the stars. He was a grizzled old coot with a kind eye and a friendly bush of clean, frizzy whiskers.

"Eve'nin', bub." He looked me over close but not in any way hostile. "Whut kin I do ye fer?"

"Couple of boxstalls, mister, and a nosebag of wet bran if you've got any," I said. "Our ponies are purty well played out."

"The buckskin ain't."

"He's half razorback hawg. How about them stalls?"

"Ye want to trade either of 'em?"

"Nope, jest feed 'em."

"Give ye four hundred dollars American fer the buckskin."

"He ain't mine, and all the pesos in El Paso wouldn't buy him if he was."

"Spanish hoss, eh?"

"Pure."

"Reckoned as much. Feller don't see too many of them real *criollos* around no more. Give ye five hundred."

"Listen, oldtimer," I eased down, wincing to my thigh muscles coming unclamped, "jest give me a couple of stalls and a bucket of bran. I'm tuckered."

"Reckon I kin see thet, too, bub. Ye look done in as a dancehall gal six o'clock Sunday mornin'." He still didn't stir, nor let up puffing his pipe. So I just gathered the reins and led Mozo and Doak's hammerhead dun in past him. "Where'll I put 'em?" I growled as I went by.

"Six and eight," he called after me. "Seven's full of broke axles and old buggy parts. Bran's in the green bin with the bucket settin' on it. Water's out back to yer left."

I got the horses put up and going good on the bran. They weren't too warm, just used up some, so I didn't bother walking them out or rubbing them down. I had just given Mozo a good-night ear-scratching when the old man limped in under the street entrance lantern. He finally had his pipe out of his mouth and he stabbed it at me like he at last meant to do business.

"Git in thet empty number seven stall, young un!" he ordered sharply. *"And see ye don't sneeze!"*

I wasn't that done in that I couldn't see he was dead serious. I slipped inside the stall and stood back under an old landau top. I had no more than made myself small, and the old man put the harness snap back on the stalldoor hasp, when I heard the jingle of bit chains and the squinching of saddle leather swing in at the street door.

The next minute I was listening to the slow walk of several tired horses down the fetlock-deep mulch of the barn aisle. They came to a halt right outside stall seven, just short of the old man who was now making out to have just shut Mozo into stall six. The first voice I heard was one I'd heard somewhere before. And not very long before.

I took a big tuck in the breath I was caught holding, and stood there with the cold sweat channeling down my backbone.

It was Sego Lockhart.

Chapter Eleven

"Old man," he said, "we're lookin' for two hosses."

"Enny partic'lar cut'n color?"

"A muddy, outsize dun," said Sego, "and a little lineback buckskin, a real *bayo* coyote."

It was a sharp distinction as to color. It marked Sego for as close a hand at calling a horse's cut as the old man himself.

Most folks lumped dun and buckskin together. Down our way a buckskin was set apart. He had to have a true black mane and tail, black stripe down his back and black points, with usually black leg-rings up to his knees in front and hocks behind. We sometimes called them "lineback" or "zebra" duns to distinguish them from regular duns like Doak's. But mostly we called them buckskins, like they did up north. It was why, when the old man had gone to $500 for "the buckskin," I'd known he was talking about Mozo and not Doak's sandy-maned scrub.

"Well," said the old man to Sego, having taken time out to fire up his pipe. "I got 'em, but they ain't fer sale."

"Ride easy, Pegleg," warned one of the men. "Sego ain't funnin'."

"Yeah," added another of them, in a voice near as young and respectful as mine. "We wouldn't none of us want to see you git hurt, Mr. Yates."

Well, I was learning things fast. Even if I couldn't see any of them, hunkered down like I was under that cussed buggy-top. Evidently the old man's name was Pegleg Yates and most of the bunch knew him pretty well, but Sego didn't. At least he didn't call him by his name and you could guess from that that he didn't live regular in Mason. It just made me wonder again at old Sec's uncommon canny gift for reading sign. Just like he had said, the leader of the bunch was a professional hardcase, but the others were most likely local cowhands and not regular gunslingers.

"Now don't ye worry, Cheyenne," Pegleg answered up. "Nor you, neither, Billie Joe. I know Sego ain't the kind to laugh hisse'f to death and I'm not workin' up to gittin' hurt. It's jest that he ain't said whut he wants of them two hosses and I'm in the business mostly to buy and sell. Now ain't thet so, boys?" he appealed to the rest.

"You talk too much, old man." It was Sego taking over again. "How long them hosses bin here?"

"Better'n half an hour," lied Pegleg cheerfully. "I'd say the boys whut brung 'em in is a'ready bedded down next door and a'sleepin' peaceful."

"Was one of them packin' double?"

"Double whut?" asked Pegleg innocently.

Above the top board of the box, I saw Sego's head and shoulders move into view as he shoved his horse forward.

Back at the barranca, one of the things about him that I hadn't been too scared to notice was that he carried a rawhide Mexican quirt. It was one of those real mean ones, loaded with buckshot in the butt and having a thin spring-steel core that ran clear to its braid-ends. It was a good three feet long and could lay a horse or a man wide open if put to them proper. I saw him swing it, now, and heard it cut into the old man. When it did, I heard the one they called Cheyenne laugh low and harsh.

"Double riders?" said Sego Lockhart.

"No." I could tell by the old man's voice that he was hurt bad. "They was only the two of 'em. Big one got off yonder at the Lone Star. The kid brung the hosses over."

"Where's the kid now?" It was still Sego, though he had eased his horse back and I couldn't see him anymore.

"Gone to bed, I reckon, like I said. He was headin' thetaway, anyhow."

"All right, old man." I could hear them turning their horses. "You'd better do the same. I don't want to see you outside agin tonight."

They were gone then, Pegleg limping after them to the door. He let down the street lantern by its pulley, blew it out and hoisted it back up again. I was right behind him as the barn went dark.

"Now ye listen to me, young un," he warned me hoarsely, "and ye do jest like I say."

"Yessir!" I piped. "I sure am beholden to you, Mr. Yates."

"Never ye mind thet! Ye've got a pardner in bad trouble yonder. I cotton to the way ye handle yerse'f, boy, and I mean to he'p ye.

"Now ye git out'n the back way and hit through the sagebresh, four buildin's down. Thet's the sheriff's office. Don't bother knockin', step right in the back door. Jest tell old Ewell Sego Lockhart's bin on yer track and is headin' fer the Lone Star.

"Ye won't need to elabryate none. He knows Sego, and he seen yer sidekick go in the saloon."

"I'm still mighty beholden to you, Mr. Yates. Likely I won't forgit it."

"Name's Pegleg!" he snapped. "And ye'd best fergit it. I wouldn't want it knowed around thet I give ye a boost. Now git!"

"I'm Button Starbuck," I said, and cussed myself the minute I did. It was the first decent chance I'd had to use my proper name, and I'd been so flustered I'd messed it up. "I sure will remember what you've did for me, regardless."

"Ye won't be rememberin' nothin', happen ye don't light yer shuck out'n here, damn ye!" he growled, and gave me a rough shove down the barn aisle.

I stumbled on through the dark and out the back way, blundering over anything and everything I could find. Yet, clumsy-scared or not, I couldn't help beginning to feel the best I had since turning yellow on Brack and Doak back in the barranca.

I had been in the toughest town in West Texas no more than twenty minutes and had hopeful reason to believe I'd already made one good friend, and maybe two. One thing was certain. I was going to find out about that second friend before *another* twenty minutes ticked away. Or ten. Or maybe even five.

He was slow-talking, soft-drawling Sheriff Ewell Blackburn.

The sheriff and his chief deputy, Tobe Edwards, were having a cup of coffee when I got there. There was nobody else in the office, at least not that I could see by spying through the cracks in the boarded-up back window. So I went on in through the woodshed door that let into the rear of the office from the alley, back. Like Pegleg had said, I didn't bother to knock, and near got myself killed for the oversight.

The woodshed was a little lean-to tacked onto the main building and had no inside door into the office. It just opened onto it with only an old cowhide curtain as a divider.

From where I came in, I could see the sheriff setting at his desk with his back to me. He was talking to Tobe and didn't appear to hear me. But the first step I took hit a loose floorboard. It let out a sharp crack and felt like it was going to give out from under me. I jumped sideways so as not to go through the floor. That was all that kept my first visit to Mason City from being my last.

That old Sheriff Ewell Blackburn was a fooler.

He was a long ways from being young. Back in the lamplight from the Lone Star's swinging doors, I'd guessed him for about sixty. But a kid seventeen naturally thinks anybody past thirty is on his way over the hill and that a man forty has long ago gone over it and ought to be unsaddled and put out to pasture before he breaks clear down and has to be shot. So Sheriff Blackburn was most likely about fifty.

But the way he came up off that chair when I hit that creaky floorboard, he could have been fifteen.

And on his way up, and around, he slung two shots square through that back door.

My ears were still ringing from the blasts when he held up with his thumb on the hammer for the third one and called out calmly, *"Quién es?"*

"Button Starbuck!" I managed to gasp. "For Gawd's sake don't shoot agin, Sheriff!"

"Well, now, Button, you come on out slow and gentle and mebbe I won't." I couldn't see his mouth under the droop of his big walrus mustache, but I could see his eyes above it. He wasn't grinning.

I moved out like he said and stood there feeling foolish as a cub bear caught sucking his paw.

"I'm sure sorry, Sheriff!" I stammered. "Pegleg, uh, Mr. Yates, he said there wasn't no need to knock, just come on in the back way."

"Pegleg's a damned old fool, boy. What you want?"

I told him quick enough. I knew that all hell was due to bust its belly-cinch up at the Lone Star any minute. And I knew that brother Brack wasn't the kind to wait for an invitation to begin his share of the busting.

"All right, Button," said the sheriff, when I'd finished, "we'll see what we kin do. You come along. Your kind either gits killed or educated awful fast. Mebbe there's yet time to learn you not to walk up quiet behind *anybody* in this man's town. Best bring the sawed-off, Tobe," he told his little deputy. "There's still nothin' like a double load of buckshot to stall off a set of sixgun artists."

Tobe reached back of the door and brought out a stagged-off, cylinder-bore Parker double. The tubes looked big enough to drop a quarter down, sideways, and when he broke it at the breech to shove in fresh shells, I saw that they were ten-gauges.

The sheriff picked his hat off the wall peg, blew out the office lamp and said, "We'll split here as usual. You come with me, boy."

Outside, Tobe set off up the street toward the Lone Star, moving slow. The sheriff and me went straight across the street and down between two buildings, moving fast. When we came out at the rear of them, he said, "Now I'll show you how to go in through a back door proper, boy. See you remember it."

A couple of minutes later we were standing out behind the Lone Star. He gave his gunbelt a hitch and for the first time let down a little.

"She's a dirt floor through the storeroom so don't worry about no loose boards." I couldn't see his face in the dark but I could hear the grin in the way he said it. "Jest don't fall into no empty whiskey barrels and don't cough without excusin' yourself."

We went in, me following him so close we got by with one shadow. He held up behind a rickety door that was standing a quarter of the way open, and gave us a good look at what was going on out in the saloon.

It wasn't much.

The Lone Star wasn't any Dallas or Fort Worth funhouse. Not like I'd heard Brack tell of them, with their flossy women cadging drinks off the highrollers, their foreign fiddle players to dance by, their draped-off cubbyholes where you could take a girl and get fresh with her, their white-coat waiters and big games going at a dozen tables and bow-tie piano players and all such fancy goings on.

In fact, the Lone Star nor anything else about Mason City was really first class. It was just that any place with more than two saloons and where they kept the lights going after dark was a big town to me. So, likely it wasn't much I was seeing through that door-crack but it was my first look at big city sin in action.

Over at the bar, Brack stood off by himself. He had bought a quart and had already lowered it four fingers. He took two more big jolts while I watched him. At the tables scattered across the room from the bar, there were a couple of little games going; one stud, one three-toed Pete. There were two painted-up girls being pawed over at another table by a couple of two-bit beer drinkers. Past them, in the far, dark corner a handsome-looking Spanish girl was getting pulled and hauled at by a drunk who meant business.

That was mighty exciting, I thought. I held up to watch it, forgetting all about Brack and Sego.

She was a mean-built girl and moved wicked with her body. She didn't have much of a dress on to begin with and the drunk was set on getting his hand down inside of what top it had. She wasn't fighting him more than enough to make sure he got to what he was going after. Just as he did, and I saw the big curvy bulge of the first breast I'd ever looked at come popping better than halfway out of her dress, I caught an elbow in my ribs that like to caved them in.

"Pay attention, boy!" muttered the sheriff. "I didn't bring you here to learn you how to buy a six-bit woman for forty cents worth of warm beer."

"Yessir," I whispered, sneaking another look anyway. "Where you suppose Sego has gone to? I don't see him no place."

"You will. Keep your eyes peeled out front. He's bin down the street to the Painted Lady, checking in for orders from headquarters. He's about due to show here, providing Buchanan ain't told him to hold off."

"Buchanan?" I said fumblingly. I hadn't told him anything about our deal or why we were down there, and it took me short.

"Rance Buchanan," he growled, eying me. "Sego's his boy. He don't go to the bathroom less'n he holds up his hand for Rance to see. And don't you let on to me you don't know it, boy, you hear? If Sego's after you and your brother, you got to be after Buchanan. That's the way it works between them two."

"Yessir," I said again, and had sense enough to shut up. That is, I reckon I had. The way things picked up in the next breath, there wasn't really time to tell.

"Watch yourself," the sheriff said suddenly. "Yonder they come."

I followed his look across the smoke and sick yellow light of the saloon, to the street doors. I could see the black shadows of the horses moving into the rail, outside. Brack saw them too. Drunk or sober, he was a hard man to come up behind.

I now saw he had picked his place at the bar, not just happened onto it.

The main light in the Lone Star came from an overhead chandelier that had a big round top-shade. It threw a circle of light around three quarters of the room, including the front of it by the doors. But back where Brack was, at the foot of the bar, he was standing just inside that light circle. He needed only to ease two steps back and he was in the corner shadow. He did it just as Sego stalked in from the street.

"Your big brother's bin around," said Sheriff Blackburn softly, and that was all.

Sego stopped just inside the lamplight, his four men spreading out behind him. He squinted to the light in his eyes, but he had Brack spotted and was looking right at him.

"I heard you was still lookin' for me, Starbuck." His chalk-scrape voice broke me out in goose bumps all over. "Well, I reckon you're seein' me. Are you hearin' me?"

"Come a little closer," said Brack out of his shadow. "My ears ain't too good."

Sego chopped his head sharp and quick. He started to move on in. Behind him came his men.

It was the first look I'd had at him down off a horse and in good light. And for the third time I thought of old Sec Gonzales and his dead-sure sign reading.

Sego was only medium tall but he had the longest legs I ever saw and took the stride of a man who would top him a full head. With his tremendous barrel chest, short body, thick hunched shoulders, big stary-eyed face, warty skin and legs bent bowed worse than a rickety Indian's, he didn't look like a man. He looked like an ugly lunker bullfrog trying to look like a man.

And as he came for Brack I saw the one other thing about him that made me know the guns were going to go off for sure.

He limped bad in his left leg.

Not ten feet from Brack he held up, his long arms dangling loose and awkward looking. But it was the awkward look of a big grizzly reared up on his hind feet and swaying gently and set to swing so fast a man would never know what hit him.

"Close enough?" he said to Brack.

"Close enough," came his answer, quick and soft.

But it didn't come from Brack.

It came from Mason County Sheriff Ewell Blackburn.

Chapter Twelve

The sheriff stood just inside the well of the lamp-light. He was three steps to the right and at an angle to Brack and Sego. In the jump and flicker of the tilted chandelier, the three of them made a harsh and scary picture.

"Now, Sego," said the sheriff, "let's move slow. Starbuck, ease off. And step out here where I can see you. I got a little speech to make."

Brack moved into the full light. He didn't say anything. Neither did Sego. Both of them were too busy with their eyes. They snaked their looks from each other, to the sheriff, to the side tables, to the barkeep and back to themselves again. They checked everything in the room that they could without turning their heads.

You didn't have to be a gunman to read their thoughts. They were searching for that last-minute break on the part of somebody caught in the show-down. The break that would give one of them the eye-bat advantage of the first clean shot. The sheriff didn't even break stride over the stall.

"While you're lookin' around," he said, "don't fergit to check the front door."

Sego's men, bunched behind him, took the hint

first. When they had, they melted away from him like he was a strychnine wolf bait. This cleared the line of vision to the street doors for all of us but Sego; and he could read the bad news in the spread and shift of Brack's eyes.

Standing just inside the entrance, half in and half out of the lamp shadow, his back to the cracked adobe of the front wall, was Ewell Blackburn's mousy little deputy. The important half of him was lined sharp and clear by the sputtering coal-oil light. "Go ahead," the sheriff urged Sego. "Take your look. I'll watch Starbuck for you."

Sego turned his head, just far enough to bring Tobe Edwards into his eye-corners.

You could see the tension go out of him. He came uncoiled, slow and careful, like a sidewinder that's decided not to strike. All of a sudden he didn't look any more dangerous than a garter snake.

Nor did Brack.

They both just stood there looking lonesome and useless as two stray sheepdogs caught in a hostile cowtown.

It's funny how a sawed-off shotgun will do that to a tough man. Especially when it's ten-gauge and not loaded for quail. And when the hunter who's got it leveled at your belt buckle is fifteen feet away with his thumb laying light on the double hammers.

Neither Brack nor Sego wanted to get cut in two for the sake of keeping up appearances.

"Well," nodded the latter to Brack, "I don't know about you, Starbuck, but I pass." It was the first time I had seen him grin. It put me in mind of the way a human skull looks like it's grinning at you, no matter how the man died that it came from. "I check to your raise, Sheriff," he leered. "Let's see the spots on your cards."

"Starbuck?" said the sheriff.

"Yeah, me too. Lay 'em down," growled Brack.

The old lawman looked them over, nodded slowly.

"All right, they read this way. Sego and his boys are goin' to turn around and git out of here. They're goin' to git on their hosses and head straight out of town, south. If they're half smart, they'll keep right on ridin' till they hit Buchanan's ranch and their bunkhouse bedrolls." He broke off, swung sharply my way. "Come on out here, boy."

I came out, afraid to look at Brack and afraid not to. I knew what he would be thinking about me fetching the sheriff on him. And he was. The single look he threw me would have withered a split-oak fencepost.

"Comin' to you, Starbuck," the sheriff took up with Brack, "you and your kid brother are goin' to climb your ponies and point 'em north. Unless you were busy in the backhouse when the brains was passed out, you'll not bother lookin' back. You kin stay the night but you're to be up and out of town come daybreak. Any questions?"

"One," said Brack.

"Name it."

"You all done with your little speech?"

"I am."

"All right. Then I aim to make one."

Brack stepped to the bar and picked up his

bottle. He poured himself a tall shot and downed it. When he came around, the whiskey was burning dark and ugly in his pale eyes.

"Every one of you sons in this saloon mark down what I say. You kin use it for evidence agin me at the trial. I'm goin' to kill Sego Lockhart and hunt down every man that walked through them doors with him tonight. Him and them shot down my old daddy in cold blood up along the Brazos two days ago. They done it on the orders of Rance Buchanan to keep us from takin' delivery on 1600 head of steers thet our daddy contracted for way back last winter.

"Me and the kid are down here to git them cattle. And we're goin' to git 'em.

"Once we have, I'm comin' back here to Mason. All alone. Sego's goin' first, Buchanan next. The rest of you, in whatever order I ketch up to you.

"Meantime, me and the kid are stayin' at the hotel. We'll be comin' for them cattle first thing tomorrow mornin'. Anybody wants to git in line ahead of schedule kin do so by applyin' in person between here and Buchanan's ranch."

He stubbed it off as blunt as he'd begun it. He didn't say another word. Not to me, not to any of them. He just shoved past Sego and stalked on out the doors and across the street to the hotel. He didn't look back, once, and nobody in the saloon left off watching him, nor said anything, until he was into the hotel and out of sight.

Then it was Sheriff Blackburn who cut into the big quiet, slow and soft like he said everything.

"Git goin', Sego."

His men were watching Sego to see what he

would do. The only one of them that was looking
at me was the young one I'd heard speak up in the
livery barn. He was just a kid, hardly more than
my age, and he acted near as scared and worried
as I did.

Sego folded.

He stared at the sheriff a minute, then nodded
and grinned, "Sure, Sheriff. Jest don't set with
your back to no doors from here on." He turned
around and limped out. His men tailed him and
Sheriff Blackburn tailed them. I trotted along at
his flank, anxious as a dogie calf that's stumbled
across a friendly nurse-cow and doesn't mean to
take any chances on losing her in the herd.

Outside, the sheriff watched Sego and his men
mount up and start down the street out of town.
Then he turned to me and I could see his big
shoulders let down and the hunch go out of them
and could hear the tiredness in his voice so deep
his words sounded like all one heavy sigh.

"Come on along, Button, I'll walk you home."

He put his arm, thick and strong as an ox yoke,
across my shoulders, giving me a quick squeeze
and a couple of fumbly pats. Then he dropped it
away, quick and awkward, and started off across
the street.

I went with him. We walked close and quiet and
neither one of us said anything more.

Next morning, bright and early, me and Brack set
out for Rance Buchanan's Lazy RB Ranch. The hotel man had told us where it was—ten miles out
on the new Austin City road—but we never made
it. We splashed through the crossing shallows of

the Llano, where it ran just south of town, and that was about all. When we rounded a big bunch of bottom brush just past it, there sat Sheriff Ewell Blackburn and his little deputy, square in the middle of the road.

"Mornin', Button. Mornin', Starbuck."

We sat there, reining in our horses. They were fresh and wanted to go. So did Brack.

"What's the rustle, Sheriff?" he rasped.

I didn't dare say anything, so I let on like Mozo was giving me all I could handle and then a little some.

"Oh, I dunno," shrugged Blackburn. "Mainly to see the peace ain't upset, I reckon. What's yours?"

"I made my speech last night!" snapped Brack.

"So did I," said the sheriff quietly.

"So what!"

"So Sego done what he was told."

"And?"

"You're doin' the same."

You could see he wasn't fooling. His and Tobe Edwards's horses were standing quiet. They had been someplace, and got back, before ever we got up. You could read that in the sweat on their withers and in the grateful way they grunted and blew their bellies out against their cinches every few breaths.

"Am I?" said Brack.

"I think you are. What would you say, Tobe?"

He turned to his deputy with the question, for all the world as though he meant, actually, to leave it up to him.

Which in a way, I guess, he did.

Tobe must have slept with the shotgun. At least he still had ahold of it the same way we had last seen him the night before. Which was to say he had it pretty well pinned on Brack's gunbelt buckle.

"I'd say you was right, Sheriff."

Tobe didn't talk much. But, mostly, he made good sense when he did. Even Brack could see that. He did his level best to get the scowl off his face and the fight out of his voice.

"Listen, Sheriff, I come down here to take legal delivery on a herd of contract cattle from Rance Buchanan. I got our deposit receipt and a bony-fidy letter of credit for the balance, from the Stockman's National Bank in Dallas. I mean to use both of them and to use them this mornin'."

Typical of him, he let it stand right there.

So did Sheriff Blackburn for a minute.

Then he nodded in his friendly, easy way and surprised the both of us.

"Sure, and I mean to he'p you do jest thet, Starbuck. I got Mr. Buchanan waitin' at the bank right now. Talked him into stayin' in town last night and openin' up early this mornin'. You got a legal claim to them cattle, you're goin' to git it served legal. It's another part of why I'm paid."

You could have brushed Brack off Doak's dun with a turkey-feather duster. But he got over it in a hurry. He never could handle anybody that treated him decent. He always looked for the bad in everything and everybody. Mostly he found it, like a man will that thinks that way.

"What you *mean* you talked *him* into openin' up

early this mornin'? He *own* the damn bank or somethin'?"

The sheriff was full of surprises that morning. Some good, some medium bad.

"He does," he said evenly. "And the hardware and the feedstore and the Painted Lady Saloon."

"Why don't you jest say the whole lousy town?" growled Brack.

"Might near as well, I guess. What he don't own outright, he's holdin' the first mortgage agin."

"Jesus," said Brack through his teeth, "now ain't thet sweet!"

"You're right, it ain't," agreed the sheriff. "Let's git a move on."

"You don't give a man much choice, do you?" gritted Brack.

"You figger you got any comin'?"

Brack looked at the sheriff, then at the shotgun.

"Never could figger past two-times-ten." He grinned suddenly, chucking his head toward the old doubles' rusted muzzles. "After you, Sheriff. Age before beauty." He bowed, pulling the dun politely to one side of the road.

"Wouldn't think of it, Mr. Starbuck. You first."

Brack heeled the dun around. Before I could move Mozo to follow him, Tobe Edwards cut his little bay in between us. He lined him out on the dun's heels, held him on a chop-walk right behind him. I found myself riding back with the sheriff and kind of halfways glad of it.

"How you feelin' this mornin', Button?" he asked me after a bit.

"Gee, I dunno, Sheriff." I didn't, either, that was a fact. "I reckon I should have stayed home with the rest of the womenfolk. I ain't hardly big enough to be playin' with the older boys."

I was trying to make it sound like I was just saying it, not meaning it. It didn't fool him any. We rode quiet for a ways, then he nodded without looking over at me. "You want to tell me about it, boy?"

I opened my mouth to say no, but that wasn't what came out. Instead, I blurted out the whole story, from start to finish, bearing down hard on what had happened to Dad and Doak, as was only natural. When I'd finished, he let the quiet take over and run on for another spell and until we had crossed back over the river and were coming into the foot of Main Street.

"Well, Button," he said at last, "you've lost a lot and it ain't much you'll ever find to take its place. All the same, I figger mebbe you and me kin make a little deal thet might he'p."

"I don't foller you, Sheriff."

"I'm sure hopin' you will, Button."

"Sir?"

There was a long pause.

"I had a boy about your age. Year or two older."

I could see he was thinking back. Likely, from the far-off stare in his eyes, a long ways back. And likely, too, from the set of his jaw and the sudden stiffness that put him ramrod straight in his saddle, a painful ways.

"I was a deputy then, down in San Antone. Boy got hisse'f mixed into a stage heist where there was a shotgun rider kilt. He come to me and turned hisse'f in with the full story. We went after the man who had laid the job out and led it and gunned the rider off the driver's box. We never got him but he came back later and got my boy for talkin' to the law."

I couldn't think of the right thing to say, so I didn't say anything. Which was the right thing to say.

"It's why I come to Mason," he went on. "I figgered sooner or later he'd turn up here." He came around, looking at me. "I figgered right, Button. He did."

I couldn't stand it any longer. I had to say something, or bust. "But ain't you scared, Sheriff? I mean scared he'll git you too?"

He shook his head slowly.

"He didn't know it was my boy he kilt. He don't know it to this day."

I was foundered for something to say again, so I dug back to what he'd started off with.

"Well, where's our deal come into it, Sheriff? The little one you was sayin' we could make. I sure cain't he'p you git him, kin I?"

"It ain't me gittin' him I'm thinkin' about. *It's him gittin' you.*"

It hit me right between the eyes.

There wasn't but one man within a hundred miles of Mason County he could mean. Neither of us needed to name him. But the old sheriff nodded just the same, to let me know I'd guessed right.

"Yeah," he murmured, looking away from me and telling it to the space between his horse's ears. "I lost one boy to him, Button. I'm askin' you to give me the chance and right to see he don't make it two. What you say, son?"

The way he said it, he didn't mean "sonny," he

meant son, and I couldn't say anything. I just jerked my head "yes" and gulped and grabbed for my bandanna and blew my nose.

"Good an answer as anythin'," said Sheriff Ewell Blackburn softly. And swung his sorrel gelding to follow Brack and Tobe Edwards toward the hitch rail in front of the Mason City Bank & Trust Company.

Chapter Thirteen

Rance Buchanan was a real letdown.

He was a little man, all of forty, forty-five years old, with a face like a persimmon that's hung on the tree all fall. He was dressed in eastern city clothes; cast-iron collar, four-in-hand necktie, coat and pants the same color and so on, and wore pinch-nose eyeglasses. He looked mild as a crock of summer buttermilk, acted about as rambunctious as a nearsighted nanny goat.

All of which said a great deal for me as a judge of human nature.

But at the moment, all I could do was gape at him with my mouth hung half open like the village idiot seeing the schoolmarm's dress go up past her ankles for the first time. That, and stand there wondering where in the world Brack had ever got the idea Buchanan was "a pure bad one."

"These here are the Starbuck boys," said the sheriff. "They claim they got a dicker with you for May 7 delivery of 1600 head of market steers. Thet right, Starbuck?"

"Four-year-olds or better," quoted Brack from Dad's contract. "No heifers, herdbulls, dry cows nor old stags, and all rounded up and road-branded at the ranch on or before midnight, May 6."

When he had said it, he stepped clear of the sheriff and away from the door we had just come through, leaving nothing between him and Buchanan but a few layers of the latter's cigar smoke.

"Thet agree with your figgers, Mr. Buchanan?" asked Sheriff Blackburn.

"It does," answered the Mason City banker, just as carefully.

That was the first warning that told me to back up and take another look at the little man in the gold-rimmed spectacles. For a wonder I caught it and paid heed to it. Our old daddy had always taught us to "watch out for the man who don't waste words, he's the one knows there's a quicker way of killin' you than talkin' you to death." Thinking of that, now, I began to smarten up and listen to what Mr. Ransom Buchanan had to say.

"Well, then," the sheriff went on, "is there anythin' standin' in the way of closin' the deal here and now?"

"Not a thing," said Rance Buchanan, "except $25,000."

The sheriff nodded. "Thet right, Starbuck?"

"As rain," rasped Brack.

"You got it on you?"

Brack moved in on the desk behind which Buchanan was sitting. He fished the letter of credit out of his vest, slapped it down in front of the little banker like it was the third queen to a full house of three ladies over double tens.

"Read it, Mr. Buchanan," he said. "But don't weep. I cain't stand the sight of a strong man in tears."

"I don't think you'll have to, Mr. Starbuck." He didn't even bother to look at the letter of credit. Only eased back in his chair, put the tips of his fingers together and sat there.

I could see the blood go dark in Brack's face.

"What's thet mean?"

"It means," said Rance Buchanan, "that I'm calling for cash."

"You're crazy!" hissed Brack, turning white. "Who'd be packin' thet kind of money in cash!"

"The man who gets those cattle," said Buchanan.

Sheriff Blackburn had eased up behind Brack without any of us realizing he'd done it. His big hand shot out, nailing Brack's wrist as the fingers of his gunhand went to hooking.

"It's legal, Starbuck," was all he said.

"It's sandbag poker and I'll kill him for it!" snarled Brack.

"You won't kill nobody," said the old sheriff. "Man wants to call for cash on a cattle deal, it's legal."

"Like a chippie goin' to church on Good Friday!" Brack's lips drew back to show the wolf-trap set of his white teeth when he snapped it out, and I began to get scared again. As usual, I would rather see any other man fall down and foam at the mouth than to see Brack stand there and grin.

"Yeah," said Sheriff Blackburn. "Same idea. Legal, but a little late in the day and not too lovely."

"Well," breathed Brack, "all right."

He picked up the letter of credit, put it back in his vest pocket.

"Seeing Mr. Buchanan wants to play it cozy, them's the rules we'll go by. You heard of the Stockman's National Bank in Dallas, Mr. Buchanan?"

"I have."

"You'd say mebbe it wouldn't strip their udder to stand back of this letter?"

"I would."

"You allow it's good as mint gold in a gov'ment vault?"

"Any banking day in the week and up to noon Saturday."

"Well, mister, *you* cash it then! You're in the banking business!"

Buchanan took his fingertips apart, nodding pleasantly as though he meant to do it. Sheriff Blackburn let down a little, nodding right along with him to show his relief. "Thet sounds legal too, Mr. Buchanan. Any objections?"

"None in principle, Sheriff, only in practice."

"How's thet?"

"I assume Mr. Starbuck can read."

I saw Brack go white again.

"You keep assumin', Buchanan, you're goin' to assume yourself square under six feet of fresh sod."

"No offense, Starbuck." He had a big legal ledger open on the desk in front of him. He turned it around and pushed it across toward Brack. "This is purely a business matter with me."

Brack scowled down at the ledger. "What's there I'm supposed to read?" he gritted.

"This month's audit of the capital assets and

cash-on-hand reserves of the Mason City Bank & Trust Company."

Brack tried bluffing it a minute, peering and squinting and moving his lips as though he could read and was doing so. Then he gave it up and looked around for me. I nodded and stepped over to the desk. I couldn't make heads or tails of the arithmetic but I could read the bookkeeper's feather-pen writing that went with each set of figures. And down at the bottom of the page there was one statement circled in red ink that a six-year-old second-grader could have deciphered with one eye shut.

I looked back at Brack.

"It says here that they ain't got but $3675 in ready cash," I mumbled.

Buchanan shrugged, palmed his slender white hands, apologized to Brack. "It's a small bank, Starbuck. We do a risky business here in Mason County. Our reserves are never allowed to get over $5000."

So that was it.

I thought Brack was going to strangle, the blood got that heavy in his neck. But the sheriff was still standing next to him and it was plenty clear by now that even if he wasn't in actual cahoots with Buchanan, he wasn't about to buck him on our accounts. Not then, nor any other time.

That was a pretty hard fall for me, coming right on top of the close talk him and me had made on the ride into town. I took it bad. Ten minutes before, I'd have said Sheriff Ewell Blackburn would do to ride any river with. Now I wouldn't let him side me across a ten-foot creek.

Nor would Brack, naturally.

"Well, Button," he said, "we've bin boxed. Let's go."

I had only time to nod, not to move, when Buchanan waved his hand nonchalant as though he was brushing aside a bottlefly. "There's no call for any great upset that I can see, Starbuck," he said. "You've four full days yet. Plenty of time to get to Dallas and back by regular stage. Isn't that right, Sheriff?"

"Sure is, boys," agreed Ewell Blackburn anxiously. "All you got to do is go git your letter cashed and come back. Dallas stage goin' north, hits through here from Austin City about noon. Gits you into Lampasas for supper, Fort Goodwin for breakfast and Cleburne for noon dinner tomorrow. You kin easy be back here by dusk of the sixth, even layin' over the night in Dallas. What you say?"

Brack looked him over, his lips lifting again. But this time there was no grin and none intended. It was a pure snarl without noise.

"I say we'll be on thet noon stage for Dallas *and*—" He just left it up in the air like that, deliberate, causing the sheriff to squint and cock his head at him.

"And what?" he asked curiously.

"And nobody better try stoppin' us from *gittin'* on it," said Brack, and wheeled around and stalked out of Rance Buchanan's office.

Nobody did. The stage was on time, rolling up in front of the hotel right at noon.

We were ready. I had been down to the livery

and arranged for Old Man Yates to tend Mozo and the dun till we got back. He'd said he would.

While I was there I had a hunch to put a trust in him. I remembered Dad saying that the only way to tell about a hunch was to saddle it up and ride it till it dropped. So I told old Pegleg about Sec Gonzales and how him and his Mexican friends and relatives might be along soon to help us get the cattle home. I asked him to tell Sec where we'd gone, and how come we had, in case we weren't back by the time he showed up. He promised he'd do it, keeping his mouth shut about it meanwhile, and I'd gone back to the hotel feeling a little better about everything.

The sheriff hadn't let us out of his sight since we had left the bank. That is, except for a few minutes that Brack took me up to our room and told me a few things in private, just before the stage pulled in. He was still with us now, while we sat on the veranda waiting for the fresh teams to be brought out from the barn next door and hooked up, and the two lady passengers for Lampasas to get done with their sprucing up in the hotel bathroom.

I had seen one of those two women pretty good. She was a big fat old mestizo squaw in a dirty black *rebozo* and a Caddo blanket. She had got off the stage and waddled into the hotel as I came out of the livery barn. But the other one I'd got only a glimpse of. That was because she was walking with the mestizo woman and on the far side of her. And anybody walking on the far side of that old broadbeam might as well have been going into the hotel back of a barn door. But from what little I had seen, she looked real slim and exciting, walking light and dainty enough to make me think she was maybe no more than a girl and a powerful pretty one at that.

I was going to be eighteen in two months and was more like Brack than Doak when it came to girls. I had an eye for them, though nothing like his nerve to go with it. You might say I was sinful interested but mortal backward and sneaky about showing it.

So I was thinking a little bit about that slim girl when Brack got up all of a sudden and eased down off the veranda. He was edgy and keyed up, acting as though he had seen something he'd been waiting for and worrying about. I watched him a minute but couldn't see what was spooking him. The street was near empty. Everybody in Mason that wasn't leaving on the Dallas stage, or seeing that somebody else left on it, had hunted up a strip of siesta shade. It was a real scorcher for that early in May.

Brack had no more than walked away than Sheriff Blackburn crinkled up his eye-corners, leaned his head toward the hotel door and said, "She's every bit as trim from the front as she is from behind, too, boy."

I got red as a turkey gobbler's neck in strutting time. That old devil of a sheriff just didn't miss a trick. He must have spotted me eying that girl from clean over to the livery barn. But I didn't let on he'd centered me, nor answer him a single decent word. I wasn't trusting him anymore after him buttering up to Buchanan like he'd done so shameful over to the bank.

He knew that too. You just didn't fool him for

five minutes. So when I put off on him like that, his ripply smile smoothed out and died away like the circles from a stone dropped into deep, cold water. He talked low and a whole lot faster than I'd heard him before.

"Now you listen to me, Button. I know whut's goin' on inside thet bullhead of yours and I don't cotton to it. You hear me, boy?"

I only kept looking at him, sullenlike.

But he wasn't watching me, he was watching Brack. And talking even faster as he saw him break off his staring across the street at the alley behind the Painted Lady Saloon, and start back for the veranda.

"I told you once you got a hell of a lot to learn and a damn short time to learn it in, providin' you're goin' to stay alive long enough to git back home. Now, damn you, you let up on thet mulehead sulkin' and you git a few things straight."

It was the first and last time he ever cussed me, and the first time I'd heard him cuss anything. I got my lip up off my chin and started listening.

"I make a deal," he went on, "I don't never back out on it. I give a man my word, he kin bet his life on it. Now you and me made a deal, didn't we?"

I nodded unhappily.

"And I give you my word on it, didn't I?"

I bobbed my head again, more uncomfortable yet.

Brack was coming up the steps now. The sheriff put his knobbly hand on my knee, said the rest of it so fierce and low-voiced I scarce heard him.

"All right then, Button, there's just the one thing more you got to git straight in your mind.

And to keep straight no matter whut happens or how things I do might look to you. Now you agree thet we made a deal and thet I give you my word on it. Right?"

"Yessir," I said, muttering it under my breath and keeping my head down so Brack wouldn't see I was talking to him. "Thet's the first of it, what's the rest of it?"

"The rest of it is thet you're bettin' your life on the first of it," said the old lawman softly, and got up and nodded friendly to Brack and smiled. "All right, Starbuck, let's go."

Chapter Fourteen

He herded us into the coach ahead of the ladies. Brack said we would take the forward seat so that the latter wouldn't need to ride backwards. That threw me because from the way he'd been acting, I would have thought he'd want us to set so's we could watch the road ahead. I said as much and he grunted for me to mind what he'd told me in the hotel room and let him fret about the rest of it.

Pretty quick the big fat woman and the girl came out and climbed aboard.

I had been waiting for the chance to sneak a look at the girl getting in, as I knew she would have to show a little ankle doing it. But when the big minute came I got flustered, as usual, and glued my eyes out the far window, letting on like I didn't know she was alive and likely pretty as a jersey heifer. So I still hadn't had my first good look at her when Sheriff Blackburn banged the door shut and hollered up to the driver to get going.

He did. And right here I want to say a word against the Abbot-Downing Company of Concord, N.H. They made the best heavy stagecoaches in the business. They weighed up to 2500 pounds, sold for $1250 and more. They would carry nine passengers inside, as many more out-side as could scramble up and cling to the roof. And I will take my dying oath that if the devil had set up all winter drawing over their designs he couldn't have improved them one solitary cinder.

They were slung on two sets of leather thorough-braces running from a pair of iron standards over the front axle to the boot bar. And when one of them took off back of six fresh horses, half empty like ours was, it was enough to knock your back-bone right out through your belt buckle.

The drivers didn't help. They all liked to hit into and get out of a town in high style. Once away, and into the sagebrush, they would steady down and let the teams take a decent road gait. But God help the greenhorns, meanwhile.

Brack had ridden plenty of them—and stopped a few, too, I guess. Me, I'd never been on one be-fore in my life. He said he forgot to warn me but I know cussed well he didn't. He knew what was going to come off and no doubt figured it couldn't happen to a better boy than me.

One minute I was setting on my far-side seat staring haughty out the street window showing the girl my uppity profile and cutting her as cold as if the mestizo squaw had been her natural mother. The next breath, the driver had kicked off the brake, notched his leaders' ears with his fifteen-foot blacksnake, let out a screechy *"Heee-yaahhh thar!"* that would have scared a gila mon-ster out of his spring skin in February—and I was flat on my hands and knees in the bottom of the coach with my face jammed halfway up between the girl's knees.

She let out a yell, as was only her right, and clamped her knees shut like a bulldog bench-vise. I near tore my ears off getting my head loose and clawing my way back onto my seat. Nor was that the worst of it. She still had my hat pinned betwixt her knees, not even noticing it until the squaw pointed to it, then grinned and said something that sounded dirty in Indian.

The poor girl got wild red, grabbed the darn thing and threw it at me like it was a jacket-busted potato just raked out of the firebed coals. I caught it as though it hadn't cooled off any being flung across the coach, jamming it on over my ears like I meant to pull it clean down to my ankles.

I reckon I must have looked awful damnfoolish.

At any rate, instead of getting huffy about it she all of a sudden busted out laughing. Not to be out-sported by any pigtail snip of a girl, I let down and went along with her.

Well, that cleared the air just fine.

When we'd done with our laugh and had sat back to get our breath, Brack just shrugged and said, "Well, Button, you fell pretty hard and I al-low it's all my fault but I jest couldn't stand the strain of you two oglin' each other out'n your eye-corners for the next forty miles. I'm right sorry, miss." He touched the brim of his big hat when he said it, flashing her that rare dark grin of his that would melt the hinges off any woman's hope chest. Or turn a good girl bad for ten cents where she could easy ask and get a dollar and a half.

It worked, too. Just like I'd seen it do a dozen times of a Saturday afternoon in Mineral Wells or Salesville. She straightened back, prettied up her dress, gave him the smile back with a sunflash of white teeth that not only took my breath away but held on to it so long I almost passed out.

And that's how I met May Otero.

I took my first real look at her while Brack, with his easy way, kept her laughing and got her to talking about herself. She rambled on gay and bubbly as though we were kissing kin on our way to a hill-country wedding.

She was just sixteen and on her way home for summer vacation from a convent school down in San Antone. She was an orphan, living with her old grandfather Jesús Otero on a little Mexican ranch a few miles north of Lampasas and west of the main road of Cleburne. The old man ran a few steers, hoed a little corn, dried a dozen strings of chili each fall and was happy doing it. It was all he wanted or needed of the world, outside of seeing that May got educated proper. The Church took care of that, for free, as it took care of everything for its mestizo *reducidos pobretes*, it's "poor little halfbreed devils."

But was May Otero, herself, a mestizo? A half-blood Mexican Indian?

She didn't say it and she didn't act it, but did she need to? Couldn't you tell it with your first hard look?

Those breed women had a fierce, wild look to them, even the little kids just sprouting their nubbins, that no white woman was ever born with. They got their breasts and hips before they were thirteen. They were fullbodied by fifteen, thick in the waist by seventeen, all-over broad as a first-calf heifer by twenty. But they still had that savage

Indian something to the way they walked and held themselves and caught a man's eye without blushing or blinking that stamped them, whether they were thirteen or thirty-eight. And once in a great while one of them, taken in her full flower, would turn out as tawny beautiful as a tiger lily.

Was May Otero one of those?

She looked it. She was slinky blonde as a mountain lioness. Her long hair was the ripe color of September corn yellowing in the crib. Her eyebrows were arched and delicate, pale as a feathery head of summer wheat, her lashes thick and glistening as tassel silk with the morning dew still on it. Her cool, slanty eyes, too, were those of a slim, sun-lazing big cat. They had that peculiar colorless jade green to them, half dreamy, half warning, all beckoning, that calls to a man soft and dangerous, "Come a little closer, come a little closer. You can see what you want if you come a little closer!" Her mouth was an Indian mouth. Wide, full lipped, dark, dark red. Her nose was straight and short, her face an angular oval, high cheekboned, clean jawed, flawlessly cut. But the most striking thing about her was her skin.

It was that rare golden-glow chestnut color that came from crossing highblood horseback Indian and hidalgo white Spanish. And in the same breathless minute that it made of her an impossibly beautiful girl, it marked her deep and ugly with the mestizo bar sinister.

And it put her just as far out of the hard, proud Starbuck world as though she had been born on another planet.

You could look at her, sidelong, and feel your

blood hammer and your heart pound and your secret thoughts for her and you fly high and wild as a homebound V of northering geese. You could do it from that minute on and until you grew so old your mind could no longer carry you back to it. It would still do neither of you any good. Not then, not ever.

You were a Starbuck. May Otero was a half-breed.

I hadn't reached the decision about May's mixed blood by more than a minute when Brack leaned out the coach window and hollered up for the driver to pull over.

The driver did it, but with some language not meant for ladies, pureblood or otherwise.

We were only just out of sight of town, maybe a mile or two, no more. He had got his teams eased down and lined out at the gait he wanted for the long haul to Lampasas and was anything but happy at being held up.

"What the hell's the matter?" he bellowed down. "Somebody sick?"

"No, nor not about to be," answered Brack, kicking the door open and stepping out. "Move over, I'm riding shotgun for you the rest of the way."

"The hell you say! The heat got you, mister? This run don't carry no shotgun rider. We ain't holdin' no Wells Fargo franchise. Last time this stage was stuck up you wasn't old enough to vote."

"Well, I am now," said Brack. "Shove over."

He put his boot on the hub, hauled himself up out of sight. I heard some more mumble-voiced complaining from the driver, to which I didn't get

Brack's answer. But I did get the flinty laugh he backed it with. So did the driver.

Brack wasn't the kind most men argued with.

The old hull gave a wild lurch, settled back onto the thoroughbraces, took a set and jumped forward into the wheelers' whiffle-trees. Banged hard in the hocks, they took out like scared cats, the swing and lead teams digging to get out of their way. They made it. Inside of thirty yards the whole hitch had hit and settled back into its rocking road-gait gallop.

There wasn't any more talk in the tonneau after Brack left. Not from my side of the seats, anyway. The girl and her fat old *dueña* said a little bit back and forth in some kind of Indian, most likely Caddo or Comanche, then even they shut up and went to looking out the windows the same as me.

I didn't know what quieted them down, but I sure knew what did it for me. It was thinking about what Brack had told me back in the hotel room.

At first, in the excitement of having the girl along, being knocked into her lap and then turning all hot and shaky inside from sneaking looks at her while she and Brack were laughing and carrying on, I'd pretty well forgot his warning. But when he yelled that driver down and got out and climbed up onto the seatbox with him, levering his Winchester on the way, it came back to me, full force.

There wasn't any doubt about it, the way Brack saw it. It was dirt simple.

Buchanan had already had two men killed to

keep us from taking delivery on that herd. He wasn't going to hesitate any to make it three. And from where Brack sat, the rest of it was clear as a bottle full of Boston gin.

Somewhere between Mason City and Dallas, and most likely between Mason City and Lampasas, that old Abbot-Downing coach was going to get relieved of a paying passenger. Then that passenger was going to get relieved of the $1000 deposit receipt and his true copy of the Starbuck-Buchanan delivery contract—the only legal proof that Rance Buchanan didn't still own that $40,000 worth of four-year-old beef. After that, Mr. Passenger was going to get left right where he gave up the evidence. His only receipt would be a bullet hole between the eyes. Or, if Buchanan sent Sego to do the job and Sego shot all Starbucks alike, two in the belly.

Nobody would ever know what had happened to that number three man. He would just disappear and his kid brother, if he turned yellow and stuck inside the coach like he'd been told to do when and if the shooting started, could sneak on home to the Brazos and make one last entry in Mother's old Bible: *Brackton Bueford Starbuck; August 9, 1843—May 3, 1874*

The chill of that last thought had plenty of time to settle in.

The dusty hours banged and jolted interminably away. The flat, hot, fly-droning miles fell behind. The sun centered, slid west, downed swiftly. The shadows started to turn purple and run long across the road. I had just looked at Dad's old stemwinder for the hundredth time since noon when I heard the driver yell and felt the lurch and clamp of the backwheel brakeshoes squeal and bite into the rusted rim irons.

It was 6:32 P.M.

Chapter Fifteen

It was just barely twilight, not five miles from Lampasas on the main-traveled road. The men wore calico bandanna masks and old Confederate cavalry coats. There were three of them, all riding common bay horses, unbranded. They had stopped us in a bad place.

We were in a shallow cut going down to cross a small creek just ahead. The top of the cut was only a little higher than the coach's luggage rail and choked solid with heavy brush and sandstone outcrop. But from what he had told me back in the hotel room about being ready for them, and from the fact there were only three of them instead of the half dozen or so he had expected, I couldn't understand why Brack didn't cut loose the minute they showed.

Then a horse whinnied and it wasn't one of the three they were riding and I saw why Brack was setting tight.

There were more men, a big bunch of them, six or eight anyway, staked out along the top of the cut. You could see their rifle barrels and hat crowns poking out from the rocks and, behind them, their reins-tied ponies standing shadowy and tail-switching quiet back in under the big mesquite and chaparral scrub and the scraggly chinaberry trees.

That was about all I had time to notice.

All three of the men blocking the road had their Winchesters in their hands, covering Brack and the driver. It was plain enough they knew there wasn't anybody to worry them inside the coach. Nevertheless, when the left-hand rider glanced my way the next minute, he shot from the hip. The bullet whanged across the door post, ricocheted off the strap-iron jamb, whined away up the cut.

"Git your damn head back inside until you're told different, Junior!" ordered the man, then punched his gun back up toward Brack and barked, "All right, mister, you unload first."

Brack didn't answer him.

I looked across at the two women. The girl was white in the face but setting still, behaving herself. The old squaw was muttering in a scowling mix of Indian and Mexican and crossing herself every other growl. The girl kept staring right at me, shaking her head kind of puzzled and slow with her pretty mouth half open and her lips puckered, as much as to ask why didn't I do something to help my big brother out.

Outside, the road agent giving the orders had allowed Brack all the time to answer that he was going to.

"Driver," he said, "we don't want nothing of you, nor the stage company. We don't aim to bother your inside passengers none, neither, savin' fer thet shavetail kid thet jest poked his head out'n the window."

He was a cool cuss and clearly didn't mind taking the time to talk. After bobbing his head to indicate me, he went on to the driver.

"All we ask, friend, is thet the boy and your pardner up there on the box climb down peaceable and *pronto*. After thet, you lace into them hosses and don't bother lookin' back till you git to Lampasas. We got a little personal business with them two and we won't be needin' any witnesses to the nature of same. You understand, oldtimer?"

That driver was all right. He had been there before and where you might have him beat, you didn't do it with any cold-run bluffs. He wanted to see your cards.

"It's a stick-up!" he snapped back. "Thet's all I understand. Cut 'em anyway you want and deal 'em double, it's still a stick-up and thet's the way it'll be reported to the company."

"You call it anythin' you want after you git to Lampasas, pardner," said the talkative bandit. "Jest don't argue about it, meanwhile. You understand *thet?*"

The highwayman nodded up to him and levered out the empty he had snapped at me. I couldn't make out what the driver mumbled back but it must have added up to yes.

"Thet's more like it," grinned the road agent, and switched calmly back to Brack.

"Now you jest toss your saddle gun down and climb down after it, mister, you hear? And you, kid," he swung on me again, "you jest come out with your hands empty and you won't git hurt none at all. Hurry it up, now the both of you."

"Sure, mister," I heard Brack say back to him

easy and soft. "Mind if I take time to give the kid a little piece of advice first? He ain't used to bein' out by hisself after dark. Don't rightly know how to handle hisself in a crowd like this. Jest don't want him to git flustered and make no damnfool plays. All right?"

I knew as well as if I could see him that he was grinning, and it made my heart ache. I had my own fancy little Winchester right under my hand, setting wedged between my knee and the side of the coach. All I had to do was grab it and start blasting out the window, to give Brack the half-second break that might mean his life.

But it might mean mine, too. And I couldn't move.

"Sure, go ahead," agreed the masked man, just as easy. "We don't want to have to mess him up anymore than you do. But make it quick. We don't mean to hang around here long enough to git a crop in, either."

"Button—"

It was Brack calling me. It surprised and startled me, real bad. Yet it wasn't the surprise or the start that had me froze to that seat, with my tongue locked like it was stuck in a squeezepole branding chute. I was sick again.

"Button? You hear me, boy?"

I managed it somehow then, the shame so heavy in me I could hardly breathe. "Yessir," I quavered. "Yessir, I hear you, Brack."

"You remember thet time I pinned your ears back for putting off on me? Thet time I knocked your front teeth loose?"

All those years ago! I thought, and he hadn't

forgot it. And me so hurtful certain, all the angry while, that he'd never given it another minute's memory!

"Yessir," I choked. "I do."

"I'm sorry about thet kid. I bin sorry about it a long time. I'd like it if you'd try to remember it thet way."

I tried to force an answer up past the lump in my throat but before I could, the boss bandit broke in, bad riled.

"Fer Christ's sake, we didn't bargin fer you to be makin' any farewell addresses, mister. You got some advice to give the kid, give it to him and git the hell on down off thet box!"

"Comin' to thet right now, pardner," said Brack, the easy grin still back of the offhand words. "Button, you listenin' yet?"

"Yes sir."

"You heard the man tell you to get down and stand quiet?"

"Yes sir—"

"Well, boy," he tailed off in a dry, burring snarl as sudden and scary as the buzz of a rattler's tail, *don't you set one goddam foot outside thet tonneau!*"

"Brack—!" I busted out, but he had said what he wanted to say, and I never got to finish.

His first shot drilled the man who had done the talking—and too deadly much of it—high and square in the chest. He was dead before he got done sliding off his horse. His second winged the rider in the middle, smashing his shoulder and knocking him clear back over his pony's croup. But his third went high and wild and whistling off into nowhere. The brush and rocks along the top of the cut had exploded a dozen times before he could aim or squeeze it off.

I went crazy.

I was hanging half out the window yelling and screaming up to Brack, not even knowing I was doing it. My only answer was the clawing topple of his body off the seven-foot height of the seat-box. And the sickening instant of utter stillness that followed its scraping fall along the coachside and into the ankle-deep dust of the Lampasas road.

I thought he was dead. But you don't kill his diamond-back kind short of final sundown.

Before the remaining man in the road ahead, or his bushwhacking friends atop the draw could throw another slug, Brack was staggering upright and blasting the cut-edge brush above with both Colts. The dumbstruck killers up there had to flatten down and eat dirt for the five seconds it took him to empty the twin .44's. And that was more time than Brack had ever asked of any man. Within its heartstop span, he drilled his last shot upward and lurched heavily back toward the coach.

I was pawing, out of my head, at the doorstrap to get out and run to him when he seized the seat-box handrail, got his boot arch into the step iron, hauled himself up out of the road and gasped to the driver to lay on the leather.

The driver, as brave a man as ever rolled a six-horse hitch, yelled to his wheelers and poured the split-thong poppers to his leaders. I had to grab at the half-opened door to keep from being pitched out headfirst. Before I recovered myself, the coach was across the creek and careening up the far-side grade. And Brack was already bellied out among the roofdeck baggage, levering the driver's old Model '66 Winchester.

In twenty seconds we had topped the little climb at a full gallop and all I could do was strain my eyes back through the dust settling out beyond the creek and watch the holdup gang swarming down from the cut into the empty stage road behind us.

What I saw back there was a sight that was going to wake me up sweating many a still dark night in the lonely years to come. But at the actual moment of taking it in, I was conscious of only three frightening things: Brack was as good as dead, I was a craven coward, and the squat, frog-bodied rider who had led the rush of the hidden horsemen out of the brush and down the cutbank was Sego Lockhart!

Sego and his bunch didn't even make a stab at running us down. They had had a bad taste of Brack back yonder in that cut and evidently figured that one man dead and another down and shoulder-broke was putting the price of twilight stage heists a little too high even for such hardtails as them.

The last we saw of them, they were catching up the loose horses and packing the dead man and the wounded one aboard them. That meant, for sure, they were through for the night and were intending to make tracks of their own and not worry, right then, about dogging ours.

I shivered, and didn't blame them.

As long as Brack was alive and there was shooting light enough to sight a Winchester, it would have been as certain slow music as a Texas Ranger murder warrant to have tried any horseback run-ups on that Lampasas stage in the open stretch of road we were now rolling along.

I had never seen Brack with the Colts before. I knew he was wicked with a rifle, both from the countless boyhood times of seeing him use one around the ranch and from the two times in the past forty-eight hours I had seen him scatter Sego's gang with the saddle gun. But in all the years I had never seen him pull a handgun except to use it for a hammer, fence-mending and suchlike at the homeplace.

It followed that it was only kid-brother natural that I had got to wondering if he was really as good as Doak had hinted, and as my own suspicions of what he'd done for a living before Dad had brought him back home to the Brazos ranch had made me imagine he was.

I wasn't wondering anymore. Nor imagining.

I had seen him for myself.

Shot to pieces and falling seven feet off a Concard seat-box, yet making his feet and flashing his draw and throwing down on Sego's ambushed bunch with the full dozen rounds in both guns before a one of them could think to get his own iron in action.

He was the fastest man with a beltgun I ever saw in my life.

It made a picture to turn you dead sick inside, that memory of him lurching back to the coach with the blood pumping down his chest and with that fearful blank fish-white look on his face. But it made your throat swell with wild dark pride, too, to think you were kin to a man like that.

A man who did not know the meaning of human fear. Who had lived his whole life without dropping his eyes to anybody on earth. Who had never walked around a bad spot in any trail, or backed down to a cold bluff from any bully, or drawn out on any friend or even any stray underdog he'd ever found in trouble too big for them to handle. A man who had been born brave and who, you knew from that one terrible look at his bloodless face outside the coach window, would die that way before another sun came up.

That was your brother Brack.

Even through your shameless tears, and above and beyond your empty-bellied dread of what you knew would come that night, that one proud thought burned bright and clear and high within you.

You were Brack Starbuck's brother.

You couldn't be a coward!

Chapter Sixteen

Brack was still conscious when we carried him into the doctor's house just outside Lampasas.

Ordinarily, it would have been real luck to find a medical doctor in a little town like that in those days. But this time there wasn't any use for such luck. Brack didn't need a doctor, he needed a Bible.

The driver helped me ease him down on the bed, with the doctor moving quick ahead of us into the musty back bedroom to throw an old army blanket over the clean spread before we did. It had been only minutes since the shooting and Brack was still bleeding something fierce and not clotting at all yet.

I started to pull his shirt off but a hand came in from behind and clamped my wrist, real gentle. I looked up and saw the doctor shaking his head.

"No call for that, boy," he said softly. "You and Charlie wait out in the parlor. Go along now. I'll call you."

I pulled roughly away from him, leaning over Brack. "Brack, kin you hear me?"

He didn't open his eyes. It was like he knew it would take strength he needed to make his lips move.

"Button," he whispered back, a flicker of the old grin passing painfully. "Kin *you* hear me?"

"Yessir, I can."

"Then you do as the Doc says, damn it. You're in the way here."

Charlie, the driver, nodded quick and like he knew what Brack really wanted.

"Come on along outside, kid. Leave Doc have his look. He won't let nothin' happen."

He took my arm and guided me into the sitting room. I didn't make any fuss. Brack had sounded like his old self cussing me that way. For a minute I got the crazy thought that he was going to make it after all.

The thought lasted long enough for Charlie to pull out and check his rusty railroad timepiece, and to mumble something about Doc Sampson being the best sawbones in central Texas and about his schedule getting ahead of him and his lady passengers needing to make some kind of connection in Lampasas.

Then he clumped out, awkward and clearly wanting to say something else that would help me hold up. But knowing, too, that there wasn't anything he *could* say that would do that. And, in the end, being simple western man enough not to try making a patchwork of empty words out of something that was better said with a quiet nod and a straight-eyed look.

He did stick his head back in the door long enough to say he would send the sheriff out as soon as he got shut of his passengers, and for me to come along back in with him if I meant to ride my ticket out to Dallas. He didn't say so but the idea was clear that his schedule wasn't set up to accommodate any road-agent delays. And that the stage would pull out for Fort Goodwin and Cleburne on time no matter which way the dark wind blew for his number four passenger, yonder in the bedroom.

After Charlie was gone, my wild hope that Brack might pull through started to flicker out. It flared up when Doc Sampson came out of the bedroom, then went out for keeps the minute I saw the look on his face. "He's wanting to see you," was what he said, but I knew it wasn't what he meant.

"How is he, Doc?" I blurted. "Has he got a chance?"

"To say good-bye, maybe, son. Not much else. I don't see how he lived ten minutes."

Something in the calm unfeeling way he said it twisted wrong inside me. I couldn't see clear and my own voice sounded hoarse and strange to me.

"He'll make it, Doc!" I cried, grabbing his shirt-front like I meant to tear it loose from him. "He's got to, he's got to! Brack cain't die, you hear me? He ain't the dyin' kind, Doc. Honest to God, he ain't—!"

He didn't move to get away from me, nor to break my hands loose of him. He just shook his head slow and gentle and said, "Your brother *is* dying, son. And there's nothing you, nor I, nor God can do about it." He paused as my hands dropped away from him, then added sharply. "Now you'd best get in there and be quick about it. He's waiting for you and he doesn't have long to wait. You understand that?"

"Yes sir," I mumbled. "I think so."

I started, staring-eyed, for the door and felt his hand touch me on the shoulder. I came around, white-faced and shaky.

"Don't be afraid, boy," was all he said. *"He isn't."*

I'll never forget that long-gone moment there in Doc Sampson's sitting room. In those six simple words a total stranger to him had summed up Brack's bitter life finer than any bookwriter could have done in a six-volume set. And far finer than I had ever been able to do in a whole hurtful boyhood of kid-brother trying.

Somehow I knew, as I stood there looking back at him, that Doc Sampson had just spoken the last, best eulogy that Brack Starbuck would ever have said over him. I was mortally grateful to him, then and for the rest of my life, for what it meant to both Brack and me.

"I know he ain't, Doc." I thanked him quietly, and went on into the lamplit bedroom.

It was over merciful quick in there.

Brack was lying easy, not breathing heavy nor fighting hard anymore. There was a little tired trace of the old hard grin on his face and that was all.

I stood by the bed, twisting my hat and blinking back the tears I was determined he wouldn't see. Pretty quick, he felt I was there and tried to widen the grin a little. I saw the muscles jump and twitch with the effort, but the pale set of his lips stayed the same.

"Git down and set a spell, Button," he whispered, trying to point to the bed alongside him. "We got ten years to make up in two, three minutes."

"No we ain't, Brack," I choked, easing down by

him and patting his hand awkward and clumsy. "We ain't nothin' to make up, you and me. Not ever anymore, we ain't."

"I'm glad about thet, Button. Real glad. I ain't never done you nor Dad nor the Doaker a minute's good. Specially you. I allus thought you was no use, kid. Soft. Runt-size. Spoiled rotten. No real Starbuck blood in you—"

"Brack!"

"Shet up, boy. I mean to say it and I ain't got time to argue it. I had you branded wrong, Button, bad wrong. And I rode you thet way from the start. I see it different now. They say a man does thet jest before he goes. Sees things right and straight and like they really are. You believe that, Button?"

"I dunno, Brack, I dunno. Please, now—"

"Well, I do. And it's true. You believe me now, Button. You remember it after I'm gone, and you see thet it makes you ride tall as any man in Texas. You're the last Starbuck, boy, *and you're the best one!*"

"Dammit, thet jest ain't so, Brack!" I was crying open now and couldn't hide it. "I'd trade places with you this minute, if I could. I ain't never gonna make half the man you've bin. You know thet well as I do. You got more insides in a minute than I'll have in a hundred and eighty years!"

He tried to grin again but no smile came. In its white-lipped place I saw the dark shadow grow.

"It takes more than guts to make a man, kid," he gritted. "Hell, a steer's got guts. A hundred and forty pounds of 'em. You got somethin' better than thet inside you. You're like Dad. You got—"

"Hush up, Brack, please!" I pleaded. "You got to rest now."

"I know, I know. God! but I'm tired, Button. Where's your hand, boy?" He reached blindly with the words, and I knew his sight had gone. "Here," I sobbed, gathering his groping fingers into my two cupped hands and holding them tight against me. The blue-veined chill of them struck my heart still, but they closed on my hands with sudden strength.

"Button, you've got to go on to Dallas, you hear me? Right now, tonight. Don't miss thet stage. You do, by God, and I'll break the buggywhip on you."

He held up and I could see his whole body move fighting for the strength to go on. "Now listen. Fetch my hat yonder. It's got the papers stuck under the sweatband inside. Get 'em and put 'em in yours. Travelin' money's in my billfold. Inside coat pocket. Put it under your hat right along with our letter of credit and Buchanan's bill of sale. Don't let on to the sheriff nor nobody else thet you got a dime nor a document of any kind on you."

He had to stop again, and I could see his breath coming different now; fast and thin and panting-shallow, like the pulse in a lizard's throat.

"Now git this last carefullest of all, boy. It's the most important. Here's the—" He broke off once more, straining pitifully to get the words out past the hollow bubble of the thin bright blood that was pushing up from his punctured lungs. "—Here's the way I want you to ride the rest of it, after you git to Dallas. You go to the bank and you—you—"

"Brack!"

It burst out of me, a smothered cry of terrified

little-boy fright and loneliness that held all of my broken heart in its desperate plea. But Brack did not answer and, suddenly, I knew that he never would.

I held his loosening hand hard to me, treasuring it fiercely against my sweat-caked shirt. Bending my head over it and saying it through the blind flood of the tears, I prayed that he would hear my whispered promise.

"I'll do it, Brack. For you and Dad and the Doaker." Then, even softer and quieter and because it was my real good-bye to him and to all that I had realized too late that he had meant to me, I told him, *"I'm not afraid anymore!"*

I will never know if he heard me or not. Yet, somehow, I will always think he did. For when I raised my eyes and put his hand gently back down on the faded army blanket, Brack was smiling again.

And this time there was no shadow of pain nor dark struggle of deep hurt left in it.

I got the papers from his hat and the money from his coat, hiding it all inside my own ragged Stetson like he had wanted. When I left him I did it like he would have; dry-eyed and not looking back.

Outside in the sitting room, Doc Sampson was as good and wise and kind with me as though I had been his own son. When I told him of my brother's asking me to go on with the journey we had started together, he said that was the best thing I could do. He promised to see that Brack got a preacher service and a decent marker with his full family name on it, and said he would take care of his things and keep them safe, should I ever want to come back for them. He advised me to take the gunbelt and matched .44's along with me. But I told him that I didn't feel like it just then and that I would some day come back to Lampasas to see Brack and to pick them up and to thank him, Doc, fit and proper for all he had done for my dead brother and me.

He said he hadn't done anything, as there hadn't been anything he could do, and for me to just go on along forgetting that part of it, right off.

Then he allowed that if my mind was truly made up to go on to Fort Goodwin that night, we had best hook up his surrey and drive on into town without waiting for the sheriff to come out. The latter would for sure want to see me, he warned, and if we could save him the ride out to Doc's place he might be happier disposed toward the whole thing. The sheriff was a mighty thorough man, Doc said, and liked to ask a lot of questions. Any least time I could save by reporting into him, I could add onto my chances of making the stage out of Lampasas.

I knew enough about cow-country law and smalltown lawmen to know that Doc was right. Accordingly, I didn't argue the idea any.

I helped him back the mare into the shafts and we set out down the road about seven o'clock.

The night air was clean and sharp. It started my mind back to working before we had jogged forty rods. The shock of losing Brack was still on me hard and heavy, but it was beginning to lift. Enough, and then some, to remind me where I was. And, more to the immediate point, where I would be when we got to town.

The bad flurry of nerves which that last thought brought on settled swiftly down to one dead-sure certainty. As it did, all the brave new courage I had found in that last grief-struck minute at Brack's bedside faded away and was lost under the brisk clip-clop trot of Doc's old buggy mare.

With Brack dead and his body left behind for burial in Lampasas, Sego Lockhart would know he had only one more Starbuck to go in his search for the Buchanan bill of sale.

That Starbuck's name was Button.

Chapter Seventeen

I wasn't given too much time in Lampasas to worry about Sego and his bunch knowing I had on me what they wanted. The main reason for that was a little stageline war that was going on at the time.

Texas was on the boom. The bad days after the War had worn themselves out. The big panic of '73 was already being talked about as though it had happened to some other folks a hundred years ago. The big cattle drives to the Kansas railhead towns were hitting their all-time peaks and things in general were really hopping down in the Lone Star state.

Result was that competition in the travel business was getting stiffer than a proddy steer's tail. The railroads were talking of running spur lines out from Fort Worth and Dallas at the rate of forty miles a minute and the stage companies were scrambling for what little tidbits of paying passenger traffic might be picked up before the track-layers put them out of business for real keeps.

The line I was riding, The San Antonio & Central Southwest, was hanging on to its franchise by trying to make the iron horse look rusty. To do it they drove right on around the clock, pretty near as wild as the old Butterfield outfit in the early days up north. And with just about as much chance of holding on.

But no matter. When our stage hit into Lampasas that night of May 3, the war was on. Our driver was going to get on up to Fort Goodwin and Cleburne on schedule if he killed all six of his fresh horses doing it. So we got an hour in Lampasas; no more than long enough to change teams, have supper and give the county sheriff a spotty rundown on what had happened in the holdup.

Naturally, the sheriff came first.

He seemed to me like a fairly good man, some younger and a lot livelier than old Sheriff Blackburn. But somehow I couldn't bring myself to go against Brack's scowling instructions back in the Mason City hotel room not to tell anybody anything, should something happen to him and I had to go on alone. And now, of course, I had his last-breath warning about the same tight-mouth policy, from Doc Sampson's bedroom just in the past minutes. Not only that, but I was still an awful long way from home and kept thinking about one of the things Dad had always pounded into us boys from the time we were old enough to go to the outhouse by ourselves. "Don't never trust nobody but yourself," he'd said, "and don't be too damn sure of *him*." So I kept quiet and let the Lampasas sheriff do the talking.

He did quite a lot of it.

He kept prying and pushing at the fact that, being Brack's brother, I ought to know a little something about what the men were after who had shot him off the stagebox. He and his deputy went over me, of course, making me turn out my pockets and put my things on the desk and suchlike.

Not finding any, they first wanted to know what I was using for money. I said we'd used our last for stagefare out of Mason and were expecting to borrow what we needed to get on home from kin in Dallas. After that, they still weren't satisfied about Brack so I gave them a little stretcher about how he'd had the brush with the rough bunch in the Lone Star Saloon and been told to get out of town by Sheriff Blackburn. Then, when I'd told them that, they wanted to know had I any idea who might have been in that rough bunch. I said I hadn't but that I'd later heard the main one of them—the one my brother had argued the most with—was a man named Blockhard, or Lockherd, or something like that.

The sheriff and his deputy looked at one another.

"You mean Lockhart?" said the sheriff.

"Yessir, I do believe that sound like it, all right."

"Sego Lockhart, mebbe."

It wasn't a question, he was telling me it was Sego Lockhart.

"Yes sir!" I said, trying to let on as though I wasn't quite bright and that it had just rung a tardy recess bell for me. "Sure enough, by gum, that's the one. I remember Sheriff Blackburn saying it now."

"Seems to me, boy," said the sheriff, "that you don't remember too well unless you want to. Now you better be pretty damn sure there ain't somethin' else you've forgot to tell us."

I didn't like the way he was watching me and I wanted, powerful bad, to get back to the stage stop. I had more reason for that want than just the will to follow Brack's last wish, too.

I'd heard the girl and her *dueña* say they were getting off to meet her grandfather in Lampasas, and I had it in mind, upset and shaky as I was, to say something to that girl before she got away. I didn't rightly know what it would be. I just knew I had to find, some way, somehow, the right words to make her quit looking at me the way she had in the stage after I'd yellowed out on Brack back at the holdup. So I still put off on the sheriff.

"No sir, there ain't nothin' else I kin think of," I told him. "You see, I was plumb scairt when the shootin' started and stayed pretty well down below the doorjambs. Didn't see too much. Jest what I've a'ready said."

" 'Pears to me you're still scairt," scowled the sheriff. "Too bad you wasn't born with a little of your brother's dander."

"Yeah," grunted the deputy. "Stage driver says he was saltier than a late summer deer lick."

"Brack never saw the man he was afeared of!" I burst out impulsively. "He was the bravest man ever lived!"

The sheriff scowled again. "Well, leastways, kid, you kin say thet they don't run in the family. Guts, I mean."

I didn't have any answer to that, save to move my boots around and stare hard at the floor.

"Pete," he went on to his deputy, "you'd best git Simms and Shoemaker and go along up to Fort Goodwin with the stage. Make certain this kid gits out'n the county in one piece. I'll see you git paid trip money."

"Thet'll be a refreshin' change," grumped Pete. "You goin' out after the bunch downed his brother?"

"Got to, I reckon."

"Yeah, I reckon."

"See you, Pete."

"Sure."

The deputy turned to me, saying it like he'd just been demoted to dogcatcher. "Come on, kid. Git movin'." He gave me a shove out the door and clumped out after me.

I didn't dast open my mouth for the first few steps back up the street toward the stage depot. But about halfway there, the lonesomes got the best of me and I tried him out a little.

"Sheriff," I said, calling him that to soften him up, "what you think will happen back yonder where they got my brother? You think Mr. Egan will find any sign he kin foller?"

"None he'll want to foller, or thet would do him any good to. Keep walkin' and quit talkin', kid."

I minded the advice for about fifteen steps, then had to come out with what was really bothering me. "What about us?" I said. "Me, I mean, Sheriff. You figger Sego'll try—"

He stopped square in the middle of the street.

"Listen, boy." He tapped it out on my chest with a big dirty forefinger. "You'd best git a few things straight. I'm not the sheriff, Egan is. And I didn't plead fer this job. If your brother crossed Sego Lockhart and Sego's meanin' to keep trailin' you on out fer it, it's none of our affair. All we git paid fer is to see it don't happen in Lampasas County. And all *I'm* gittin' paid fer is to wetnurse you up to Fort Goodwin. After thet, I don't give a fancy four-letter word fer what happens to you. Now you shet up yer damn mouth until you're told to open it."

"Yes sir," I gulped, and went back to my walking.

At the stage stop, things didn't break any better. There was still a little of the long spring twilight lingering around, even though it was getting well on past seven. What I couldn't see by that, I could make out all too good by the early lamplight flooding out of the depot windows.

May Otero and the mestizo squaw were standing waiting on the boardwalk in front of the depot restaurant. As I spotted them, Egan's deputy said, "You're goin' to eat, kid, you'd best do it right quick. Stage leaves in twenty minutes, mebbe less. I'll be back in ten. See you're somewhere in sight and set to go when I do. Hear?"

He turned off and crossed the street without holding up for any answer and after a minute of toeing the gutter dust to get my courage up, I started sidling over toward May and the squaw.

I never made it.

Up the street, jolting in from the north, came a slatbed buckboard back of two skinny bays that wouldn't have made decent wolf bait in the Brazos country. Driving them, proud and proper as though he was handling a four-horse hitch of Johnny Bull hackneys ahead of a Peabody Victoria, was an old dude of a Mexican dandy who couldn't have been anybody else but Jesús Otero.

He was May's grandfather, all right, and before

I could make up my mind whether to back off or buy in, he had swung the bays into the curb and the family reunion was on, full tilt.

I wasn't more than a pebble toss away from them and not wanting them to think I was gawking at them I stepped back around the depot corner, where I could see them but they couldn't see me.

I couldn't hear what May and the old man said while they were passing their hugs back and forth but anybody could see they were natural kin by the gay, happy way they carried on. Well, I'd been told that much—that he was her actual grandfather—so that was all right. Anyway, he was a fine-looking old man for a Mexican. Near as dignified and grizzled handsome as old Sec Gonzales. From that you could see right off that he was a pureblood and that May's Indian side must have come in from her mother. The shocker came when the old man and the squaw got together.

They squeezed one another something scandalous and I plainly heard the old man call her "*hija mia*" as he patted and made over her.

That was a bad surprise and should have finished May Otero for me.

For if the squaw was old Otero's daughter and May was his granddaughter and they were all living happy together, it for certain sure meant just one thing.

That grinny-fat Indian woman wasn't May's *dueña*, she was her mother!

It was enough of a rough turn to keep me back of that building corner while they piled their luggage into the buckboard. The squaw and the old man got in but May held up on the boardwalk, looking up and down the street real anxious, before she climbed in after them. When old Jesús shook out the lines, starting his scrawny mustangs away from the curb, I stepped out onto the walk figuring the coast was clear. I wanted a last look at that girl, no matter it was only the backside of her perky little head bobbing along to the jump of the buckboard bouncing off up Lampasas's red-dirt mainstem.

I was still standing there feeling lost and lonesome as a weaner calf that's just been cut out of the cow herd, and wondering who or what May had been looking for that last minute when, fifty yards up the street, she turned around for a last glance back and I found out.

I was so intent on watching her I had forgot I'd moved out in front of the depot lights, where she could see me plain as I could see her—maybe even plainer. Anyhow, one way or another, I wasn't thinking too bright when I saw her throw up her arm and wave back my way almost kind of frantic or flustered. For a crazy minute, remembering all of a sudden that I was standing out in plain sight, I thought she might actually be waving at me. But just as quick I remembered the way she had last looked at me, and knew that couldn't be. So I stood there dumb and dismal as a fresh-sheared sheep.

Then was when she did it—sort of halfway stood up in the buckboard seat and waved again and blew a graceful kiss square my way.

Even then I didn't smarten up. I actually turned around to see who was standing behind me.

But there wasn't anybody there. Not on the boardwalk. Not inside the depot windows. Not even crossing the street at that precise minute.

That was when I woke up.

That excited good-bye wave and dainty blown kiss were mine. May Otero had meant them for me, Button Starbuck. Not for another single soul in the whole wonderful state of Texas.

My heart just laid down and quit, cold. I let out a strangled sort of a sound that was supposed to be a glad yell, and lit out up the boardwalk waving after her like I'd missed the last train for home. But I was too late. She had already turned back around and sat down and I knew she hadn't seen me. She never did.

I got only to the far end of the depot building, still running and bumping into people coming along the walk from that way. I broke across the alley north of the depot, gathering my wind to holler, "Hey, May, wait up! wait up!" and that was all. The words were still in my mind and not yet out of my mouth when three men stepped out of the alley in front of me. The leader grabbed my shirtfront and slammed me up against the depot wall. He stuck his rocky, bristle bearded face into mine and growled, "Hello, kid. Remember me?"

It was Pete, Sheriff Egan's deputy.

"Yes sir," I mumbled, "I wasn't going no place, honest I wasn't."

"Hell of a hurry to git there, wasn't you?" asked one of the other men.

"No sir," I said, for no good reason.

"Polite little bastard, ain't he?" grunted the third man.

"As peach pie," nodded Pete, giving me a shove toward the stage, just pulling across from the livery and up in front of the depot. "Git aboard, Starbuck."

"I ain't et yet, dammit!" I objected, getting up a little spunk and holding back.

"Listen to the little man cuss," said Shoemaker, the smaller of Pete's two fellow deputies. "It ain't hardly fit nor proper, sech languidge in front of grown-ups."

"It sure ain't," agreed Simms, the hulking bigger one of them. He grabbed me by the seat of the jeans and the slack of the vest. Pete swung the stage door open. Simms literally threw me into the tonneau. He slammed the door shut back of me and grinned in at the window. "Now mind you, Clarence, no more dirty talk! Papa don't like puttin' you to bed without yer supper but we cain't have you growin' up green-broke and bad-mannered."

He pulled back and Pete stuck his head in the window, but not grinning. Palming his cavalry model Colt out of his holster, he pecked its seven-inch barrel at me warningly. "You make one more break, kid," he told me soberly, "and I'll bend this across yer hat. Understand?"

"Yes sir," I said. Then, not putting off on him, or anybody else, and meaning it from the bottom of my empty puckered stomach. "Gee, don't I git no supper, Pete?"

Simms lounged back to the window, his wet-lip grin working overtime. "Try suckin' yer thumb, Percival," he sneered. "It's only seventy-five miles to Fort Goodwin."

We were under way five minutes later. Pete rode inside with me and the four new passengers getting on at Lampasas. Simms and Shoemaker rode topside with the driver, both carrying shotguns, with their Winchesters unbooted and to hand in the toprack behind them.

The moon rose, the miles rolled on. It was after midnight when I fell asleep.

Chapter Eighteen

Egan's three deputies got off in Fort Goodwin and I never saw them again.

At the last minute Pete turned middling decent. He bought my breakfast and made me take $5 pin money. I didn't want it but since I had already said I was broke, keeping to Brack's orders to shut dead up about what I had under my hat, I had to accept it.

On top of that, he went on and told me to stick close to the stage at stops and not to get caught in any talk with strangers and I would make out all right. He further said that if it was actually Sego who'd been after us, I could count on him not following much past Lampasas County because of all the warrants out for him in the thicker settled counties to the north. As to the rest of his gang, the road between Fort Goodwin and Cleburne and then on into Dallas was too heavy traveled for any broad daylight stickups, and naturally I'd be safe in Big D by dark that night.

I thanked him, feeling mighty awkward, and promised him I would remember him and Sheriff Egan.

He turned back grumpy and said to do him a

favor and not to bother. It was all in the day's
work for them, and I didn't owe them a thing but
to keep clear of Lampasas next time I meant to get
a big brother killed. Then he said a funny thing,
one which made me feel better than I had at any
time since that sick minute of seeing Brack fall
past the coach window, into the dirt. He fetched
me a rough clip on the shoulder and scowled,
"You jest fergit it, kid. What'd you expect yerse'f
to do with Sego Lockhart and six, eight hired guns
starin' at you?"

With that, he gave me a hard look, spit tough,
and turned around and walked off. I never forgot
Pete. He was a pretty good man for all his mean
ways.

We rolled on up to Cleburne for noon dinner
and new horses, making Dallas by way of the
Waxahachie Cut-off about five that evening.

I'd been in Fort Worth with Dad a couple of
times but never in "Big D" as everybody called
Dallas then. Since the banks were all long closed
for the day when we got in, I just located the Stockman's National so's I would know where it was
come opening time next morning. Then I looked
me up a cheap hotel down on the south side.

I didn't sleep much.

I got to the bank with the day janitor about
seven o'clock and had to sit out on the steps for
near two hours until old Colonel Bellingham
showed up a few minutes before nine.

I knew him from Dad's telling about his Robert
E. Lee goatee and his shiny old-fashioned landau
hack with the matched team of blood bay Kentucky coach horses and the old colored driver in

his red-and-white monkey suit up on top. I followed him into his big front window office and told him who I was and what I was after.

He treated me fine to begin with, but pretty quick got started to asking a powerful lot of questions about why Dad or one of the older boys hadn't come for the money, instead of sending a "little old tad" like me.

Right off, he like to threw me, too. He was so fine and good-natured an old gentleman, and all such like as that, that I came mortal close to breaking down and giving him the real truth. But just there I remembered what Brack had said about not saying anything, to anybody. Naturally, I'd wondered before then if he had meant to include Colonel Bellingham in that "anybody." But since he hadn't got to say he didn't, I reckoned I'd better figure he did. So I grabbed a deep breath and launched out on the chance of the Colonel remembering Dad from the old days with General Price.

I told him a straight whopper about how Dad had thought we would maybe run into trouble with Buchanan asking for cash and had sent me along with Brack and Doak for just that very reason. That was, so in case somebody had to run up to Dallas for the money, it could be me, leaving the two older boys to keep an eye on Buchanan and our cattle.

I kept getting in deeper and deeper, the whole thing tasting fishier by the mouthful—even to me. Yet I had made a blind lucky guess.

When I ran out of lies and wind at the same time and was standing there waiting for him to call the bank guards or send for the town constable, he just smiled and fired up his big banker's panatela and allowed the entire yarn fitted "Old Henry" like a kidskin glove.

"Your old daddy, boy," he expanded, "always was a great one for believin' in him, and his." He leaned back in his brass-studded leather chair, blowing a blue cloud of cigar smoke up toward the cut-crystal chandelier. "Ah kin well remembuh a time, seems like it was no more than yestidday, when we were with General Price down Waxahachie way. That was right toward the last, theah." He broke off, peering at me through the smoke.

"You remembuh your daddy speakin' of the General, no doubt?"

"Yes sir, indeed I do, sir!" I answered up, all but saluting him. "Many times. He always said he was the finest soldier ever lived, exceptin' mebbe yourse'f, sir."

"Uhh-harr-rumphh!" he acknowledged. He seemed to choke a bit about mid-draw. "Yes, yes, of course!" He got rid of the rest of the smoke, waving it away from in front of him, real busy, before he went on.

"Well now, boy, this time Ah'm speakin' of was right aftuh your brothuh Brack had joined the regiment. He was a spraddle-legged colt jest about your own age then, boy, near as Ah kin recollect. 'Course," he qualified hastily, sizing me up for the first real time, "theah was a mite more to him. But no mattuh boy, no mattuh. He was jest a little old tad, jest a little old tad—"

"Yes sir," I said.

Brack would have been all of nineteen then, but I didn't mean to make any fuss over a couple of years. Not standing where I was right then. All I wanted was to get my hands on that money and get out of there.

"Yes sir," I prompted him. "You was sayin'—?"

"Well, now, let's see, son. We were down theah around Waxahachie, like I said. We'd heard thet a sizable Yankee patrol was slippin' in between us and Foht Wuth. We needed a man to go out and contact them, if possible findin' out what they had behind them, if anythin'. Young Brack volunteered befoh anothuh man could move out of ranks.

"Well, believe me, Ah wasn't goin' to let him go and right theah is wheah your daddy stepped up and said, 'Thet's right, Colonel, don't nevah send no boy to do a man's job—*not less'n he's a Stahbuck boy!*' Now, I ask you, son. Does thet sound like your old daddy, or doesn't it?"

"Yes sir," I agreed fast, "it sure does."

It did, too. And it brought a bad lump in my throat to hear it told like that and then to have to stand there and lie about it to Colonel Bellingham. But I was in too deep to start laying back in the shafts by that time. So I just put my head down and leaned into the collar.

"How about the money, Colonel?"

He looked at me, cocking his head a little too quick I thought. But then he smiled and waved his cigar again and said, "Well suh, comin' from anybody but Henry Stahbuck, I'd say a man was crazy to send a button like you to carrih back $25,000 in cash. But knowin' old Henry—"

"Yes sir?" I muttered anxiously.

"You got a moneybelt, boy?"

"No sir." That's how green I was. I hadn't even thought about how I was going to tote all that money back to Mason.

"Well, no mattuh, you jest run down the street and buy yourse'f one and come on back heah. Ah'll have the money counted out foh you."

I thanked him and got out of there as quick as I could. I wasn't as relieved as I'd thought I would be, though. In the half hour it took me to find a harness shop and buy the belt, I got a lot more worrying done. It didn't advance me an inch, either.

I had tossed all night down in that hotel about whether or not to tell the Colonel the whole story, regardless of what I thought Brack had meant me to do. But when daybreak had come, I still didn't know.

If I *did* tell him, he was sure to hold me up until he could check on my claims about Dad being killed—not to mention Brack and Doak—meanwhile wasting precious time in going about the whole thing legal and careful the natural way a banker would want to. I knew, too, there was no way in the world ever to prove Rance Buchanan had sent Sego up to our ranch, or even that Sego had ever been there. The same went for the way him and his bunch had got Brack and Doak. So the sleepless way it had worked out for me, was that there wasn't but one surefire course to get that money back down to Mason City on time. That was to lay a smooth lie over the whole thing for the Colonel, letting on like I'd been sent for it with no question on our side, and none expected from the bank's. If the bluff worked, I would at least leave Dallas with time left to get back to Buchanan's Lazy RB Ranch with the cash. If it didn't, I hadn't lost but the little time it took me to tell the lie.

Now, it *had* worked.

I was going to get the money. I would have it wrapped around my middle, under my old cotton workshirt and ponyhide vest, within the next twenty minutes.

And five minutes after that I would be standing out on the big stone steps in front of the Stockman's National Bank in Dallas, Texas, with $25,000 in greenback cash sweat-stuck to my shrinking stomach. And with nothing left between me and that money and Mason City but one simple little question.

How was I going to get it there?

It was the one thing my brother Brack had failed to figure out for me. The one thing he hadn't told me how to do.

But the shivery fact it brought me square up against that May morning on the steps of the Stockman's National Bank, was something nobody had to tell me about.

For the first real time in seventeen years, I was on my own.

Chapter Nineteen

That was a real big question, that one of figuring out what was the best way to go about getting that money back to Mason City. But before I got out of that harness shop it turned from just plain big, to downright deadly.

It did it in a way nobody could have imagined ahead of time, or even believed, unless it had happened to him.

My main problem, as I fretted over it while the clerk was showing me some belts, was just the bare idea of anybody my age carrying that much cash down into the toughest county in Texas. That is, doing it without giving himself away, somewhere along the line, to one of the sharpers or floating highline riders the country was crawling with after the bad times of last year.

I was fairly sure, from what Pete had told me in Fort Goodwin, that I didn't have to worry about Buchanan's bunch making any serious play much outside their home county of Mason. That apparently went double for Sego, himself. So, actually, I wasn't thinking along the lines of having real trouble from that direction until I got back down somewhere near the Mason and Lampasas country. Meantime, I figured all I had to worry about was some other stray bunch, or loner, spotting me and the money before then.

I got the first glimmer of how wrong Pete could be, and I was about to be, when somebody moved up behind me at the belt counter, as the clerk went into the back of the store to bring out some more belts.

"Don't look up and don't let on we're talkin'," I heard a familiar voice say. "It's me, Billie Joe Heston."

The name and the voice jumped me over two hundred miles, back to Mason City. It was the young kid I had heard with Sego in Pegleg's stable, and seen with him in the Lone Star Saloon.

"What're you doin' here?" I heard myself asking, my own voice so tight it squeaked.

"Same as you. Lookin' fer a moneybelt."

"What you mean?"

"I mean the one you're goin' to buy. Sego sent me and two others up here to tail you away from the bank."

My neck hairs got up on end. "Gawd Amighty, how'd they know? About the bank, I mean?"

"Buchanan, what you think? Your brother showed him your letter of credit didn't he?"

"Jesus—"

"You said it, kid. Let's look at some saddles. Yonder comes the clerk."

I picked out a belt, fast, paid for it, moved along off as though to browse the saddle rack before leaving. Billie Joe was already there, on the far side of the rack. He talked fast. While he did, he kept shooting side-glances out to the street in front of the store and letting on near as spooked and skittery as I was.

"They're out front, there, waitin' fer me. They sent me in to see what you bought and how you paid fer it. They wasn't sure you'd got the money yet."

"I ain't. Who's they?"

"Morgan Counts and Beatty Grimes. Two of the four that was with Sego when he got your old man."

Even in a corner that tight, the mention of Dad's murder put a little iron in me. "Who was the other two?" I wanted to know.

"Me," said Billie Joe, "and Cheyenne Carson."

He saw the look I shot him over the bucking roll of a low-cantled bronc rig, and handed it back to me without warming it up any.

"Now, listen kid. You shet up and use your ears. Brains too if you got any. You hear?"

I nodded that I did.

"All right," he went on. "We stay in here much longer, Beatty and Morg are goin' to come in after us. They're bad jumpy. We got mebbe another two minutes. Your daddy's dead and neither you nor me kin he'p that now. So's your two brothers. All's left is you. So why the hell you think I'm here?"

"I dunno, fer Christ's sake," I said. "Why are you?"

"To he'p you if I kin. It won't be much, with them two after you, but it might leastways give you a halfways chance. Thet's more'n your daddy or brothers got. You goin' to hesh up and listen?"

"I'm hearin' you, Billie Joe!" I gulped out his

name without thinking, but knowing that in some crazy way I'd never dreamed about down there, I'd made a third friend in Mason City. "Fer Gawd's sake, go ahead on!"

He did. And in those hundred and twenty seconds he'd allowed we had to spare before Counts and Grimes got suspicious he proved that, crazy or not, I was right about that third friend.

It was just one of those things of two boys caught in a man's mess they had both been drifted into by accident. And both being lonely and scared and bad outclassed at the same time. There wasn't any other way to explain it, then nor later. Billie Joe Heston and me simply took a natural shine to one another. It was all in the world made him do what he'd done for me, and made me listen to him tell of it there between the new saddles in F. D. Mercer's Harness Shop in Dallas. And not only listen to him, but to believe him and to wish I had his guts and gumption and more, to forgive him and feel that he was my real friend—even though he had been with the men who had killed Dad and Doak and Brack. There sure wasn't any explaining that, either. It was just some more of that same lonesomeness and being afraid: that kicked around, friendly dog feeling that draws boys together wherever things are being run by hard men who have no time, nor temper, nor love to waste on anything that isn't man-grown.

So Billie Joe talked and I listened.

This is what I heard.

Ever since Sego had shot down Dad, Billie Joe had been trying to quit him and get out. But Sego was watching him, special. He had told him he was. That he suspicioned he was thinking of running out and that the minute he saw anything that made him sure of it, Billie Joe would get his. So he'd had to go along with the bunch, playing for the break that would give him a twenty-four-hour headstart, clear of Mason County.

To test him, Sego had put him with the two new men who had fronted the stage outside of Lampasas. He had been the one on the left, the one missed by Brack's third, wild shot. Letting on he was satisfied with the way he had behaved on that job, Sego had sent him up to Dallas with Counts and Grimes. But Billie Joe had an inside fear the latter'd had orders to take care of him on the way back, providing they got the money off of me somewhere short of Mason County.

The way Billie Joe figured it, having missed getting the deposit receipt and signed contract off of Brack for Buchanan, Sego was going after me and the cash money on his own. Either way, whether he meant to stick with Rance or double-cross him, Billie Joe still had that inside hunch that Sego had decided to leave him, as a weak link, safe and silent in some lonely dry wash up Dallas way.

With that in mind, he had risked sneaking into Sheriff Blackburn's office and spilling the whole thing to him.

It was Blackburn had told him to stick with Counts and Grimes, making his getaway play in Dallas. Old Ewell's deal on what came after that was that he would stand by Billie Joe in court later on for his part in the killings, providing only if he could get to me in Dallas before Counts and Grimes did. He made it real simple. If they *did* get to me and the money, Billie Joe Heston had better spend the rest of his natural life riding wide of Sheriff Ewell Blackburn. If they *didn't*, he had best spend that same time sweating about staying far clear of Mason City and Sego Lockhart.

It was the kind of a choice that was no choice at all.

Billie Joe had picked me, not even rightly understanding why he had, in my opinion.

But now, having kept his promise to Sheriff Blackburn, if he could give Counts and Grimes the slip he was going to run for his life. That was all he had to say. He wound it up, right there, took a last look out front, started to move for the door.

I caught him in the second step.

"Billie Joe, wait up a minute! Where in hell you goin' to run?"

"Dunno, kid. South, I reckon."

"Don't you do it, you hear! It's jest what they'll expect."

"Yeah, well, so long, Starbuck. I got to go."

"Dammit all, I listened to you! Now you listen to me!" He held up, hesitating a minute when I hissed that at him. I put it to him fast.

I told him to head for our place on the Brazos, and how to get there out of Fort Worth. I told him about old Sec forming up that bunch of his *mesteñero* friends to follow us down to Mason and how, if he really wanted to help me, he could do it by riding hard for the ranch and speeding them up, if they hadn't yet left. Also, whether he made it in time to catch Sec or not, I added, the Starbuck ranch would be the last place in the world that

Sego, or any county sheriff in West Texas would ever think to look for him.

I think it was that last part of it that did it. He thanked me with a kind of a head-hung nod and said, "All right, kid, I'll do it," and was gone before I could say good luck.

I gave him time to get out and back to his friends in the street.

When I went out, I turned right and took off up toward the bank. I whistled as good as I could with my spit sticking, and swung the moneybelt in my hand to keep time and to make sure anybody that might be interested could see it was empty and that I wasn't worrying about its being that way for long.

I didn't look around the whole way. But when I crossed west over the street to climb the big stone steps of the Stockman's National, I got a chance, back of a passing beer wagon, to steal a look back.

Morgan Counts and Beatty Grimes were just stepping off the east curb.

Billie Joe Heston wasn't with them.

Chapter Twenty

The first bad turn came inside, not outside the bank. When I eased into Colonel Bellingham's office, my eyes popped out far enough to knock off with a stick. Stacked on his desk, for all the world like so many little brass poker chips, was my $25,000. *In $20 goldpieces!*

"Jesus Murphy, Colonel!" I gasped. "You mean to say I got to pack all thet money *thetaway?*"

"Son," he said soberly, "with these muleheaded Texicans, theah isn't any othuh way."

The Colonel was a First Family Virginian. In his opinion, as with all those old FFV's, as we called them, that set him a good cut above the rest of the Confederacy—especially the long-haired cousins from Texas. "Theah isn't a South'un cattleman west of the Nueces Brakes will take Yankee papuh less'n he's got the homeplace mortgage due and nothin' bettuh to pay it with. Surely you ought to know thet from your old daddy, boy."

"Yes, sir, I'd forgot," I lied. I hadn't forgot at all, really. By that time in Texas, there was lots of federal paper around and folks were beginning to use it for something besides to frame and hang on the front parlor wall. It was good as government gold most places, but I allowed the Colonel was a banker and knew his business.

I allowed right.

"What would you figure to do, son?" he asked, with that bird-bright way he had of cocking his head and pecking it at you, "once you got back to Mason City with your belt full of nice fresh treasury notes and then had your Mr. Buchanan up and tell you thet when a Llano Rivuh ranchuh says cash, he means U.S. gold?"

I thought quick and bluffed a chessy cat grin.

"Well, Colonel, I reckon I'd say, 'Yes sir, that's whut Colonel Bellingham up to the bank in Dallas told me,' and start countin' him out his stack in $20 yaller chips."

Lucky for me, he bought the grin as well as the sneaky pat on the back.

"You'd say right, boy," he nodded real pleased. "Heah, now, let me he'p you with the belt. Theah's a right way and a wrong way to pack the infernal things, so they will set neat and not bulk too much under your clothes."

When we got it loaded, that belt weighed the best part of one hundred pounds. I weighed less than one hundred and fifty, soaked six days in the horse trough. I would be doing good to tote it out of sight of the bank belted around my middle like that, without it broke me square in two. How, ever, in the good Lord's name I was going to pack it all the way to Mason, I had no rightful notion.

One thing was sure. I couldn't possibly walk natural with it.

The minute anybody would see me staggering out of the bank, he'd know one of two things;

either I was early morning drunk, or had just cleaned out the vault. The "sure" part of it was that Morgan Counts and Beatty Grimes would know I hadn't been belting any bourbon in the Stockman's National.

It was time to think fair quick.

"Colonel," I said, hitching the belt up and wishing I had some hips to hold it there, "if you all don't mind, I would like to use your washroom before settin' out. I'll be on thet Cleburne stage a powerful long time without I git another chanct."

He told me where the gents' room was in the back of the bank and said, "Now you jest do thet, boy. And when you see your daddy, give him my very best regahds. Tell him Ah'm comin' out to Mineral Wells on business the lattuh paht of August and will surely expect to spend some time with him while Ah'm theah."

With that, he gave me one of those flossy old-fashioned Dixie bows and was back to his desk and his gilt-edge ledgers before I could thumb my hat and back out of the room.

That was how much sending $25,000 in gold to an old Confederate friend by way of a coming eighteen-year-old boy worried Colonel Isaiah Bellingham. He was, for sure, one of the last of his breed in the Texas banking business. To him, a man's word or his handshake or his son sent to town with a note pinned inside his vest pocket was as safe as his bond. In those days, good men still understood and trusted one another. They had to. There just weren't anywhere near enough law officers to make anything but the old western, "shake hands and hold off till the crop money is in," credit system work.

Which was the whole answer to the how and why of what found me heading for the Stockman's National washroom with better than $20,000 on me that May 4 morning, and not a set of eyes in the entire building following me. Ten years later, I couldn't have walked out of that bank with $500, short of having it secured by a $50,000 ranch.

All I was looking for in that washroom was a window.

My kidneys were way too tight puckered with worrying about those two hard-faced trailhounds of Sego's waiting out front to loosen up for the next sixty miles.

There was a window, all right. It was a big one, with a low casement, and standing wide open.

That was tolerable good luck for a starter, but in the alley outside things shrunk up considerable. It was a short, dead-end box, opening out on the street I had just come up from the harness shop. The bank was a corner building and from its front steps Counts and Grimes could see the alley exit clear as they could the bank entrance. Behind me was only the washroom window wall. Across from me was a ten-foot brick fence closing in some kind of warehouse yard with no alley gate. At the far, dead end was a little feedstore loading dock.

That was it. I was up a blind canyon. Unless something happened to get me out of it, I was in a real bad squeeze.

But something did.

Up at the far end of the alley, the feedstore owner was just coming out onto the dock. He padlocked the one door into the store and climbed up on a wagonload of bagged feed to make a delivery. I got ready.

He gave me a funny look as he drove by and I squinched up flat against the building to give him room. If he had given me another look after he got by, it likely would have been a funnier one yet. For he wouldn't have been looking at anything but a mighty empty alley. When that feed wagon rumbled out onto the side street, swung the corner and creaked past the bank, I was wedged in under a dozen tailgate sacks of Hackenschmidt's Superior Horse Bran.

The last I saw of Sego's watchdogs, they were loafing restless along the front street curb eying the bank doors. Which was fine with me.

But the last I "heard" of them was something else again. And nowhere near so fine.

The feed wagon moved by them so close I could have spit in their shifty eyes—if I'd had any spit. Right abreast of them, the driver held up his team to let a fine-looking lady in a flashy dogcart swing her nice blacks clear of our wide load. Just as she made it and before our big dray horses could dig in and get rolling again, Counts took a scowling drag on his ricehull cigarette, threw it down and ground it under his boot.

"Dammit to hell, I don't like it, you hear? What's keepin' the little squirt in there all this time?"

"I dunno," said Beatty Grimes. "But I'll tell you one thing."

"Yeah?"

"Yeah. If he ain't out of there in five minutes, I'm goin' in and find out."

I stayed with the feed wagon for a good half hour and until it stopped way over on the west side of town. I was in more good luck there.

The load of sacked bran was going to a horse trader's place, which was where we pulled up. I got out from under the bags, ducked back of a handy crib of shelled corn, dug the bran dust out of my ears and straightened myself up. Then I waited till the load was put off, the driver paid and the wagon gone back up the road into town. When it was, I stepped out and had my go at the trader.

He was a wizened up little old cuss of a quarterbreed siwash of some kind, and tack-sharp like a man in his business had to be.

He listened to me tell him what I was after, never letting up watching me the whole time I was talking. He had a face as pint-sized and dirty and sun-shrunk as an Osage orange that had ground-laid on the west side of the hedge since last August. His eyes were no bigger than new dimes, bright and glittery and sunk deep into his head. The way he used them minded me of the pet monkey a heathen Chinee roundup cook Dad had hired one fall had owned, and had kept chained to the chuckwagon tailgate. I knew from one look at him that he was the very first *hombre* I was going to have to be careful with.

"Sounds to me," he said, when I'd done describing the kind of outfit I had in mind, "thet whut you want is a fifteen-dollar hoss and a five-dollar hull."

"Yes sir," I bobbed my head, dull-like. "I allow thet's about it."

"But it looks," he went on as though I hadn't said a word, "as if you could afford somethin' a sight nicer."

"Whut you mean?" I asked, playing the dumb act for all it was worth. "I don't foller you."

"Well, foller this," he advised me, with his snaky, button-eyed blink. "You're dressed some neat fer a boy thet's down to buyin' wolf bait."

I was, that was a fact. My boots alone cost more than the horse and saddle I was dickering for. It was something I hadn't thought about till that minute, but I was sure thinking about it now. And he was watching me do it. Mighty close.

"Whut you gettin' at?" I stalled, still trying to play it like I had spent my school days setting under a pointed paper hat on the corner stool.

"Don't let it sweat you none," he shrugged. "We git all kinds of customers here. Most, like yourse'f, in summat of a hurry."

"Mister," I said, "You're sure losin' me."

"Uh-huh," he nodded, peering off up the road the way the wagon had gone. "Well, look at it this-away, cowboy. Happen I was tryin' to ease out'n town without the marshal caught me at it, I'd not figure to be see'd settin' a fifteen-dollar hoss with forty-dollar boots on. Them eggshells settle the java any fer you?"

I let down a little, even faked a half-honest grin. It was all right with me if he wanted to think I was on the dodge from the Dallas law. Still, like I say, that smirk I handed him wasn't worth more than fifty cents on the dollar. It didn't, for one sure thing, cut a tongue-lick of the sharp mustard off the unsettling fact he'd been able to pick me out for some kind of a bluff-runner, right off the bat.

"Well," I stammered, coloring bad, "as a matter of fact I was hopin' I might swap you the boots fer the hoss. You see, I'm sorta long on credit and short on cash right at the minute."

"Cash and brains," he said. Then he looked at me, shaking his head as though I'd already been shot and rolled over into the arroyo. "No deal, Buster. Hoss and saddle will cost you money. But I got some used duds I'll trade you fer the boots."

"Whut duds you got?"

"*Cholo* kid," he grunted. "Little shrimp, 'bout your size. Had him swampin' stalls and mangerin' hay up to yistidday. Marshal come a'lookin' for him on a *borracho* stabbin' over to Chili Town couple nights gone. He lit out th'ough the sage-bresh, barefoot. I'll swap you the boots even fer his stuff."

It must have looked to him like I was hesitating, for he squinted me up and down with his blinky stare and added on, " 'Pears to me you could pass for a chili picker your ownse'f. And in purty good light, too, happen you was dressed fer the part." Then, with a mile-wide grin and wink worse than the villain in an opera house stage place, *"No es verdad, amigo?"*

I knew what he meant, all right. He wasn't talking about me looking like a Mexican, either. Though, along with being called a Comanche by Brack and Doak in fun, I'd had a fist fight or two out in back of the boys' outhouse after school over getting that "chili picker" label pasted onto me, for serious, by smart kids showing off in front of the girls at recess time.

But it wasn't that that was holding me up from answering him.

I had spotted a pair of old U.S. Cavalry saddle-bags hanging back of him on the shed wall in amongst a bunch of other moldy green horse tack. They were the kind you slung across the horn on either side of your pony's withers and were mostly used by couriers to carry dispatches and suchlike in. They hung neat and flat, couldn't be jolted or worked loose, yet could be lifted off and got free in no time.

"Mister," I said, "you've almost got yourse'f a deal. Th'ow in them old cross-horn cavalry pouches and let's git on out to the back hoss pens."

We closed it there. I went into the harness lean-to where the runaway swamper had bunked, and changed into the Mexican kid's things. They were terrible mean and poor, but reasonable clean. I even took his peak-crown Sonora hat and ratty Chihuahua serape. It was a miserable outfit but the kid had been a horseman. The bow that was set into the cheap cowhide boots and worn leather "*chapareras*" leggins, fitted my own bent legs like they'd been cut for me. By the time I had followed the monkey-eyed trader out to the back pen where he kept his sorebacked packmules, bear-bait mustangs and other sick or crippled stock I was feeling pretty good.

In the next twenty seconds I was feeling even better.

That was exactly how long it took me to spot and fall in love with Gavilanito.

He was the sorriest-looking horse ever foaled north of Ciudad Juarez. But he was pure Spanish and of the breed the *mesteñeros* swore would die before they tired. Everything about him was right to my eye, and to all the secrets of the real *criollo* taught me by Sec Gonzales.

He wasn't two fingers over thirteen hands, wouldn't weigh seven hundred pounds, grass fat. He was neither Roman-nosed nor dish-faced but straightheaded and wide between the eyes, with short sensitive ears. He was barrel-bellied and spindly boned, yet thick through the fore- and hindquarters where it counted. He was ewe-necked and rattailed, knee-sprung before and cowhocked behind. And ribby and saddle-galled and spur-scarred and had a hip knocked down on one side and a stiff hock on the other. Just about everything you could hope for in a Mexican raised and rode mustang.

But mostly he had the color. Not the true *bayo coyote*, the coyote dun, like Mozo, but the only other color that was as good and maybe even a shade better. That would be the *grullo.*

The *grullo* was a slaty blue, mouse-colored horse called after the smoky-feathered *grullas,* or sand-hill cranes, so common down our way. This one, this Gavilanito, was line-backed and had the leg stripes like all true *grullos* and the best duns, but that wasn't all. He had not only the dorsal stripe and barred legs, but the rare crossline over the shoulders to make the *cruz* of the Christ-marked Mexican burros—a marking that in the Spanish mind stamped him as *"un caballo de caballos—a horse among horses."*

His name, in Spanish, meant "the little hawk," and when I called him by it, "Gavilanito! Gavilanito!" he at once threw up his head and grunted soft and happy in his throat. When I moved in on him clucking some of the gentle Coahuila words I had learned from Sec, he whickered eager and grateful, trotted up to me and shoved his homely, bristly whiskered nose under my arm with a wheezy-lunged sigh of old friend gladness that would have put a lump in any ranch boy's throat. I had bought myself a horse.

I paid for him, laced on the old high forked $5 hull I had picked out, slung on my verdigrised cavalry pouches and got out of there.

I never looked back.

Beyond the horse trader's barns and stockpens, the west road faded out into the open sagebrush the way a hill-country spring branch spreads and dies in thirsty desert sand. It was my kind of road from that minute on. I knew it and I took it, me and Little Hawk.

Ten minutes later there wasn't anything but the horned toads and chaparral birds to argue the lonesomeness of those empty wagon ruts running into nowhere due west of Dallas, Texas.

Chapter Twenty-one

It was about one hundred seventy-five miles, crows' flight, from Dallas to Mason City. I meant to ride it as close to crow-straight as I could. But an hour out of town I began to worry.

I was getting a little direction-puzzled already. Right after setting out, it had come on to rain. Not much, just a blustery, blowy spring squall. That was fine for laying my dust but the low scudding clouds which came with it cut off the sun, leaving me nothing to tell me which way was southwest. The growingly uneasy fact now was that since stopping a mile or so back to switch the gold from the moneybelt to the saddlebags, I'd had no rightful idea where I was pointed.

Suppose I got lost for fair?

I had four days on the face of it. Or perhaps the best part of them. But I couldn't figure it that loose.

I had to leave a full day in Mason. That was to get in touch with Sheriff Blackburn, barring Sec being there to help me, or to work out in whatever other way I could the problem of getting the money to Buchanan in such a way he couldn't lift it off of me in the last mile and minute.

Mainly, I was counting on the sheriff, because of what he had done for me by way of Billie Joe. Still, even with him to help me, we had to have time to set up delivery of the money safe and sure. You just didn't walk into a town like Mason with $25,000 and holler, "Come and git it, boys, or I'll throw it to the woodpeckers." It would be like driving into a Comanche *ranchería* with a wagonload of fresh buffalo meat and asking for directions on how to deliver it to their dear friends and western neighbors the Mescalero Apaches. You would be stomped to death in the stampede to be helpful.

So that cut a day off my four, leaving me three.

Two of those three would be needed just to cover the ground between me and Buchanan's Lazy RB, and that providing Little Hawk proved out sound and could make one hundred miles a day, two days' hard running.

It left me twenty-four hours slack. And all I had to do to tighten that time up so short it would strangle me was to make one wrong turn somewhere in the two-thirds of Texas that sprawled out ahead rainy gray and landmark empty, between me and the New Mexico line.

So it was no joke about getting lost. I had managed to do it within forty miles of my own beloved Brazos, out chasing mustang broomtails. Many was the long night I had slept out by a mesquite fire waiting for the sun to show me the way home. That West Texas *llano* was to a ranch kid like the ocean to a Gulf port sailor boy. Once you lost your landfall, it was all alike. You could wander for a week and wind up right where you started. Nowhere.

Another twenty minutes of what I figured was due west riding did it. I turned Little Hawk sharp left, started looking for a high spot to take a sight from. Pretty quick I found a ridge that gave me a thirty-mile view of what ought to be the south. And way down there I saw something that looked might good—a long snaky line of wagon tracks looping through the brush and creeping back up toward where I imagined Dallas to be. It was maybe six, seven miles down there but the morning quiet was so still, with just the right feathery gulf breeze lifting the shower mists and clearing the ground steam, that I could see those wagon tracks like I was looking through a telescope. The sight of them struck me as clear and sweet as the sound of a lost packmule's bell in the mountains.

I wasn't sure what tracks they were but from the southwest direction they looked to lay, they could easy be those of the stage road I'd come up on. I didn't linger up on that ridge sweating about it. I took off to find out. Whether that was the stage road or not down there didn't really matter. It was a road and it was running my way. As long as it did, I aimed to run with it.

I cut the rocks and ruts of its grade about forty minutes later. I set out down it, keeping to the easier going it made for Little Hawk. Before long the clouds broke away. When the sun came out it hit me between the shoulder blades and I knew I had guessed right about it running southwest. It was about eleven o'clock.

I held Little Hawk on a steady singlefoot until the sun was low enough to strike in under my hat brim. By five o'clock and a watering stop at a shabby rundown horse ranch back in the chaparral, I found out I was only five miles east of Cleburne.

The rancher's wife was good and lonely. She hadn't seen her man for three weeks, she said, as he was out trailing a couple of Comanche pony borrowers. I told her I was a poor orphan Mexican-American boy from Goliad, going west to look for work as a cowboy on one of the big gringo ranches. She told me a lot of things. Mostly they were her troubles with her man and getting him to make love. When she fetched me a snaggle-toothed grin and reached for me with her saggy fat arms and said what a fine, strong-looking young *cholo* boy I was and wouldn't I come along in the house and have some warm supper, I knew I had overplayed my politeness and my sprucing up at her horse trough.

I got away from there, laying some dust doing it. Yet I had got one little tip, outside of learning not to strain the Starbuck smile past a decent "howdy, ma'am" with any left-alone horse rancher's woman. That was that if I cut sharp south by a shade west just past her place, I would hit the mainline stage road about three miles outside Cleburne. That was, to the south of it. And more, too. From Cleburne, the stage road was my shortest route to Fort Goodwin. It would let me get on down that far, night riding if I wanted, without any chance of losing my way. Which was real good. For, once past Fort Goodwin, I wouldn't dare follow any nice, easy-riding stage road between there and Mason.

Needless to say, I heeded the woman's words about the short cut around Cleburne, and took it.

I figured I had a fair sound reason. Two of them, in fact. One named Counts, the other Grimes.

Naturally, that was just a flying guess. But it could prove a mean close one. Out of Dallas for Cleburne, the stageline ran in pretty open country. About two o'clock I'd had to throw Little Hawk into the handiest stand of horse-high brush, in a real tall hurry. That was to let the morning coach from Dallas, which had snuck up on me behind a long rise, hammer past. It was late, as usual, and laying on the leather to make up. I couldn't be sure, with the dust and the way that old Concord was rocking, but I thought the two big *hombres* facing one another in the windowseats on my side looked a powerful lot like Counts and Grimes.

It had been a tight call and was no more than I deserved for the hour I had wasted bucking the sagebrush west of the horse trader's. And it was why, as I guided Little Hawk up the last low ridge of the cut-off trail where it topped out above the road to Fort Goodwin, I was letting out a mighty grateful sigh of relief.

For a third real good reason.

The stage made a regular one-hour layover in Cleburne for five o'clock supper. Once you knew that, there followed a whole string of nasty little "ifs," which all came down to one nice big one.

If Counts and Grimes were on that morning stage from Dallas, as I figured they stood a good chance of being from that quick glimpse from the roadside brush back yonder, and if I hadn't had the tomfool luck to hear the stage and get hid in time to grab that glance, I likely would have chanced riding right on through Cleburne. And if I had done that, I would have run a fifty-fifty gamble of blundering square into them rolling their after-supper smokes on the veranda of the Cleburne House Hotel!

So that's how come I was letting out that big sigh and figuring I had played everything pretty smart up to now. I hadn't, and was sighing way too soon. I found that out awful quick.

Five minutes later I pulled Little Hawk in atop the rise. Over west, the sun was six o'clock low, resting tired and dusty red in Hueco Pass far out beyond the Pecos. Below me, snaking through the Bosque County brush flats, lay the soiled-ribbon trace of the San Antonio & Central Southwest Stageline's Fort Goodwin road. The light was still plenty good and would be for another hour or more.

But I didn't need any hour to see through the dustboil I was looking at.

It was low and flat and a long ways off, putting me sudden in mind of that other dustcloud me and Doak had set and watched above the Paint Rock road what now seemed like a lifetime back. But this wasn't rider dust. It wasn't coming out of the San Saba barranca and it wasn't being raised by Sego Lockhart.

It was Abbot-Downing dust. Being put up by a six-horse hitch ahead of a nine-passenger, heavy-duty coach built in Concord, New Hampshire.

It meant two things. One for sure, one for almost certain.

That damn driver had made up better than an hour getting into Cleburne.

Ten got you one that no matter how many passengers he had aboard with tickets paid through, at least to Lampasas, two of them were named Morgan Counts and Beatty Grimes.

Chapter Twenty-two

There was nothing to do but go on that night toward Fort Goodwin.

I figured I had another thirty miles to the town itself. As I sat Little Hawk on that ridge outside Cleburne, I had already been riding eight hours. That meant we had made somewhere around fifty miles so far that day. Yet the little horse had gone right well and still felt good under me. I put him on down the ridge, still thinking.

Getting to the road I crossed on over it, then decided to gamble. I remembered a good camp spot down along the stageline about five miles. I had daylight aplenty remaining to ride it easy, still leaving me time to get in some wood, build a coffee fire, let my horse graze and water and myself to snatch a little nap before getting on.

It was risky following the stage road but it was my best bearing once the sun was down. Further, I allowed Counts and Grimes had no likely reason for getting off the coach short of Lampasas. The only thing I had to watch out for was other chance riders. I figured I was getting smart enough to handle that part of it.

Besides, I was dying for some coffee.

I had traded with the horse rancher's wife for a half pound of Arbuckle's and a quart feed measure to boil it in, along with some bannock bread and cold fried fatback, before things got personal. I hadn't had a bite to eat the whole day long and when I got to thinking about the smell of that coffee steaming up in a can of branchwater, that did it.

I got to the camp spot all right. Putting Little Hawk to graze down by the creek, I got my Arbuckle's boiled and drunk. It was wonderful. The bannock and fatback weren't far behind. They went down easy and sweet as roast humpribs and buffalo tongue. They sat a little heavy was all.

I threw some sand on my fire, so's it wouldn't wisp any smoke up against the twilight sky. Then I knocked the grounds out of the feedcan coffee tin and went down to the branch to wrench it out and see to the gelding.

That little old *grullo* was smart.

He showed that, and his breed as well, by the way he was all set to go when I got down to him.

He hadn't had the bit out of his mouth twenty minutes, yet he was all through with his grass and water. If I knew his kind, he hadn't taken on more than a dozen handfuls of the one, nor three quarts of the other. He knew he wasn't halfway to where he was going. Until he got there, he wasn't about to founder himself on a sour bellyful of wet hay. That was your Spanish mustang for you. Any other horse, rode fifty miles on one water stop and turned loose on a clear branch of cold running springwater and all the prairie hay he could crop in six months of not pulling his head up, would have drunk and stuffed himself to a fatal fit of colic.

But that wise little old Gavilanito horse met me halfway up the creektrail, tossing his ragged forelock and jawing his cuspy yellow teeth at me in a way that said, plain as red paint, "Come on, pardner, let's you and me make another fifty miles before midnight!"

I grinned and gave him a good ear-scratching and a little piece of the cold fatback I had saved specially for him. He ate it and liked it. Which was just one more of the wonderful things about those coldblood, rangebred ones. They would eat anything a might hungry man would, and grateful for the favor. Turning the token around, I've seen hotblood settlement horses sold for hundreds of dollars that would starve to death where there was offtrack feed enough—like mesquite beanpods, prickly pear pulps, cottonwood bark and green willow browse—to carry forty mustangs through a hard winter.

When I slipped the bit back in his mouth, he rolled it a minute to get it set proper on his tongue, then followed me on to the camp spot happy as a Bluetick hound I'd raised from a pup.

I didn't do a thing to anchor him when we got there, save to cinch the front girth back up and drop the reins. That was to let him know we would be traveling soon and, being a Spanish horse, it was all he needed to know. He had his head hung and his eyes drooped closed before I could throw down my serape and stretch out to join him.

I slept quick and easy, knowing he would whicker a warning the minute anything more serious than a nosy coyote or kit fox got within prairie smell or night sight of us. There just never was a city- or settlement-raised watchdog, nor a ranch one either, could come within a sixteen-section stretch of a Texas mustang on letting his master know trouble was afoot and sneaking his way.

When I woke up, the moon, just two days short of lumpy full, was inching clear of the creek willows. I judged it to be about eight, nine o'clock; high time to be moving on.

Little Hawk was standing right where he had put his head down two hours ago. He gave me his muttering little whicker when I got up, and a bunt in the backside with his upper lip bristles when I took up on the flank strap. That was all. I didn't even need to touch him with the irons when I swung up. He was already moving for the stage road by the time I had eased my weight back against the cantle.

For the fun of it I didn't give him any knee or neckrein when we hit the coach tracks, wanting to see what he would do. Naturally, he did it. Without a look the other way. Just turned south and lined out straight down the ruts for Fort Goodwin.

Well, it simply had to make you feel better to have a horse like that under you. And why not?

He would have me better than halfway to Mason by sunup. That would mean a good thirty miles beyond Fort Goodwin, the last bad chance, short of Lampasas, of running into Counts and Grimes. After that, I had only to rest up a good part of the whole day, use what was left of it to bypass Lampasas in the early dark of evening, and night-ride on across country to hit into Mason safe ahead of daylight, May 6. Worked out that way, it looked plumb foolproof. Even plumb damnfool proof. I would have my twenty-four hours with Sheriff Blackburn in Mason, and to spare.

It was a beautiful thought. I was still dwelling on it twenty miles down the line.

Then, with the lights of Fort Goodwin twinkling two miles ahead and just as I was swinging Little Hawk to cut through the chaparral wide around them, the game little *grullo* stumbled and went to going lame on his onside forefoot.

I was off of him on the third limp. And all the beauty went out of that soft May night in the next ten seconds.

His left front shoe was loose, hanging by only two nails. Under it, his hard little hoof was split bad in the wall of the toe and was rock-cut and bleeding between the bulbs and the frog.

How many miles he had gone on it that way, the good Lord alone knew. For only He would know how deep and great was a Texas mustang's heart. And how far it might be to the iron bottom of a brave little Spanish scrub like Gavilanito. Yet it did not matter, now, how many miles were behind him. The frightening thought was how many he had left in front of him. And the good Lord didn't have to tell me that.

One, probably. Two at the most. Then he was done, save for one desperate "unless."

A good blacksmith could trim and pin the split hoof and have a new sidebar shoe on it, strong and good as ever, in less than thirty minutes. Unless I got Little Hawk to such a smith inside of two miles he might be lamed for life—for sure would be for the next three weeks.

I didn't have three weeks, nor three days. And there was a good blacksmith in Fort Goodwin.

"Little hoss," I said, "move careful and keep your weight off that foot."

I stayed down off him, handleading and petting him the whole way. It was a long walk across to those twinkling lights.

Out in the brush at the edge of town I held up, peering through the whitening glare of the moon, down the dusty street. It was a spooky minute.

Fort Goodwin couldn't even be called a wide spot in the road. It consisted of three saloons, a feedstore, general store, rickety stageline depot and flyspeck lunchroom, livery barn and blacksmith shop. There were maybe half a dozen smaller shanties being lived in, clustered like brushticks on a sick calf, to the cracked board flanks of the main buildings both north and south of town. That was it, other than the chaparral, the moonlight and a couple of forlorn coyotes tuning up over in the badland brakes beyond the brush flats.

The lights I had seen were mostly from the stage depot and the one saloon that had stayed open to soak up the penny-ante whiskey money of whatever thirsty passengers might come through on the late run for Lampasas. The blacksmith shop was lit up too for some reason. Other than that, the place was deader than Lazarus before Jesus got around to levitating him.

Yet, while it was for sure the lonesomest town any scared Brazos River boy ever shivered in the sagebrush outside of, it wasn't the lonesomeness of it that was putting the shake in my knees.

It was all those oil lamps smoking and blinking in front of the depot and the smithy.

And the big nine-passenger heavy Concord they were smoking and blinking at.

I pulled out Dad's old watch, checking it by the daybright moon. It was ten fifty-two. Something had sure gone wrong with the Lampasas run. I knew its schedule from having just rode it up to Dallas. It was set up for four hours between Cleburne and Fort Goodwin, with no more than a passenger pickup stop at the latter. I knew it had got out of Cleburne before six o'clock. Yet there it was still setting in front of the Fort Goodwin depot at eight minutes of eleven. The unsettling part of its being there was dead simple.

My ten-to-one guess still went. A dollar still got you a dime that somewhere down the moonlit dust of that street—bellied up to the saloon bar, or perched on two of the six stools in the lunchroom— were Morgan Counts and Beatty Grimes.

And would be until the stage pulled out.

That happy thought got me nothing but a new crop of gooseflesh. But by the time it had smoothed down, I was thinking straight again.

This way, at least, I knew where they were and could watch out for them. I would also know when they left town and I wouldn't need to watch out for them any longer. Also, it was a lucky thing to catch the smithy open that late at night. All I had to do was lay out in the brush till the stage left for Lampasas, then ease into the blacksmith's before he banked his forge and put his bellows up.

The more I thought about it, the better I got to feeling. Pretty quick, I had worked myself up to where I was getting cocky as a cactus sparrow. I figured I wasn't learning a tarnal thing standing up there at my end of the street listening to the wind whistle. The smart thing to do was sneak down along behind the depot to get a closer look at what was holding up the Lampasas run. And likely, as well, steal a peek across the street at the saloon to spot Counts and Grimes, figuring that's where they would be if they actually were on that run.

I petted and gentled Little Hawk, easing him down so he wouldn't fret over being nose-wrapped. I needn't have bothered. When I knotted my bandanna around his muzzle, cinching it up tight so's he couldn't set his jaw for a decent whinny, he didn't even snuffle or blow out his nostrils. By that I knew he had been there before and that this wasn't his first night stalk, likely by several.

It was just one more thing about that little horse to be grateful for. Every move I had made with him, so far, he had been two steps ahead of me and marking time for me to catch up. It was only the way of his breed. Ewe-necked, knee-sprung, cow-hocked, hay-bellied, slab-withered, whatever; Gavilanito was a *criollo!*

I set out, leading him through the sagebrush east of town. Lame or not, he walked quiet and cautious as a cat. All I could hear of him, behind me, was breathing being bothered a little by the nosewrap.

Back of the depot I got a good look, between it and the smithy, at the saloon across the street.

They say, down our way, that you never can tell about the luck of a leppy calf. That was me. And my cards were running high and all one color that night. There were three men leaning on the "Little Alamo's" beer-stained mahogany. One of them was the bartender. The other two were Morgan Counts and Beatty Grimes.

I drifted, quick, on down to the smithy.

It was open, front and rear, like most of its kind in spring and summer. That was to let the heat and smoke of the forge out, but right now it was mostly letting me look in. I saw, directly, what had held the stage up. It was a rear wheel iron had broke loose from its hickory rim. The smith was just dousing his braze with tempering water. He eyed the results with a careful nod and I heard him say to the driver, "She'll hold to Lampasas, anyhow. Jest take it easy on the hard turns and rocky stretches."

By the time I got back up behind the depot, they had the wheel on, the axle pinned and were knocking the jack-prop loose. Two, three men passengers were already aboard, a couple more climbing on. I slipped over to the far side of the depot and checked the Little Alamo. It was empty.

When I got back to the south edge of the building again, the depot agent was just slamming the door shut behind two more men. I couldn't make out faces inside the crowded coach, only forms. But those last two birds had got on while I was checking the saloon and had to be *my two*.

I let out a sigh that could pretty near have been heard out in the street. Half a minute later, when the driver "heeyahhed!" his wheelers and swung his leaders away from the curb, I let out another one that could have been. Maybe it even was. It no longer mattered. Counts and Grimes were on their way to Lampasas. All I had left to do in Fort Goodwin was amble down and make my deal with the blacksmith.

"Come on, little hoss!" I laughed to the *grullo*, whipping the bandanna off his nose and fetching him a big hug around his skinny neck, "let's git the hell on down the road!"

Five minutes later, the smith was rasping off that poor split forehoof and asking me how the grass had made out with the early spring rains up our way. Twenty minutes later, he had the new shoe on and was arguing that he didn't want to take the extra $5 I was pushing onto him for the fine job and late hours. Two minutes after that he had give in, we had shook and said good luck and I was climbing up on Little Hawk.

It was in the next ten seconds the clock ran out.

I had just toed into the stirrups good and solid and was gathering the reins to cluck at Little Hawk to move on out of the smithy when the two tall shadows, jumping black and flickery in the forge's dying light, loomed in the street door.

"Goin' somewheres, kid?" said Beatty Grimes.

"Yeah," grinned Morgan Counts. "Whut's yer hurry, kid? Git down and set a spell—"

Chapter
Twenty-three

Nobody moved. Nobody said anything. There was absolute quiet.

I sat there, dumfounded. The smith stood with my money uncounted in his hand. He was not an old man, nor a dull-witted one. He just didn't have any ambition to die young. He had seen hired gunmen before, knew precisely what to do. Stand stock-still and don't ask any questions. He did it. Five seconds crawled past. Counts and Grimes lounged in the doorway and let them crawl. It was my play.

I couldn't believe it. How had they found me? Where had I slipped up? What tiny little thing was it, somewhere back along the trail, that I had done wrong?

Could it be my Mex *vaquero* rig? It didn't seem possible. That gimlet-eyed horse rancher's wife had taken me for the real article in broad daylight. Earlier, I had passed the time of afternoon with two old *paisano* sheepherders and been treated like the first cousin they thought I was. No, it wasn't that. Nor anything else to do with back along the trail. It had to be something I'd done right here in Fort Goodwin. Likely still was doing.

Some damn fool, crazy thing that was so obvious I couldn't see it square under my own nose. *What was it?*

For some peculiar reason, or other, I wasn't scared. I was mad. For the first time in my life I wasn't thinking about getting hurt. Or looking for the best place to hide. Or wishing that Brack or Doak were there. I was just plain riled. And I was *damned* if I wasn't going to find out how they'd jumped me, before I lay down and let them finish it.

"These here are friends of mine," I heard myself telling the smith. "There ain't goin' to be no trouble."

"Smart boy," said Beatty Grimes.

"Real smart," growled Morgan Counts.

I nodded my silent thanks for their opinions, asking Grimes, who seemed the easier nerved of the two, for a ten-second stay of execution.

"Jest one thing before we go, Beatty," I said, trying to grin him to death like Davy Crockett with the bear. "How'n the name of hell did you two cut my sign?"

"Shet up, kid!" barked Counts. "And walk thet pony out here, careful. We kin chin later."

"Aw, let up, Morg," grinned his slack-lipped partner. "He's got a legal right to a last request. It was easy, kid," he went on. "You make a purty good Mexican but you missed up on one little detail. Men in our business got to have a fine eye fer sech piddlin' trifles—and a long mind for rememberin' them."

"What'd I do wrong?" I blurted.

By this time, I was nowhere near so curious as

I'd been when I put the lead-off question. I was scared, stalling, and starting to think. Counts sensed it. He tried breaking in on Grimes again, but his empty-faced friend was enjoying seeing me squirm.

"Nothin' you *did*, kid," he leered. "Somethin' you *forgot* to do."

"Whut you mean, Beatty?" I figured I had nothing to lose going heavy on the old first-name trick to soften him up. It worked a little this time. His grin spread.

"Somethin' you had on you, and should of took off. Somethin' you *still* got on you, kid. Take a look."

I couldn't help but glance down at myself, yet even then I didn't see it.

That struck Grimes real funny. He laughed like crazy. And I mean, *like crazy*. It was the first time I had noticed that his two eyes didn't track and that he didn't look quite smart.

"Kid," he cackled, "you'd a made a hell of a outlaw. Honest to Christ, you're dumber'n I am!"

"It ain't possible!" snarled Counts. "Dammit, git it done with, Beatty. This ain't the way Sego'd want it did."

"The hell with Sego. This here's my show and I'm arunnin' it to suit myse'f." He swung back on me with his loony grin.

"Well, kid, you see me and Counts we left our hosses here on the trip up. We was jest amblin' by outside to git 'em out'n the livery corral next door when Counts he looks into the blacksmith's here and holds sudden up. 'Beatty,' he says, 'you see somethin' familiar abouten thet Mex kid in yonder? Somethin' he's packin' he ain't got no right to?' "

Grimes wagged his head, let his grin out another slobbery notch. "Well, sir, I take my squint at you and yer crowbait hoss, and sure enough I see it. I says, 'Morg, you're absolutely correct. What're we waitin' fer?' and in we comes." He shrugged, pleased and happy as a halfwit with two wings tore off a hand-grabbed horsefly. "Like I said, kid, you made a right convincin' *cholo*, savin' fer the one small thing."

He stood grinning another minute, letting me sweat a second pint down the back of my saddle, then put it to me with his scary chuckle and wally eye-roll. *"I ask you, kid, you ever see a ten-cent chili picker totin' a hundred-dollar hand-carved Winchester in a two-bit scabbard on a six-bit hoss?"*

It hit me like a heel-clod from the horse ahead of you in a hard race. Or a whippy branch slashing close behind a man you're following through heavy brush in a tall hurry. Smack between the eyes! And stinging my mind awake.

Of course! Dad's little Christmas gun! The one thing I hadn't had out of my hands since leaving home. The one thing I was so used to carrying with me, wherever I went, I wouldn't in a million years have thought to ditch. It was exactly what I had figured in the first five seconds of facing them: I had forgotten something that would be the most obvious thing in the world to everybody else but the one who had it on him and was trying to think what it was.

"Come on," said Counts, dropping his hand to brush his Colt handle and stepping clear of the smithy door to give me room to move Little Hawk through it. "Git thet damn pony movin'."

"Yeah," smirked Grimes, moving on inside the smithy and chucking his head at the glistening butt and rich-engraved breech of the Winchester, "but first, shuck me out thet purty little popgun. I'd admire to stick it under my own laig fer a spell."

I put my hands up, high and pious. "No thanks," I said, real sober. "I ain't agoin' to tech it. You might mebbe think I was aimin' to make a play with it. He'p yourse'f, Beatty, I don't want no trouble."

He slobbered another grin, calling over to Counts, "Kid learns fast, stupid as he looks. Mebbe he ain't as dumb as me, after all."

In the end fraction of that last second, I was praying I wasn't. And was easing my right boot free of the offside stirrup. Counts was standing on the far side of Little Hawk and couldn't see it. Grimes wasn't looking for it.

When he reached for the little gun's shiny stock, I kicked him square across the bridge of the nose.

I spun the startled *grullo* hard left, jerked the Winchester myself, snapped the chamber shot at Morgan Counts from the hip. It was high but made him hit the dirt. Before he could dig himself back up out of it, or Beatty Grimes could knuckle the blood from his broken nose out of his eyes, Little Hawk had me out the open rear of the smithy barn and seventy yards into the sagebrush.

I never even looked back at them firing at me from that rear doorway. I was no shucks with a sixgun myself, but I knew old Sam Colt hadn't invented his famous equalizers with a cat-fast mustang and two hundred and eighty feet of glary

Texas moonlight in mind. They never were worth a damn at anything over fifty yards in broad daylight and you could make that fifty feet for most men that used them, and still not get hit one shot in three.

Counts and Grimes knew that as well as I did.

They slung after me only what shots they had loaded in their cylinders, which was no more nor less than anybody would have done that had been kicked in the face and made to eat smithy dirt by a snip of a boy they'd tried to be decent with.

No, *after* the shooting was when I began to get worried. That is, when it got quiet back there behind the smithy. And when it was still quiet after about a mile of slowed-up hand-galloping and standing in the stirrups to look and listen back, *that* was when I hit for the only little ridge in sight, and was forever glad I did.

I could see a far, lovely piece from up there. It was a beautiful, beautiful night. I don't ever remember the moon shining so still and bright. I couldn't only *see* Counts and Grimes clear as telescope glass, I could *hear* the grunts of their horses and squeaks of their saddles, just as good.

Which wasn't too strange.

They weren't over one hundred and fifty yards behind me.

There was nothing to do but run for the hills. Counts and his wall-eyed friend were too close for anything else.

Their horses must have been standing ready-saddled in the livery corral. Probably they had seen to them, right off, when the stage pulled in.

Any two good cowboys would have done the same, before looking to themselves. So they'd had only to dodge out the rear of the smithy, pile onto them and trail my dust over the tops of the tall brush. I hadn't seen their dust because they were riding careful and had the blackness of the town's buildings to their backs. When I had slowed to climb the ridge, was when they had poured it on.

Now it figured to be a flat-race. One that would make an old man of any boy, in the first five miles. *If it went that far.*

I kicked Little Hawk around, pointing him south down the ridge toward the open flats between us and the far hills. He took off like a stomped-out brush bunny.

Below us, Counts and Grimes heard him go, and held up to follow the sound. Next minute, the brush along the ridge thinned. They had me spotted. They wheeled their horses, digging them hard to cut me off where the ridge spurred down onto the flats.

They missed me there by a hundred yards, for two reasons. Little Hawk had headed them by a dozen jumps before they saw him; the going along the top of the ridge was downhill and not so rocky as that at its base.

On the flats we lined out. The run for the $25,000 Fort Goodwin Handicap was on.

Chapter Twenty-four

I had to gamble big on a way to ride it.

Counts and Grimes would have good horses under them. Likely they would be Lazy RB cow-horses, bred up from native stock by good eastern studs, the same as Dad had been doing with our horse stuff on the Brazos. Most of the smart cow outfits were doing that. I had to figure Rance Buchanan wouldn't be running anything but a smart outfit.

If that was so, their mounts would have the early speed on mine. With all his wonderful qualities, your true mustang was not a fast horse under five miles. It was exactly why the up and coming ranchers were using the blooded Missouri and Kentucky stallions on their range mares—to give their foals more size and early speed.

I looked ahead, figuring hard.

We had at least three miles to the hills where I hoped to have a chance of losing them. Their faster horses meant they could haul me down in half that distance, unless I could get away with running a cold bluff on them. I already had the bluff in mind.

They had seen Little Hawk, could read his breed

as quick as the next good cowman. They would never expect him to be fast, only durable. So my best play was to convince them otherwise—to trick them into thinking Little Hawk had more starting speed than any mustang they had ever chased—and would need to be walked, not run down.

The big gamble came on whether they would buy my bluff and fall back on the pace, or match it and come on to take me in the second mile.

I settled down on the little *grullo* and laid the spurs to him. He flattened out and went.

The ground was clean and open, not jarring hard nor draggy with sand, but just right. And Gavilanito could go! I knew the minute I opened him up that he had real speed, and it sure surprised me. He was likely the second fastest horse I'd ever sat, old Sec's Mozo being the first. He turned that first mile in such good time that I knew, even as I eased him up to look back, that Counts and Grimes would have done fine just to hang on, let alone making up any worrisome ground. At the same time, I knew they better not have made up any.

Real horsemen know that no horse can run more than a quarter of a mile at absolute top speed. Letting Little Hawk go like I had, the full mile, had about blown him. If they had managed to stay up with him and were still coming on the pace, my big gamble was as down the drain as slime water out of an unplugged stock tank.

They hadn't, and my gamble was good. I got that, and my second surprise of the race, when I stood up in the stirrups to look back.

Past missing me at the bottom of the ridge spur, they hadn't even tried to run me. They were at least a quarter mile back, moving at no better than a rolling lope. My heart jumped. I had outslickered them! They had been bluffed out by Little Hawk's amazing early foot. They had bought my gamble. They were going to trail me out, not try to run me down. The hills were looming ahead. I would be into them in another ten minutes. It would give me a little more time, some small, further chance. It was all I asked.

Then, suddenly, the excitement died out of me. Little Hawk was moving rough and the realization of what I had done to him, and to myself, hit me in the pit of the stomach. I knew, then, why they hadn't come after me. *Really*, why they hadn't.

My burst of speed had had nothing to do with it. My brainy bluff had been the stupidest thing I could have done. I knew it the second I felt the little *grullo* roughen up under me, but it was already too late. They had outsmarted me dangerous bad and the *real* reason they had quit running was enough to send a cold chill clear down to my spur shanks.

Counts and Grimes were medium-sized men. Saddles and guns, included, their horses weren't packing over two hundred pounds, each. And they were livery-barn fresh. With me and the gold and the old-fashioned hull I'd had to take from the horse trader, Little Hawk was carrying close to two hundred and sixty-five pounds; better than a third of his own weight. And he had already been under saddle for twelve hours and eighty-odd miles.

Trying to think the way old professional hands like Morgan Counts and Beatty Grimes must be thinking, your end question came out painful clear.

Why hurry?

Digging desperately for a decent answer to that thought, for some silly, offtrack reason, brought to my mind one of Dad's favorite object-lesson yarns, the kind he used to spin us kids to teach us what he called "the hardtail facts of life," the likes of which, he claimed, "was never learned in no school."

The story was about two rangebulls, one young and mighty ready, one old and some wore out. Seems the young one spied a nice bunch of breeding-age heifers on a hillside over across a considerable stretch of country. The young bull snorted and pawed the ground and threw a lot of dust and bellowed, "C'mon, oldtimer, let's run over yonder and git us one of them heifers!" But the old bull, he only rolled his eyes and got up slow and rumbled easylike, "Hell no, son. Let's jest walk over and git us the lot of them."

I had never rightfully understood that story, nor had a good use for it till that minute.

But, looking back through that scary moonlight at Counts and Grimes loping their big strong horses in no rush whatever and not caring a hoot how far I had headed them across that "considerable stretch of country," I sudden found a plenty good use for it.

Why hurry, indeed, if you were them?

They were going to get what was coming to them, and get it without breaking out of a walk. I was going to get what was coming to me, too. A bullet in the back, or the front, either way I wanted it, just as sure as it came daybreak and good shooting light tomorrow.

It was what a young bull got for fancying he could outfigure two wise old ones.

I made it to the hills. Or, better, what had looked like hills far off in the moonlight. They turned out to be more just a bumpy stretch of prairie, deep-cut with barrancas and little blind trails leading a dozen ways at once. Bright moonlight will do that to you in a strange country.

No matter, my luck held. I struck a good wide drywash leading straight ahead. It had a level bottom, free of big rocks, and seemed more to cut through the patchy stretch than to climb up into it. Also, it proved twisty as a stalking cat's tail. That was good, too. Those switchbacks would keep Counts and Grimes honest. They wouldn't know around which corner I might decide to linger and wing a shot at them as they came around.

I went on along, letting Little Hawk pick and choose the way ahead, while I got out my Winchester and watched the backtrail bends, behind.

Nothing happened. We made a mile, then two. Still nothing. Little Hawk kept moving on his all-day running walk. He made no sound in the wash sand. None came, either, from Counts and Grimes behind us.

Another mile padded past. The wash hadn't started to climb any. By that, I could be pretty sure it did cut clear through the prairie roughs, and more, too. So far, I hadn't seen a solitary sidewash.

The wash trail, which I could have got off of any one of fifty places in the first mile, was now walled off by fifteen- and twenty-foot banks of red mud and sandstone that would have given a whitetail buck trouble. A horse, even a *cruz*-marked *criollo*, could just forget them. And they were getting steeper all the while. I had no choice, whatever, save to go on, keeping the Winchester ready.

Then we rounded a last bend and I had my choice.

Ahead, the wash split. The main cut kept going, level and due south. The side channel came in from the right. It angled off, southwest, climbing fast onto the higher ground. In the same minute I saw the split, I felt the footing firm up under Little Hawk. We were on bedrock.

For the second time since lining out ahead of Counts and Grimes, my heart jumped with hope.

With the trail forking and clean sandstone underfoot, they would have to guess which way I had gone. Providing naturally, that I could get across the little open flat ahead and on into the fork of my choice before they broke around the bend behind me. If I could, I had a chance. For, bright moon or not, that water-scoured rock wouldn't hold any hoofsign they could sight-trail.

But the choice was tough. Which way *was* I going? Not rightly knowing, and beginning to panic a little, I held up, confused.

Little Hawk didn't want to wait. He let me know it, too. For the first time since I had climbed on him back in Dallas he fought the bit. He wanted his head and no two ways about it.

When he showed me that, it triggered off a desperate thought in my mind. Which one of those cuts would a chased mustang, one that knew he was being run, take of his own free choice? I knew it was reaching pretty far, but it did seem to me, stampeding like I was starting to, that the little old *grullo* pony was as good as saying, "*Cuss it all, boy, leave me git the bit-bar in my teeth! Time's a-wastin' sinful fast!*"

It was. That was a fact. I gave Little Hawk his head and let him go.

He took the righthand cut, scrambling up its narrow track nimble as an antelope doe. We didn't get far. The cut turned damp and brushy in the first fifty yards. It benched out another fifty yards above, in a little cup of land that held a few scrub trees, some scant graze and a live, ground-seep spring. My belly pulled in. True to his broomtail instincts, Little Hawk had headed for what his wonderful nose had brought him news of down below—sweet grass and clean water.

And in doing it he had climbed me square into nowhere.

Behind the little bench, three sides around, was nothing but sandstone outcrop going ten and fifteen feet straight up. We were trapped.

Chapter Twenty-five

Grimes and Counts came into the open flats of the wash forks five minutes later.

I clamped my hand on Little Hawk's muzzle and took a big mortgage on my next breath. It paid off. Where it was a good hundred yards up the sidewash to our bench, the cut twisted around so, in climbing, that we weren't over forty feet above Sego's two gunslingers. On a moon-still night a dropped pebble will carry twice that far to a prairie-trained ear.

I kept ahold of my breath, muzzling the *grullo* with my left hand, running the fingers of my right along the soft hollow under his jawbones to keep him standing quiet. Down below, the two riders sat their horses. The seconds dragged by. They continued to sit, saying nothing, just using their eyes and ears. Studying the fork. Looking first on along the main wash, then staring up at the bench.

Pretty quick Counts said something guarded and low. I couldn't make out what it was, but I could make out Beatty's loony chuckle answering him and could tell from that that whatever it was, Beatty wasn't buying it. Then a light wind stirred up the wash from behind them, twisting my way and carrying the low-voiced rest of it to me spooky clear.

"By God, I ain't so sure. He's made dummies of us once tonight," complained Counts.

"Naw!" Beatty cackled again. "Not a chance, Morg. Hell, you kin see from here thet gully don't go nowheres. Jest up onto thet little blind bench. He ain't thet stupid, to ride hisself into a box like thet. Not with the whole of Lampasas County in front of him. He's gone on out the main wash, fer sure."

Counts wasn't convinced. I could see him plain as if he was standing across the main street of Mineral Wells in good lamplight. He kept looking up at the bench, rubbing his three-day beard and wagging his head.

"C'mon, fer Pete's sake, let's drift," urged Beatty. "Past this stretch of cut-up stuff, we got fifty miles of open country to nail him in."

"We cain't chance it." Heating up to the argument, Counts was talking a little louder. "You cain't tell fer sure if thet damn gully lets on out up there or not. Not without ridin' up to see."

"By God, thet's so. Well, hell, let's split up. You take the main wash, I'll mosey up yonder and have a looksee."

"No, dammit all, we done messed it up enough a'ready." I could have hugged Counts then, ugly as he was. For he said it like he meant it and like he meant to stick to it. "We got to hustle on down to Cheyenne's shack and pick up Sego and the boys."

"Christ Amighty, Morg, thet's the same as clean down to Lampasas. Barrin' six, eight miles, it is."

"Cain't he'p it if it is. We miss this boy again, Sego'll kill us. Way it is, we dassn't tell him we had him cold and lost him. We'll jest say we picked up his trail in Fort Goodwin and then hit on ahead for Cheyenne's place to give him the *qué vive*. Likely he'll buy thet and spread out to nab the kid between Lampasas and Mason." He held up, slewing around in his saddle to glare at poor Beatty.

" 'Course," he snarled, laying it on a mile wide, "iffen you'd ruther I rode on down alone and told him how beautiful you bossed the job back yonder in the blacksmith's, jest say the word."

Beatty broke out his halfwit laugh ahead of his answer and just as he did the wind dropped off sudden and I couldn't hear what he said. But I could see from the way he was jabbing around with his hands that he was still arguing the idea of splitting up. Beatty wasn't bright but when he got ahold of a notion, he hung on to it.

In straining forward to try and pick up what was eating him, I must have let my hand go slack on Little Hawk's muzzle. For sure, I forgot to keep scratching him under the chin. He didn't cotton to the neglect.

The next thing I knew he had bunted his head half free of my hand and cleared his clamped nostrils with a muffled blow-out snuffle. I had to move quick to hold on to him and in doing it my boot turned under me, starting a little rock trickle that rattled and slid real nice through the dead quiet that followed me getting his nose shut down tight again.

By the time I got my eyes bent back down to the flats, Counts and Beatty were both sitting stock-still in their saddles, their heads swung straight my way.

It seemed to me they sat there twenty minutes

without moving. Actually, it couldn't have been more than that many seconds, for I was still holding the same breath I'd gulped when I jumped for the *grullo's* nose.

"Buck deer," said Counts, loud and clear. "Must have bin watchin' us and jest got our smell."

"Yeah," agreed Beatty, quick and dumb-sure. "Wind's funny in these side-cut washes. Full of dead spots and backflows. Likely he seen and heard us the whole time."

"Likely. Anyways, he's gone, judgin' from thet rock trickle."

"Yep. Snuck on up the bluff-face yonder. Them bastards kin climb like a cat when they're a mind to."

"They kin and thet's a fact." Counts shortened his reins. "Well, we'd best be shovin' along. Thet is, less'n you'd ruther go deer huntin' than git on down the line and square things with Sego."

Again Beatty's crazy chuckle covered up his answer. But this time I didn't care about not hearing it. The simple reason being that I was seeing it. The two of them swung their ponies and put the spurs to them, with never a backward look. The last muffled beat of their kicked-up lopes died away down the main wash inside thirty seconds.

I let out that breath I had been misering and took a fresh one. It was time for Button Starbuck to look up and let the good Lord know how thankful he was that Beatty Grimes was as fearful of Sego Lockhart as any bad-scared boy from the Brazos. And that neither him nor Morgan Counts could tell a pinched-off mustang snuffle from a buck deer snort.

When I had stared up at the stars and done just that, I pulled everything off Little Hawk and turned him loose. I didn't even try to find a soft spot to spread my serape, just slumped down right where I was. The next thing I knew the sun was in my eyes, four hours high.

I saddled Little Hawk and hand-led him down the gully. Down below, out on the sandstone floor of the main wash, I held up a minute just to look around at that bluebird-beautiful morning and to tot up how mortal fortunate I had been the night before.

Looked at in the broad daylight, it didn't seem possible I had got away with it. That gully-head spring and clump of trees seemed close enough to chuck a rock into from down there. But moonlight was a heap different than daytime, I knew. Both as to looking and listening. Moonlight always made things seem farther off than they were. More than that, no matter how many times he learns better a man just never can seem to believe how far his voice will carry clear and true on a white moon night.

Thinking of that and feeling almighty thankful for it, I took a last deep breath of the morning-fresh prairie air. Then, feeling good enough to box a bear or kiss a Kiowa squaw, I legged up on Little Hawk and headed him on south out of the main wash.

Just past where it left the gully junction, the wash narrowed to swing hard left. At the same time the walls got higher, shutting out the sun dark and sudden. Ahead, I could see where it flared wide again, letting the sun back in.

I touched up the little *grullo*, not liking the close feel of the walls and wanting to get free of it as quick as I could. He shifted into his rolling lope, banking around the sharp turn quick and frisky as a green-broke calf horse.

Clearing it, he set his forelegs and shot his haunches up under him so fast he nearly put me over his head. I pulled back up in the saddle, set to cuss him six ways from Sunday. Instead, my mouth just stayed wide open.

Ten feet away, his chunky bay swung slanchwise to block the trail, slouched in the saddle with his left boot hooked around the horn and his Winchester wandering my belt buckle, sat an old friend of mine.

"Mornin', kid," grinned Beatty Grimes. "Where's the fire?"

I was just so simple dumfounded I forgot to be afraid.

"Beatty!" I gasped. "Now how in the hell—"

"Nothin' to it, kid," leered the slow-witted gunman. "Let's jest say we ain't none of us as dumb as we look. Or better yet, happen the moonlight's quiet enough, thet some of us kin still tell a horse snuffle from a buck deer snort."

I was already too shocked and thinking too hard of a way to stay alive to flinch to the news of my own dumbness. That imbecile Beatty was crazy like a loafer wolf. Him and that damn hardtail Counts. They'd read me like a mail order catalogue, the minute me and Little Hawk had made a sound up on that bench last night. Beatty had laid out to nail me coming down with daylight, and Counts was no doubt already halfway to

Lampasas and Sego's hideout. But I couldn't let on I saw it that clear.

"Where's your friend?" I gulped, trying to make it offhand pleasant and wanting time to guess at my chances of jumping the *grullo* past his sleepy bay, before he could wing me.

Beatty lost his grin fast. "Don't try it, kid!" he snapped, seeing my hands tighten on the reins. "And lay off thet blue-eyed little-boy stuff, you hear? I got my belly full of thet innocent act of yours and some to spare, back yonder at the blacksmith's. You know where Morg's gone, damn you. You heard our big mouths goin' last night, you little bastard!"

He was furious mad, all in a minute, and I thought he was going to kill me then and there.

But he fooled me again.

His broad face came unclouded and turned frowning serious, just that quick.

"Now you do what I tell you, will you?" He asked it as though it was a favor, knitting his eyebrows and chewing his lip like he was real concerned. "I was told to blow your damn head off, but I dunno. Somehow it don't seem right gunnin' a kid. Now Morg he'd do it. I jest cain't, though. So you do like I say, huh?"

I knew from that minute that Beatty Grimes wasn't just ordinary foolish. Or village halfwit simple. There actually was a piece of his poor mind missing. I knew something else too, in the same minute—I could thank God that there was.

"All right, Beatty," I said soberly and letting the reins go slack with the careful nod. "What do you want I should do?"

"I want you should git down off'n thet pony, leavin' his reins trail." He growled it like he was mad at himself and couldn't understand why. "Then jest turn around and start walkin'."

"You gonna set me afoot, Beatty?" I stalled.

He shook his head. "I'm gonna start countin' to ten right now. If you ain't off'n thet pony and back past thet turn in the wall by nine, I'm gonna kill you."

I got off Little Hawk, stepped clear of him, dropped the reins.

As I did, Beatty kneed his bay in between us and bent to grab them up.

For as long as it would take a flipped quarter to turn over twice in the air his eyes were off of me. It was then the idea hit me.

It was a fact of cowhorse life that you could count on with any proper-broke stock horse ever foaled. And Beatty Grimes was riding an eight-year-old Lazy RB-branded cutting horse that was proper broke from hock to fetlock. I didn't wait for the thought to get any farther than that. I just let out a yell and dove for the ground and rolled in under the bay from his offside and with my hands and feet flying wild as a gear-stripped windmill.

The old gelding came apart on all four corners.

He went up in the air and out from under Beatty and away from above me like he'd stepped on an uncoiled sidewinder. Which was exactly no more, nor any less, than any good cowhorse would have done in his place. That was, just simply, to break his own poor neck if he had to, to keep from stepping on the least, helpless part of a loose rider fallen or thrown under his feet.

Beatty came down hard, not over three steps from where I came rolling back up on my feet without a scratch. He was bad shook up and hadn't any more than got his hands and knees under him when I came down on the back of his head with a chunk of sandstone the size of a green muskmelon.

I put my head to his chest and was glad to hear his heart still bumping along, a little rough but good and stout. I hid his belt-gun and Winchester, left him his loose horse and got out of there. It was maybe a foolish thing to do, yet actually I owed him my life. I figured the least I could do was leave him a mount. Besides, there was one other thing almighty sure about my good deed.

By the time he came around and caught up the bay, Beatty Grimes would be the faraway least of Button Starbuck's worries.

To make certain of that, I put the pressure on Little Hawk without letup. We rode south and we rode hard and we rode long. By late afternoon I was ten miles north of Lampasas, skirting the stageline road to the west and just about to turn away from it to gain the open country I would need to go wide around the town. I was in heavy mesquite and high brush cover, a good mile off the road, when I started my circle. I hadn't gone a hundred yards when I saw it, drifty and thin and yet quite a ways off, but moving fast and dead my way.

Horse dust on the Lampasas road.

Chapter Twenty-six

It was a funny feeling. There was no doubt to it, no hesitation. I took one look at that dustcloud and knew it was Sego and his bunch, coming for me.

Humans are sort of remarkable that way. They go along their whole lives thinking they're something special, forgetting they're animals the same as a dog or a horse or a cow critter. If they get a funny feeling, they call it a hunch. It's not. It's animal instinct. It's why a coyote will stand and watch you no more than a rock toss away when you haven't got a gun. And will cut and drift from half a mile off when you have. Or why a fat buck you've got centered in a pair of field glasses six hundred yards over on the next ridge will throw up his head, stare your way and take off for the state line like you had reached out and touched him on the shoulder.

That's the way it was with me in the first five seconds of seeing that dustcloud. In that little time the whole layout was as clear to me as though I had sat in with them on planning it. Right from the spooky coyote part of it, down to the deer and the field glasses. *Especially*, the field glasses.

For the past hour I'd had that eerie feeling of

being watched. I had three times climbed a little high ground to see what I could see. Each time it was the same. Nothing. I had wanted, then, to cut and run. But no. We get so used to fighting down our hunches we go ahead and reason ourselves into traps a dumb animal would smell a mile off, upwind. Yet, strange enough, once we're in the trap we quit thinking and try to fight out of it on pure instinct. Which is simply God's little way of giving us half a chance.

By the time the first two of those five seconds had ticked away, I knew it was Sego and his bunch and that they had spotted me. With the second two gone, I knew how they had done it: picked me out of twenty miles of rough country with field glasses; gone for me with a straight-out rush, knowing there was no place I could head for that their big fresh horses couldn't beat my tired little *grullo* to.

But with the fifth second faded away, I was all done thinking. Putting the spurs to Little Hawk, I took my tail-end cut at the Lord's last slim chance.

I ran for my life like a hunted animal.

Inside of half a mile, quartering southwest, I hit a dim wagon-track leading west. It was good grassy track, used only enough to keep the sagebrush down. It led into what looked like rougher, more cut-up country ahead. I took it. Where you've got the devil grinning at you from all four points of the prairie compass, you've got no more choice than with Thomas Hobson's horses. You just take the one standing in the stall nearest the livery barn door. For me, that one was the grassy little wagon-track wandering due west into the dusky red of the dropping sun.

For the first mile there was no elevation in it which would let me look back. Then I hit a slight rise and could see a good five miles behind me.

I didn't loiter any over the sight.

I had good eyes, most as good as Doak's. The sun was to my back. High prairie air, in late afternoon of a wind-still day, is the clearest in the world. You can see through it like trout pool water. It's what fools eastern dudes, making them think fifty miles is five.

It didn't fool me. I knew how far it was to the Lampasas road. Three miles. I could see where my wagon-track cut away from it and how far along that wagon-track my cloud of horse dust had come. Two miles. I could do even better than that. I could count the rider dots moving under that dust. Eight. Sego Lockhart and seven men. Not over a mile behind me.

I did all I had the will left to do—gave Gavilanito his head and let him go.

He showed his breed then, the breed that will die before it tires. With all the extra weight and all his bone weariness, he gave them a race.

In the second mile they gained but a quarter on us. The little horse was still running fairly steady as we went into the third. But within a half of it, he was sobbing for air and I could hear the hoarse roar of the windbreak building in his raspy lungs. Beneath the sweaty clamp of my legs, he was beginning to shake. At the three quarters he stumbled, almost going down. After that, he could not find his stride again. I knew he was going his last quarter.

I looked back.

I could see Sego hunched like a great, short-necked toad on his powerful bay. He was within three hundred yards of us. Behind him came his men, strung out in a loose pack like hound dogs running crippled game. All eager, all straining to be in on the kill, but some just not so fast as others. In the little time I watched him, Sego closed another fifty yards. He was pulling his saddle-gun, when I swung my eyes back to the road ahead.

I wasn't looking for anything but a decent place to die. Some spot to which I could put my back. A little barranca, a rainwater ditch, a stand of *madroñas*, a clump of mesquite, a rock half the size of Little Hawk—anything. Just so it was big enough and close enough to get behind in time to charge something for Dad's gold.

I had a price in mind, too.

For some reason I was very clear on that. There were seven shells in my little .38-40 Winchester. Unless he got me in the back before I found my place, I was going to sell that gold to Sego Lockhart for seven slugs of lead. Or three, or two, or one. Whatever I could put into his bullfrog belly, before he rode me down.

I never got to make the deal.

As my eyes swept the brush ahead I caught, off to my left the flash of a little log and 'dobe jacal and thatch-roof ramada. In the same glance I saw the faint set of buckboard ruts branching off to go down to the little Mexican spread. The *grullo* read my mind. I never touched him. He just changed leads and went for the jacal.

What is it that will make a man, or a dumb-brute

animal that's used to being with a man, run for a house if he can?

There's many a better and cleaner place to die. Many a stronger and safer defense in the natural open. Still, a man, or any animal that's been broke by him, will scrabble and run for a mud-dobbed wickiup or a willow-stick goat corral that wouldn't slow up a beanshooter quicker than he will for a good rock outcrop or clay cutbank that would stop a howitzer.

I never gave it much thought before but—funny thing—as Little Hawk galloped those last steps, I knew the answer. It was because those flimsier things were built by another man and no man, not the bravest one ever lived, wants to die alone. Not by choice. It's nothing more than a mirage, that idea. A cruel, bright lake of water that isn't there, beckoning ahead. Yet many a man before me had died feeling better just for trying to reach it.

In this case, though, it was a mirage that knew how to shoulder and hold steady an old Model '63, .52-caliber Sharps buffalo gun.

I knew that gun and its hollow boom like an old friend. I had cut my first big-caliber teeth on one of those Model '63's—my own dad's.

I saw the greasy mushroom of the familiar black-powder smokeburst bloom outside the paneless window in the log wall ahead. I ducked as I heard the whine of the big slug whistle over me. I heard, behind me, the soapblock smack of it going home in something a sight more solid than sagebrush. Heard, too, the whinnying scream of Sego Lockhart's mortal-hit bay, and the cursing yell with which his rider went down with him.

I had no time, then, and precious little want, to look back. Before me, the heavy planked door of the jacal was swinging open. The murderous *anciano* with the buffalo gun was breech-loading another round into it, waving its forty-inch barrel out the window and yelling at me all in the same excited Mexican minute.

"La puerta, amigo! La puerta! Monta Usted, por la puerta!"

"Mil gracias, patrón!" I yelled back, reining Little Hawk right where he had invited me to, square through the held-open door. As I did, I heard three slugs smash into the lintel over my head, then the snarling crack of a .44 Winchester opening up from the second hut window, beyond the door. Before the weathered planks were swung to, I caught the angry shouts of Sego's men as they broke wide and scattered for cover from the .44's fire.

Then I was down off the gasping Little Hawk and seeing three dark-skinned ghosts from the streets of Lampasas.

The old man in the first window, with the Sharps, was Jesús Otero. The slim youth in the boy's *buscadero* belt and home-tanned *chapareras*, manning the second window and the sharp-barking Winchester, was his granddaughter May. The fat shadow with the villainous white-toothed grin and calmly bracing the doorplanks with her broad rump was my old friend the *dueña*.

"Buenas tardes, señor," said the old gentleman in unsmiling, high-class Castilian. "Please consider my poor house as your own." He touched off a shot at one of Sego's cowboys, who apparently wanted to make sure the old man hadn't been just

lucky in drilling Sego's bay. "You are welcome here for as long as you may wish to stay. What little I have is yours to command. I am Jesús Otero."

"I know who *you* are," I rasped in harsh gringo English, feeling for some reason cheap because I had fooled them with the Mexican boy's clothes in the first place, and my Spanish yell in the second, "but I reckon you've called my color wrong. *I'm Button Starbuck.*"

I saw the girl's gray eyes widen. Even the grinning squaw trapped her thick lips into a straight line. The old man bent his head, peering through the jacal's dirt-floored gloom. He took a long time, going from my rough Chihuahua boots to my peaked Sonora hat, two times over, before nodding and saying in a voice as slow and gentle as summer rain, "When a man is in trouble, my son, he has no name."

It was my turn, then, to look at him a lengthy spell. *"Ya lo creo, patrón,"* I said at last and humbly. "I truly believe it."

I turned and went to Little Hawk, jerking the Winchester out of its scabbard. I came back to him at the window and he stood aside for me. "I will get you something to eat," he said.

"I will see that you are not interrupted," I replied, throwing a shot at what I thought was a piece of black hat crown moving behind a brushclump.

"We are men who understand one another, my son," was all he said. And, *"Ya lo creo,"* was all I could add to that.

Chapter Twenty-seven

While I ate, the squaw took my Winchester and my window.

The food was stone-ground tortillas and *frijoles refrescas;* cold fried beans, and beef. Fresh venison liver and wild turkey couldn't have topped it. But before I had got halfway through it, I flinched to the familiar thin crack of my own little rifle and jumped for the window. María, that was the squaw's name, waved me back with her evil grin. *"De nada, niño,"* she shrugged, spitting on her thumb and rubbing the front sight. "One of them tried to get behind a better rock, *así no más.* He is more comfortable now."

Something in the way she said it took me on to the window. I slid along the wall, snuck a look out. A long hundred and fifty yards up the buckboard trail a man lay on his face, fingers knotted in the wiry grass. He wasn't moving. It was Morgan Counts.

"Ya lo creo," I muttered for the third time in ten minutes, and turned back to my supper.

As I did, the girl's frowning eyes caught mine. *"Ya lo creo, ya lo creo,"* she mimicked. "Is that all you can say, boy? Do you believe everything?"

"When the horse has cost nothing," I quoted her the old Coahuila proverb, "do we complain of his cusps being worn away?"

"*Ya lo creo!*" she surrendered, and her smile lit up the jacal like a flicker of heat lightning.

I could see the old man smiling too, at last, and was conscious of the squaw watching me and the girl with her sidelong, crooked grin. Somehow, I all of a sudden felt as though I hadn't just rode one hundred and thirty miles without but two hours sleep and a snack of cold bannock and fatback. I felt mighty fine.

But no man, nor any 135-pound boy, for that matter, can keep his eyes open on smiles. By the time I had scraped clean my third plate of beans, I was looking around for a couple of wood matchsticks to prop my eyelids apart with. They all saw how it was with me.

So far, none of us had had a minute for Little Hawk. Now, as I finished my supper, the old man picked up his Sharps, went over to May's window, touched her on the shoulder and said something I didn't catch. She gave way to him, came over to me, smiling for me to come along with her. I didn't argue it any. When she picked up Little Hawk's reins and led him out, I dragged along after them beat down and obedient as a birddog that's run forty miles flushing prairie chickens.

That little jacal had been built a good many years before, in a time when the red brother was still wild and inclined to what Dad had called "Comanche mathematics." That meant that in Indian arithmetic you could multiply horses faster by stealing them than by waiting eleven months for nature to supply your answer out of a foaling mare. So whenever the moon got cantaloupe-full—a *Tsaoh* Moon was their own name for it—they would creep in and lift what they wanted of white or Mexican horseflesh off the outlying ranch spreads.

By the same sneaky token, the ranchers got smart with the way they tacked their corrals right onto their houses, so's they could drive in their choice horse stock whenever the nights got bright enough to where there was a Comanche Moon hung overhead.

This little jacal was like that.

It had a ramada on each end. You got to them by doors big enough to pass a saddled mustang cut in the solid walls and hung over with only an old cowhide or army blanket to shut out some little of the stock smell.

The Otero ramadas were wiser built than most. Most were nothing more than four poles set in the ground, roofed over with whatever was handy that would shut out the sun. But these had only a thin lace of dry willow over them. Just enough to kill the sun but not enough to kindle a fire-arrow blaze big enough to catch the jacal logs. They weren't wide open to the prairie breeze on the sides, either, but were walled up to five feet with the same pole-and-plank construction as the living quarters—ample high enough to keep any disappointed Comanches from shooting the stock they couldn't get their thieving hands on.

In one of them, the east one, the Oteros kept their sacked beans, dried corn and chilis, Spanish sausages and suchlike. It held something else, too, a sight more precious to anybody who might be under Indian siege for up to a week at a time—a live spring that had been rocked in and ditched out under the back wall. The west ramada was fitted out to hold four horses and what little cut hay they might need to stay alive five, six days. Right now it was empty save for a little lineback buckskin mare. This was Poquito, the girl told me, her mare, handfed and bottle-raised from a wobbly broomtail orphan and who hadn't spent a night in the open in the seven years May had had her.

With Little Hawk and Poquito it was the same as with me and May Otero.

The little *grullo* was smote hard and deep.

Naturally, the mare didn't take it the same way. Not right off. When he went to shoving his nose at her as May led him past, she eared back and cut loose at him with her heels. She could have kicked him square in the head, he wouldn't have felt it. You could tell he was plumb overcome and that barring being tied up short on the far side of the ramada and long ago gelded, he would have got busy right then and there doing his scrubby bit to increase the *criollo* population.

I didn't give him more than a cussing swat in the rump and a tail-twist to move him on by her. I reckoned I knew how he felt but I was too damn tired even to think about May and me, let alone him and his sudden buckskin lady love.

By the time May had him snubbed up to the far-side manger and his saddle and bridle pulled, I was looking for a soft spot in the stacked hay to spread my serape.

"I got to sleep, girl," I told her. "You're jest goin' to have to take my watch till moonrise."

"*Buenas noches*," she murmured, keeping her head down. "I will awake you then."

I don't even remember her going out. The sweet smell of the hay reached up for me and I was dead as a stuffed dodo bird inside two deep sighs. When I opened my eyes again, the moon was shining into them a full hour high over the ramada wall.

"*Es una noche, muy bella*," said May Otero softly.

I looked at her leaning gracefully against Little Hawk's manger, Winchester cradled carelessly in her slim arm, her dark-lashed glance first for me, then for the outer stillness of the sage. I looked at the night sky, clear and silvery above, deep and mysterious along the low curve of the far land to the west. I looked at the moon, smelled the fragrance of the prairie hay, heard the rustle of the night wind in the ramada thatch. And, last, I looked at May Otero again.

"*Dice Usted, una cosa muy verdadera*," I agreed happily.

It was, indeed, a very beautiful night.

We talked a long time, there in the moonlight.

The night was quiet. Sego and his bunch had pulled back out of range into a rocky draw up by the main wagon-track. We could see their fire up there and the hipshot shadows of their horses standing beyond it. There was no doubt a man posted up on the little rise of ground between us and their draw, where he could watch both the back and front of the jacal, but that would be about all. María's snapshot of Counts in the buckboard tracks, yonder, had sobered them up considerable. It looked like it was going to be either a starve-out or stand-off now, and why not?

Either way, Sego won.

If he wanted to stick by Buchanan, all he had to do was keep me pinned in the jacal another forty-eight hours. That would clear the contract delivery date. If he meant to play it loose with Rance, grabbing the gold for himself, he needed only to set out there and stretch those forty-eight hours till I either broke and ran or came out with my hands up.

So it was quiet out there and we knew it was going to stay that way, at least till daybreak. Jesús was on watch in the far ramada. María in the main jacal. It was a time made for lonely kids to watch the moon in long quiet stretches and to get shut of a lot of stumbly, awkward talk in between.

Yet, after a lively spell, me and May ran down.

I had told her everything there was to know about Button Starbuck. She had traded me back, fifty-fifty. Or, anyway, forty-fifty. When she was all done, I realized she hadn't told me anything I hadn't already heard between her and Brack in the Dallas stage. That nettled me, since I was by this time really wanting to know for sure if María was her actual mother. But I didn't complain. The things we *had* talked about were a lot more important—even if I couldn't, for the life of me, think back later to what a single one of them was. That didn't bother me either. It wasn't what sixteen- and seventeen-year-old kids said under a Texas moon of a soft, balmy spring night. It was the way they said it.

And May had a way of saying it.

It was maybe five minutes after the talk had run out that we quit our stalling and our staring out at the sagebrush and came around to look at each other.

We did it at the same time. May was facing the moon. Our eyes locked up long and slow. Her lips fell apart in that lazy, slack way she had of smiling as though she knew a lot of things you didn't. And wasn't going to tell you a one of them. Ever.

I didn't have that long to wait.

She was the first girl I ever kissed.

And the last.

It must have been hours later. I could only judge by a startled look at the set of the moon. Old Jesús made a decent commotion in the jacal—coughed wheezy like an old man will late at night, grumped a few things deliberate loud to María, stumbled against a chair on purpose—to let us know he was coming.

When he pushed the cowskin aside, we were apart; May back at the wall with the Winchester, me staying where we had been.

I stirred around in the hay, clutching for the serape and trying to let on like I was thick with sleep. *"Qué pasa? Quién es?"* I mumbled. "What's going on? Who's there?"

Over at the wall, May laughed at me and I could have killed her. But that was the Mexican in her. And the Indian. To a first-woman white boy, it was a wondrous magic and midnight thing, what had happened there in that moonlit ramada. My stomach was still shaking and my heart still pounding with it. But to a mestizo girl it was only something to look back at and laugh soft and cynical about.

I didn't get to more than glare at her, though, before old Jesús was standing over me. "It is I, my son." He nodded quietly. "Did you sleep well?"

"Así no más," I shrugged, ill-natured. Then still scowling, *"Qué pasa?"*

"Nada, it is only that the girl should sleep a little now, too. You are refreshed enough?"

"Dispense me Usted, patrón," I muttered, getting to my feet and giving him the proper little courtesy bow I had learned from Sec and which was so dear to all those Spanish-blood people. *"Por supuesto."*

I turned to May, making the bow a stiffneck sneer. *"Buenas noches, niña. Mil gracias por el favor."* It was bad Spanish, said just about backwards, but she got it. *"Por favor!"* she laughed bright and hard. Then, as quick to turn from ice to fire as any half-breed, she stepped over to me, handed me the Winchester and said it for me only, her lips so close the husky whisper brushed my cheek like a kiss. *"Buenas noches, caballero—!"*

She was gone then and I was alone in the ramada with the old man.

He waited for the cowskin to stop moving behind her, put his thin hand on my shoulder the same way Sec had always done when something was giving me more trouble than my bull head could handle.

"What can one say, *hombre?* She is a woman."

It was simple, like everything else about the old gentleman. Yet dead right. A family Bible full of Paul's fanciest advice, or Solomon's best decisions couldn't have said it any sharper.

"*Nada, patrón*," I grinned gratefully, and headed for the lookout wall.

He followed me over, his gentle voice continuing.

"Keep a close watch now. They should be changing their guard out there within the hour. When they do, get your pony ready. Meanwhile, look to him to see that he is not lame or stiff. *María has a plan.*"

I only nodded to let him know I had heard him. I wasn't thinking about him, or what he had said about looking to Little Hawk. It was crawling on toward one o'clock. A little chill was settling into the early morning air. May was gone and the moon was fast getting out of my eyes.

I was all of a sudden thinking about nothing but sunup and Sego Lockhart.

Chapter Twenty-eight

The new chill that the prospect of Sego and first sunlight put to cat-footing up my backbone wasn't any part of the early morning nippiness. It got to me so bad after a spell of staring out into the dead-still sage that I started scratching around in my mind for some excuse to go into the jacal where I could be with some company better than my own worked-up nerves.

Shortly, I figured that asking for the makings would be a good reason. The need for a smoke was taken for granted in any language.

I started for the jacal cowhide intending to hit up María, who I had seen puffing one of the bitter black Spanish *cigarillos* that those south of Texas and Mexican border Indians used so heavy. My idea was set up to work two ways: asking for the seegar would save me from fumbling around with the makings, letting her see I wasn't a smoking man and was after something else; then, with the seegar lit and likely her having one with me, maybe we could talk a little and I could find out something about her and May. Which was only no more than 50-50 fair, anyways. I had already told them all about me and what I was packing in those army saddlebags, while I was eating and out of simple gratitude for their dangerous play in backing me against Sego. As a matter of fact, I had told them that if I got out of this box-trap alive, a good part of the gold would come back to them as soon as I could get it there. So, to me, it figured as only equal shares that I should know a little more about them.

It turned out to be a good idea, better even than I thought. I didn't even have to go inside the cowhide, nor half strangle myself on a Spanish seegar. I found out all I wanted to know on the double-dealing subject of fat half-breed *dueñas* and slinky-bodied mestizo girls without leaving the jacal.

I was just reaching to pull aside the cowhide when I heard María's low mutter and May's soft answering laugh.

There was the same mixed-blood hardness about that laugh of hers as the one she had flung at me when I was trying to bluff old Jesús after nearly being caught in the hay with his precious little granddaughter. I checked my reach and held up, listening breathheld.

They were at May's bunk, and her bunk was built against the jacal wall I was standing behind. I slid along it, away from the doorway, looking for a chink in the logs. Whoever takes care of damp-eared white boys about to get took for two-bit dummies in Mexican mud huts was on full duty that late spring night. I found my chink and it was a good one. I could not only hear May and the squaw, I could see them; a-grinning and whispering for all they were worth in a stray slant of moonlight from across the room.

"*Pues, little one,*" the squaw was shrugging in Spanish, "one cannot have everything in a man. We women know that. He is a pure *Tejano,* that is surely something. If you can have him, you had better think hard about it. Do you want to spend the rest of your life in a jacal?"

"*Por supuesto* no!" said the girl, losing her smile. "But neither do I want to live my whole life with a weakling!"

"A weakling!" sputtered María. "Bah! Show me the man who is not one!"

"A coward, then!" scowled May defiantly.

María softened. "Ah, you mean about the poor brother? The fierce light-haired one? Aye, there was a *caballero. Qué hombre, muchacha! Ai de más,* a man for any woman, that one. But, then, there is the difference. He is dead. This one is alive!

"Besides," she flashed her evil grin again, "I like this one too, in his way. If it was a mother he needed, I would consider him myself."

"You had better do it then," sulked May. "For that is what he needs."

"Ah, no, *niña.* He needs a woman. If not you, then another. Be very sure of that."

"I am. It will be another. I do not want him. One must have love, *madre. No es verdad?*"

Madre! I thought. Then the squaw *was* her mother! Up to that moment, hard as María's calculating words had hit me, I had still been thinking May was all right. She was saying straight out what she thought of me and wasn't going along with her mother's cold-deck scheme to use me and the gold to get the girl shut of jacal life and leave the mestizo brand far behind.

Now, the certain knowledge of what I had feared but really refused to admit all along—that May was a half-blood and María was her actual mother— jolted me clear down to my eavesdropping toes.

But I hadn't got my last jolt yet.

"Love!" snorted María, picking up May's honest question. "What is that? Some man's arms around you? Any *hombre's* body on the blanket by your side? *De nada!* When it is dark, a man is a man. You don't see him, you feel him! All women close their eyes at that time, anyway."

"I don't," said the girl quietly. "I love with my eyes open."

"Aye!" winked the squaw, the moonlight flashing from her white teeth. "So I noticed, so I noticed."

"*Madre*—!"

"Tut! Don't '*madre*' me, *muchacha*. You are not the only one around this jacal who keeps the eyes open when making love. Remember that."

"*Madre*, you couldn't! You didn't—!"

"*Muchacha*, I could, I did," mimicked the squaw flatly. "Now tell me again that he is a weakling and a coward and that you have no use for him."

May's mood changed as swiftly as her mother's.

"It was the moonlight, I swear it!" she laughed. "It meant nothing."

"It did to him," grunted the squaw, not echoing the laugh. "It meant you can have him if you will— and you are a fool if you won't!

"Now you listen to me, *niña*. I have a plan—"

I saw her look around quickly to check old Jesús, nodding on guard at the front window, then drop her voice even lower. But as I gritted my teeth wanting to strangle both of them, and as I set myself to hear the rest of it, regardless, Jesús got up from his guard-spot and came across the room.

"*Qué pasa aquí?*" he grumbled. "What is all this mumbling about? Let the girl sleep, María. What is it that is so important here?"

"*De nada, de nada,*" smiled María, smoothing May's hair and patting her creamy cheek. "Just woman talk, *así no más.* Nothing an old man would understand."

"An old man understands many things," said Jesús softly, and I wondered if he knew what was in María's mind.

"Well, old man," she laughed, "you would never understand this! Now you better look in on the boy and see that he is not asleep again."

"Aye," nodded Jesús slowly. "I will do so. He is a good boy, brave and generous. I wish him well."

"You are an old fool," said María. "Go and see that he is getting himself ready, as I ordered."

Jesús nodded again and moved obediently for the cowskin. On my side of the partition I hesitated only long enough to see María start in on May again about her precious plan. Then I slipped swiftly back over to the ramada wall and my sagebrush watching.

"*Qué pasa con Usted?*" said the old man, coming to my side. "Is it yet quiet out there?"

"Very quiet, *patrón*," I answered politely.

"That is good. You are preparing yourself as I asked? You have looked to your pony against the time when they will change the guard?"

"I was about to do so, *patrón*. I was only taking a last look out there to make sure the new man had not yet come down from the fire."

"That is well and right. Everything must be done with the greatest care. I cannot tell you what it is that María will do for you. She has forbidden it. But she is an Indian, my son. It will be something worthwhile, something real."

"I thought María was a mestizo," I said, partly curious but mostly just to make talk and keep his company a little longer.

"She is a pureblood Mescalero Apache, my son," he said quietly. "She is my daughter by marriage only, and she is the true mother of the girl. *Buenas noches—*"

"*Buenas noches*," I muttered back unhappily, and felt the bitter loneliness close in like a shroud behind the dropping cowskin.

Chapter Twenty-nine

A long hour later, I could see the man coming down to take over from whoever was on watch up on the rise. He walked right down the buckboard trail till he was near the spot where María had nailed Counts, then ducked into the brush. Pretty quick I saw the other man come out of the same brush and head for the fire in the draw above. The guard was changed.

Minding what Jesús had told me, though not understanding it or even thinking too much about it, I got Little Hawk ready. If María had a plan for getting me on my way, no matter if it involved trying to sell me to May, I wasn't going to spit in her eye about it. Not, leastways, till I'd heard the full details. Meanwhile, I looked to Little Hawk as Jesús had told me to do when the new man came on guard.

That little *grullo* was a never-ending wonder.

I checked him over careful before saddling him and slinging the gold back in place. He seemed perfectly all right. His breathing was easy, with no rasp of windbreak in it whatever. When I backed him and moved him around to see if he had gone stiff or broke down in any quarter, he stepped around loose and free as though he'd been just decent warmed up, not anywheres near rode to death. You would have thought he'd been stabled for a month, was full of rolled oats and raring to get rid of them.

It seemed to me then, and it still does, that Texas ought to forget about Sam Houston and Stephen Austin and Jim Bowie and Crockett and old Colonel Travis and the rest of those Alamo boys and just build herself a life-size statue of a 700-pound mustang to stand in front of the state capitol. It would be closer to telling the truth. It may have been a six-foot San Antonio man that hung that lone star up there in the old Republic's flag, but by damn he was standing on the back of a thirteen-hand Spanish pony to do it.

I had to admit, though, that I was prejudiced in favor of horses. Especially the linebacked coyote-colored ones, from *grullo* blues through roany duns to pure butter buckskins. There never was a man of any color could hold a guttered candle to them.

I let Little Hawk know as much with a good ear-scratching and a long hug of his skinny neck. Then I tied him to his manger and went back to my sagebrush staring.

After that, it just got quieter and quieter out there.

The bullbats had long ago given up their June bug hunting and gone to roost. I heard a fox yap down in the little spring-branch bottoms behind the jacal. The usual coyote talk was bickering back and forth out beyond him. A little cactus owl floated around for a spell, waiting for a field mouse or kangaroo rat to come out of the east ramada where old Jesús stored his tortilla corn and where María kept her *metate* for grinding it. He didn't have much luck. He lit over on a rotted-off corral post, shook out his feathers and fussed at me as though I was to blame for the lean hunting. Then he sailed off down the branch to see could he find a young cottontail dance going on somewhere where the moon was brighter and there wasn't any man-smell around to spoil things.

When he had gone I couldn't hear a sound save Dad's watch ticking away inside the Mexican boy's ragged jacket. I pulled it out, slanting it to the moon. One-thirty. I went back to staring at the sagebrush. I remember looking at it once more at one forty-five. The next thing I knew I still had the watch in my hand and it was ten after two and old Jesús was calling softly from the jacal.

"*Hijo!* Come in here. There is something for you to see. María has brought you a little something. Come quickly."

I ducked in past the cowskin, almost knocking May down. She was going into the ramada as I came out. She was lugging a grubsack and two old army canteens. She didn't say anything. All I thought, from that, was that she had got what she wanted from me and that she and the others, for some fresh reason, were in a powerful hurry to get shut of me. I let her go with no more than a hurt scowl, went on over by the east window where Jesús and the squaw were waiting for me.

The moonlight was streaming in good and strong there. I took what the squaw handed me, paying her off with a scowl as mean and ungracious as the one I'd just given the girl. It was a

heavy *buscadero* belt with two late model Colt .44's
hanging in its twin holsters. I didn't get the drift. I
thought maybe she was wanting to trade me the
Colts for my little .38-40 Winchester, and was just
about to tell her to go to hell, when she grinned
and reached over to tap her finger on the belt's big
hand-carved buckle.

I looked at it. It was Mexican silver, overlaid
with some goldwire chasing, and for a peculiar
uneasy reason looked sort of familiar to me. I held
it sideways to the moon, making out the initials
C. C. cut oversize and bold into it.

"C. C?" I grumped aloud, in my puzzlement
thinking and talking in English. "Thet supposed
to mean somethin' special?"

If it did, to María, that was, she never got her
chance to say so.

I had no sooner asked the question than I didn't
need her answer to it. I had my own. It came to me
in a scary flash. I *had* seen that belt buckle before.
It was in the Lone Star Saloon in Mason City. And,
previous to that, in the lantern light of Pegleg
Yates's livery barn. And more. In both cases, it had
been wrapped around the lean middle of Sego's
righthand man! That C. C. stood for Cheyenne
Carson, the tall bitter-eyed gunhawk who had
warned Pegleg to watch his manners just ahead of
Sego quirting him—and who had laughed when
the knotted rawhide laid the old man's cheek
open to the bone.

"Where did you get this?" I asked, back in
Spanish again. "I know this belt, I have seen it before. Where did it come from?"

"From one who no longer needs it!" laughed

María. "Feel it, there, where it passes around the kidneys."

Without thinking, I slid my hand around the back of the belt. It came away sweet and sticky. I felt sick. "You—?" I whispered.

"And *him!*" she grinned. When she said that "him," she palmed the eight-inch gleam of a Comanche skinning knife out from under her old black *rebozo.* She tapped and patted its clotted blade like she would the curly head of a child who had behaved well. "But mostly him," she conceded modestly. "It was nothing, once the guard was changed and I saw just where to go."

She must have seen the color drain out of my face, even in the moonlight. For when she saw my look, she shook her head and held up her hand as though worried I'd got the wrong idea.

She was a woman of morals. She made that clear.

"Do not think I am a common thief, *niño,*" she reproved me. "When one borrows from a friend who is not home, one leaves something in exchange."

"How is *that?*" I asked. "What do you mean?"

"A belt for a belt, *niño,*" she shrugged. "*Así no más.*"

"What belt?" I snapped. "*Qué cinto, por Dios?*"

"Your belt, *amigo.* The one you bought to carry the gold in." I swung my eyes across the jacal, to the wall-peg I had hung the empty moneybelt on. It was gone. "I thought you would have little need for it, *niño,*" she apologized. "So I filled it with sand and stones and left it around him, up there."

Well, what could you say to that? I buckled on

the *buscadero*. "All right," I began, "what is the rest of it? *Qué pasa ahora?*"

"*Nada,*" grinned the squaw. "*Hay no más.* It is all arranged. You can go as soon as the girl has the mare saddled."

"The *who* has the *what* saddled!" I exploded in English, the mention of May and the little buckskin mare jolting me out of my shock of that great ball of fat having gone out and knifed Cheyenne Carson without even the little cactus owl knowing about it.

"The girl," put in Jesús Otero quietly. "She is going with you. It is a rough country to the south. You will need a guide who knows its night trails."

"No," I said at once. "She does not go with me, *patrón*. I am grateful to you and María. I will never forget you, but the girl stays here. I can follow the stars."

"Can you also follow them when they are not there?" he asked.

"*Qué dice?*" I said uneasily.

"Look to the south, my son, and to the east."

I looked. Way down by the Gulf, a sudden cloudbank was building. Even as I watched it, the first faint flashes of the heat lightning lit up its black underbelly and the distant growl of the thunder muttered across the darkening miles.

I shook my head. Stars or no stars, I wasn't going to let him send May along with me. Not with what I knew about why she wanted to go.

"It makes no difference, *patrón*," I insisted. "You cannot permit her to do it."

He smiled a funny, sad smile then, lifting his hands in that hopeless way a Mexican uses to ex-

cuse anything he figures ought to be left up to the
Lord.

"But it is not my doing, *hijo*," he said. "There is
no matter of permission in it."

I was tying down Cheyenne's holsters when he
said it. "What do you mean?" I said, picking up
my Winchester.

"The girl, my son. She said she was going with
you, that is all."

"Yes? And what does that mean?"

"She will go."

"Just like that, eh?"

"*Sí. Por supuesto.* She says the gold is heavy and
that two ponies can carry it better than one."

"You wouldn't even *try* to stop her?"

"Would you, my son? Would you, if you were a
very old man? One who has not long to live now?
Would you deny to yourself, and to her, what is to
be so easily read in the way she looks at a young
Americano? Would your selfish tongue and lonely
heart say no, where your weary old eyes can see a
tender first love saying yes?"

"I do not know what you mean, *patrón*," I stammered.

"Let her tell you then," he murmured. "You will
have a long ride for it. Much time to talk."

"Bah!" broke in María roughly. "They won't, if
you mean to stand here all night cackling like an
old hen over her last sickly chick! *Niña!*" she
hissed toward the ramada, "come at once! Do you
hear me, good for nothing!"

May came out, leading both ponies. She handed
me Little Hawk's reins and I took them without a
word. It was all way too deep for me. I was clear

out of questions and answers. I knew only two things for sure, right then: May was going with me and María had given us a possible three-hour headstart by knifing Sego's lookout.

Past that, it was anybody's guess. But I figured I could come reasonable close on the first try. It would begin to turn light about four. If Cheyenne didn't report back when it did—and you didn't have to guess that he wouldn't—they would come looking for him. When they found him they would know that it meant their $25,000 Brazos bird had flown the coop and was off and winging for Mason City. They would be circling the jacal for our tracks no later than five o'clock at the best. Sixty seconds after they found them, they would be running them at a flat gallop.

We walked the ponies out through the east ramada. There was a drop-bar gate in its south wall, letting into the ranch yard behind the jacal. Outside, we held up and listened for a long minute, then swung up.

May and María and her grandfather must have said their family good-byes in the jacal, before old Jesús had called me in from the ramada. There were no weepy hugs nor sad words in the yard. The old man just said, *"Tengais cuidado, niños,"* and patted both Poquito and Little Hawk on their rumps and stepped back. María didn't say anything at all.

May turned her little mare, starting her for the spring-branch gully. I put Little Hawk after her. *"Un momento,"* called Jesús, waving to me. I checked the *grullo* and he came up to stand at my offside knee. "I did not want her to hear," he said quickly. "A man will understand these things. *No es verdad, hombre?*"

"*Sí, patrón. Qué es?*"

"You will love her, you will be good to her, even though she is mestizo?"

"Yes." I said it before I even thought. It just came out. I wasn't really listening to him, I was watching May. She had checked the buckskin and was waving for me to come on.

"I had to know that," murmured the old man. ".She is my whole life. The sole child of my only son, who died long ago. We are pure Castilian, *niño*, of the highest blood in Old Spain. But then there is María and the dark blood. I am sorry for you, my son, truly sorry. Yet, still, *qué mas hay?* She is my granddaughter and I am very proud of that."

He said the last of it low and fierce and with his fine old head held high, and I knew he was not apologizing for May but for me and the whole haughty idea of the *Americano* blood behind me.

I looked at him, wanting powerful bad to say something just right in answer. It wasn't in me. I never had a way with words, nor with a properly decent thought when one was needed. So I just put it the way he made me feel it inside me.

"I, too, am proud that she is your granddaughter, *patrón*," I told him in Spanish, and put the spurs to Little Hawk and got him out of there.

Chapter Thirty

We were well down past Lampasas by daylight.

All through the dark hours just past, May and me had ridden with no more talk than was necessary for her to give the trail orders and for me to understand and follow them out. The whole time my mind had been turning like a chased coyote trying to figure out what she was thinking and why she had come along with me, seeing she felt the way I knew she did. I hadn't come up either with any answers nor with the nerve for any questions. Now there wasn't time for any.

Old Jesús's storm had never got away from the Gulf. I had been praying it would, to lay our dust and wash out our tracks. When it didn't, I knew it was going to be a straight race for Mason and told May as much without any covering up.

That's when she really started to shine. She laid us a line of tracks across that faceless country that couldn't have been straightened out with a surveyor's transit. My object, now, was to cut into the stageline where it left off running due south out of Lampasas and angled southwest toward Mason City.

The idea was that we could make better time on

the stage road. That and the fact we knew where Sego was and knew he wasn't between us and Mason.

Anybody else we bumped into would be welcome company by comparison, nor was that all. Following the road would give us our best chance of running into that somebody else—say like Ewell Blackburn or Sec Gonzales, for prayerful instance. Providing, always, that either of them had got a posse together and was out looking for their young friend Button Starbuck.

We struck out on a steady lope.

Every couple of miles, regular, we held up to blow the horses and switch the gold. Each time we would pick a high spot so that we could look back and spot any trailing dust. The first two stops there was nothing. The third, there was.

We could see their dust lift up and drift away from them, telling us they had held up to look ahead. I got that funny feeling of being watched and knew they had the field glasses on us. To make sure, I told May to follow me quick. We took our horses on over the rise, then swung them up through the sagebrush and cut back to look over the hill. The dust was rolling again. Our way.

We got out of there. I kept Little Hawk in hand, holding him to his natural lope. The buckskin mare stayed with him easy, not straining any. I didn't say anything to May right off. I was too busy thinking.

We were still thirty miles from Mason. Sego and his men were only a short six miles behind us. They figured, in any over-the-stretch run, to make something like seven miles to our five. That was because of their better horses and because they had no need, like May and me, to be trading that hundred pounds of gold back and forth.

Unlucky for us, there wasn't a blessed move we could make to improve either one of those facts.

Much as we loved our little mustangs for their guts and gumption, they simply could not outrun those bigger, bred-up, Lazy RB stockhorses. And if we let either Poquito or Little Hawk pack the gold steady, the one that did would break down miles quicker than the other.

The answer was easy. We could give or take a mile and not worry about carrying the final figure out any set number of decimal points. Somewheres around fifteen miles short of Mason City, Sego Lockhart was going to run us a dead heat for our $25,000.

There was only one thing we could do about that. The least thing. Go ahead and ride it out and let him know he had been in a horse race.

We were getting into Llano County now, a piece of the prettiest prairie in Texas. It minded me of our lower pasture up on the Brazos, but it didn't make me homesick. Just sick.

There wasn't a stick of timber in sight tall enough to shade a snake. Nor a hump of sod high enough to shelter a sandgrouse. We couldn't split up to make them gamble on who had the gold, and maybe chase the wrong one. Their field glasses fixed that. For the same reason, we couldn't hope to hide unless it was in a prairie dog hole. We couldn't even find a rock outcrop or gully-wash big enough to get behind and make a stand that might buy us an hour of time to let somebody friendly show up along the Lampasas road.

We had not only run our string out, we had snapped it. We were as caught as two tumble bugs in the middle of crossing a forty-mile cow chip.

I called over to May and told her as much. She rode on it a minute, frowning hard. Then I saw she had thought of something. There was no missing that wonderful sunburst grin of hers. She rattled the reason for it to me, as we crowded stirrups with Poquito and Little Hawk matching strides like they'd been team-broke in a circus ring.

We had a tag-end hope to hang on to. About twelve, fifteen miles east of Mason City, the Llano River broke its southeast course to wander up north in a lazy ten-mile curve before turning back down south again. At the high point of the curve, it came within half a mile of the stage road. I wouldn't have noticed it on the trip up, she told me, because the prairie climbed to the south of the coach route, putting the stream and its telltale fringe of willow and cottonwood behind a bend-cut bluff.

Those bluffs—they weren't really bluffs, at all, May said, but only sizable shelfbanks that dropped off steep—ran for maybe a quarter mile along the north side.

At the point she had in mind, from a childhood trip she had made with old Jesús to bring up a little herd of Tamaulipas calves through Laredo, an old cattle trail crossed the river. Coming from the south, low side of the Llano, the crossing was marked by a small upstream island that cut the river into two channels, slowing and shallowing it to make the old Mexican ford.

Sego might know of it, and he might not.

Either way, it gave us a chance to hold out for a stiffer price than we could hope to ask out there on the pancake flat of that cussed Llano County prairie. Once into the trees of that little island, May promised me, her gray eyes flashing, they would have to come at us across open swimming water. It was that, or camp up on the bluffs and starve us out.

The fever of it got to me. I sat a little straighter in the saddle. It was a chance, by damn. And no raunchier than any one of a dozen others I had already run in the past three days. I grinned at May and reached over and squeezed her hand and told her we'd take it.

It was a strange, new feeling I had right then.

I wasn't *scared* anymore. All of a sudden, I just *wasn't*. And more. I *hadn't been* for some time. Not since the minute I had slid off Little Hawk in that mud-floored jacal and turned around to see May smiling at me.

The thought of that made me do something I hadn't done in a long spell—laugh. I stood up in the stirrups, looked back to check our lead, slewed back around, set myself careless in the saddle—*and laughed!*

"Come on, May!" I yelled. "Let's show those Texican scrubs what a couple of real *criollos* kin do!"

She laughed back, put the quirt to Poquito, lit out in the lead. I touched up Little Hawk and let him go.

The run for the river was on.

* * *

We made it.

With a mile and a half and five minutes to spare.

Our two little *criollos* couldn't have run another furlong without killing themselves. As it was, when they had swum down to the island from up-current with us hanging on to their tails and holding our *buscadero* belts out of the water on the ends of our Winchester barrels, they were the next thing to dead, anyway. They just tottered out on the up-stream sandspit, spraddled their trembling legs, stood with their heads down and their jaws yawping for air. It made my stomach crawl to do it, but I had to take May's quirt and actually lay their rumps open to make them move on into the trees.

Once under cover, we pulled everything off of them picketing them with our *reatas* and praying they could gasp in enough breath to stay alive till dark. We were half wild with the excitement of having beat Sego and his bunch to Ten Mile Bend. We were so worked up we were talking crazy. We already had a plan going to bury the gold on the island and try swimming out downstream with the horses should the Gulf storm, now muttering and growling off to the east again, come on to give us fast, high water and heavy rain cover after sun-down.

But our wild talk died sudden away.

Sego had ridden into sight up on the bluffs.

It was him had the glasses. He put them on the crossing the minute his naked-eye sweep of the empty *llano* to the south told him his two mustang riders had evaporated into ten miles of wide-open nowhere.

We could see the sunwink of the lenses as they picked up our tracks coming down to the ford, and turned to follow them up the wet sand of the north bank. Then another sunflash as they jumped the north channel water to pounce on the wobbly line of Poquito's and Little Hawk's hoofmarks leading along the midstream sandspit.

We saw Sego's tensing head move clear around the near side of the island, raise slightly to put the glasses on the sand of the farside bank beyond the south channel. We knew what he was seeing over there. Nothing. And those lenses wound up staring straight at the only place left in the east half of Mason County that could hide two cornered kids and a pair of rundown Spanish *mesteños:* the cottonwood clot of Ten Mile Island.

It was like Sego, what he did then.

No deals. No offers. No arguing of any kind.

He just took down his glasses and started stationing his men.

He put all five of them over on the south bank. That was a bad startler to begin with. Bad for one main reason.

As of my last look the afternoon before, Sego had had seven men with him. María had then centered Counts and knifed Cheyenne, making it five. Now I counted six again. Then, even as I did I recognized the sixth one—Beatty Grimes.

The crazy devil had come to and followed me down from the Fort Goodwin wash, then tracked Sego and the rest of the bunch along the wagon trail from where they had jumped me over by the Lampasas road.

Well, seeing Beatty back in business was unsettling enough. But it wasn't the worst of what was bothering me. What really had me trying to get my tongue back under the bit was why Sego was sending him and all the others south of the river. It didn't make sense, yet we could see them swimming their horses across way down below the ford, then spreading out and working back up through the brush and rocks to cover both ends of the island with their guns.

I still didn't get it.

For some crazy reason of his own, Sego was staying alone up on the north bluffs.

Why?

The question no sooner formed in my mind than Sego himself answered it.

"Starbuck—!"

I had been watching Beatty and his bunch getting into position. The sound of my name in Sego's scrapy voice jumped me hard. I flinched around, peering up through the cottonwood screen to locate him. He was afoot, standing on the crown of the bluff across the north channel. In his right hand dangled a sawed-off shotgun.

"Kid," he called, "you and your lady friend rest easy. You got till dark." He paused, letting it sink in. Then, cat-and-mousing it in a way to put a chill into you till next spring, "After thet, I'm comin' over there after you. *All alone, boy.*"

He stepped back and was gone from sight.

I gulped but couldn't swallow.

It wasn't a threat. Threats weren't Sego's way. He was just telling me what he was going to do. The same as he had told Sheriff Ewell Blackburn that night in the Lone Star when he'd warned him not to set with his back to any more doors from then on. And what he was going to do, now, was come across to the island with that shotgun when it got dark and hunt me down like an egg-sucking rat in a settlement chicken shed.

Chapter Thirty-one

Quiet? It was so quiet it made your ears ache from straining to listen to it.

The river lapped along steady and sleepy, eddying and back-swirling by the island, cutting and digging at the north bank where the current ran deep. Once in a while a chunk of the bank clay would break away over there and slide into the water. It was the noisiest thing that happened all morning, those little pieces of bankdirt slipping into the Llano without a sound.

May and me talked in whispers like people will do when they're alone in church, with nobody but God and the empty pews to listen to them.

There was a thousand things I wanted to tell her but I couldn't get proper started on a one of them.

Being a woman, she did a little better.

For a beginner, she told me what she knew about herself. She kept it short.

She had been born on a big plantation out west of San Antone. The owners were rich folks and had got hold of a part of one of the original Spanish grants. It was one of those pieces they figured in sections rather than acres, and by the number of days it took to ride around it, horseback, instead of

by survey map miles. But in one of the last big Comanche raids that far east, the main ranch buildings had been burned out and everybody in and
around them, killed. Everybody, that was, except
the *mayordomo* and the *cocinera*, the plantation
cook. Them and the little baby girl who had been
born to the cook and her husband only days before.

The husband had been the cow-boss on the
place; a wild young Spaniard named Mayo Otero.
Of course he was that only son Jesús had told me
about. Just as naturally the *mayordomo* had been
old Jesús, the *cocinera*, María, the baby, May herself.

They had all three got off with their lives because María had been brought up a Comanche.

Bred and born pure Mescalero Apache way over
in New Mexico, she had been captured by the
Texas Lipan Apaches when she was a little girl.
Then traded by them to the Kwahadi Comanches
and raised in their customs in a Pecos River
ranchería till she was past twenty and had met up
with and married Jesús's boy. She could rattle off
Comanche like a pureblood, looked more like a
Kwahadi squaw than any of the women with the
raiders. She had wrapped May in her old black
rebozo and Caddo blanket, the same ones she still
wore, and let on loud and big, Indian fashion, that
Jesús was the baby's father and a full quarter
Chiricahua Apache in his own right. The red ras-
cals had bought her noisy bluff and left her and
the old man their hair.

The two of them had then taken May and fled
north in a hurry. María's Comanche connections

were known in the settlements and they were afraid there might be some ugly trouble when it was found out they were the only ones survived the burn-out. They had ended up finding and hiding out in the deserted old jacal northwest of Lampasas, where I had found them. It was the only home May had ever known, or wanted to know.

She trailed off kind of sad and I couldn't help but wonder why, till she shook her head and added real soft, "I never heard that full story myself till last night. I've always thought María was just the Indian cook who saved Jesús and me. I never knew she was my real mother, though I called her *madre*, until I heard it from Jesús after he had talked to you in the jacal."

She paused, then went on, quieter still.

"He said that he had to tell you because I was going with you, and had then to tell me for the same reason. He said we both had to know I was a true mestizo and not his pure Spanish granddaughter as I had always thought and as you and your brother might have been led to believe from thinking María was only my *dueña*. But I would rather have died than to have you know that about me."

She trailed off again and I took hold of her hand and held tight onto it and blurted out, "Why?"

She glanced up, made awkward and shy by the way I was squeezing her hand, and murmured, "Because."

"Because what?" I asked, just as embarrassed.

"Because you are white," she said, and I could see the hot tears gathering.

"What difference does thet make?" I whispered back, not wanting to see those tears spill over.

"You're still the old man's granddaughter. That ought to make you proud. It does me. What's more, I told him it did, too!"

She looked at me quick and funny. "When did you tell him that?" she asked.

"When he called me back, jest as we was startin' off last night. Why? What does it matter?"

"It matters a lot—to me—" she said, and I could see she didn't want to talk anymore just then.

But I couldn't let it rest. I had to know what was in her mind that she wasn't telling me. When I pressed her about it, she really busted loose. It came out of her in a wild, tear-stained flood; the whole story of María's wanting her to hang on to me and the gold, exactly like I'd heard it back of the jacal partition. She didn't leave anything out nor change anything to make herself look good. But when she had finished, I for some strange reason felt calm and right and peaceful in my heart about the whole thing, and I told her so.

"Well," I said, nodding to her sober-faced and keeping my voice down like you do when you're talking to a nervous pony, "you see, May, all thet don't matter a bit to me. You didn't say nothin' about me thet wasn't true, nor you didn't look to be buyin' any of María's ambitions about usin' me to git shut of thet mud-floored hut. As for her, you cain't blame her a nickel's worth. She was only thinkin' of you, her own kid. And look what she done fer me, goin' out and knifin' Cheyenne like thet.

"No, I reckon María's all right and I *know* you are. The only thing thet's botherin' me is how come you to change your mind and come with me. I know durn well it wasn't me or María or the money. Just what was it, May?"

My long easy talk had quieted her considerable. When she looked up this time the tears were being blinked back and that smile of hers, that was so like her mother's in the quick dark way it broke, was beginning to put its exciting curve to her red lips.

"Maybe," she said, blushing a little, "it was that dive you made into my lap when the stage started out of Mason City. Or the lonesome way you looked standing there in Lampasas the night I waved back to you from the buckboard? Or yet the way you looked at me last night in the ramada. *Quién sabe, caballero?*" she finished it up tauntingly in Spanish and with that shoulder-shrug nobody but a Mexican can make say more than a million words without their lips moving.

"No, May." I shook my head, not smiling back. "It wasn't none of them things. What was it?"

She changed to serious quick as light, the teasy curve going out of her lips, her gray eyes finding mine and holding them steady.

"My grandfather." She nodded humbly. "He knew my heart better than I did. And my thoughts better than María. It was he that told me."

"Told you what?" I scowled, not following her now and suspicioning that she was starting in on me again with her cold-blooded Indian tricks. But I was wrong. And was never so wrong again in my whole bullheaded life.

"*That I loved you,*" said May Otero softly, and dropped her eyes to hide the swift return of the tears.

We went back to listening to the river and to watching the south bank rocks and the north bank bluffs after that. There was no more talk of any kind. The sun centered, began to slide west. Nothing moved in the rocks. Nothing stirred on the bluffs. Two o'clock came, then three, then four.

The wind began to move about five.

It was a southeast wind, blowing up from the Gulf. It began to get dark with the sun still over an hour high. We looked east and saw it coming, the sullen front of its rain-swollen belly moving across the prairie miles swift and silent as a buzzard's shadow. It was going to be a real grass bender; a gully washer and a goose drownder.

And all of a sudden our crazy talk of getting away under its cover was not so crazy.

If you lived in that country, you knew those fierce prairie storms. They could blow up out of nowhere, closing in on you faster than any horse could run you away from them. They could shut out the sun and have the back country barrancas running brimful before you could more than look around and hit for the nearest high spot. They could take a beautiful balmy late spring afternoon like this one and turn it into a roaring hell of black rain and blind wind inside of thirty minutes.

If that storm came on like it was coming now; if it shut down around us as it looked like it was going to; we could load the gold on our horses and swim them and ourselves off that island on the roll of the downstream rise, with no seven men in the world being able to stop us doing it. It would be like trying to see and grab two burnt bottle corks bobbing past in a bat cave river at midnight blindfold.

May and me knew that.

So did Sego Lockhart and his six men.

Sego showed up on the bluff the minute the wind began to move. He yelled across to Beatty Grimes to get busy and smoke us out. He would stay up on the bluff and drill us if we broke cover on that side. I heard Beatty's idiot laugh answer him, then heard him, Beatty, yelling something at his men. I couldn't make out what it was but knew what it amounted to—close in.

There was no need for any more whispering. The wind was making too much noise and the time was getting a little too late in the afternoon. I hollered at May to try and keep Sego pinned on the bluff, then scuttled across the island to the south side.

I saw Beatty at the same time he saw me. We traded hipshots on the run and both of us dove for the dirt. Behind him. I could see the others break from their rocks and move up. I snapped four aimed shots from back of a big cottonwood drift-log and got a piece of one of them on the last round. I saw him spin down, swatting at his shoulder like he'd been bee-stung.

But my burst had let them know where I was, which was all they wanted. While Beatty kept me pinned so close to the log I couldn't get my head up to aim decent, the others spread and ran for still better spots. I nicked another of them in the leg with the last shell I had for the Winchester. Then I had to shift to Cheyenne's big Colts. From that minute they had me and they knew it.

It was the way that damn island lay cuddled in the steer's horns curve of the south bank that made it a deathtrap, once they decided to take my fire and come on in regardless.

From Sego's side it wasn't so bad. The water was wide and moving fast over there and there was no brush or rock cover along the base of the bluffs. But the south channel was actually no more than an old backwater slough. There was no current in it to speak of and it wasn't more than a hundred feet from any point of the island's edge to the mainland. And that wasn't the half of it. The horns of the main bank curved out on either end of the island to give cover to anybody with the guts to make a dash for them. Once they got a man out on each of those horntips, we were done. They could pin us from both sides of our cottonwood spit while they took their murderous time firing down the middle of it from both ends!

I could see they were going to make it, too.

In the same minute I did, May's .44 began to bark for the first time and I heard her yelling excitedly for me to clear out and come over with her.

That did it.

Sego was making his move and May was in real trouble. There was nothing to hold me back of that old cottonwood log anymore. And nothing could have. The only thing that mattered to me in that last minute was to be with May Otero.

I broke and ran, bluffing Beatty's bunch with a wild right and left burst from both Colts.

When I got to May she was just squeezing off another shot at Sego who, for some reason, was ducking and running around like he wanted powerful bad to get shut of that blufftop all of a sudden. May's shot was close enough to clip his hat and I saw him grab at it to keep it on, and dive for the handiest rock. Then May was levering her Winchester and spinning out her last empty and making no move to reload.

And with the sweetest right not to you ever heard in the prairie world.

Other Winchesters, and plenty of them, were taking up where hers had left off!

It was that simple. It had happened just that way and that fast.

Drawn in by the shots carried to them on the whistling southeast wind, Sheriff Ewell Blackburn, Tobe Edwards and Sec Gonzales, with Billie Joe Heston and a six-man posse of Brazos River *mesteñeros* passing by on the Lampasas stage road, had ridden over to see if the shooting could possibly have anything to do with their missing boy, Button Starbuck!

The second part of it went just as swift and sure.

Over across the Llano Beatty Grimes and his five men lost interest in getting rich without working. The minute they spotted and recognized Ewell Blackburn and his shotgun-toting shadow, Tobe Edwards, they mounted up and took out for the Rio Grande and the Coahuila line without bothering to wave good-bye. Much to my surprise, the sheriff let them go.

In a way I was kind of glad that he did.

I didn't care about the others, since they hadn't been mixed up in Dad's death, but somehow I felt a little different about Beatty even though he had been. I always thought that in his crazy, twisted way he had sort of taken a shine to me, no matter that I knew he would have killed me had I pushed him to it. One thing was certain anyway. I owed him my life, twice over, and was glad to see him get off with his, regardless of my surprise at the sheriff just standing there and letting him and his pals make it clean away.

But the old Mason County lawman wasn't getting soft in the head. And he didn't let me stay surprised very long. His reason for letting Beatty and the others go was deadly simple. I tumbled to it the minute I saw him turn away from the river and sweep his eyes back up toward Sego.

He had what he wanted, cornered in those rocks atop the north bank bluffs.

Chapter Thirty-two

Ewell Blackburn handled the rest of it like a lion hunt. When you've got the big cat in the rocks, with the hounds all around, he's killed his last calf or dragged down his last colt.

With Beatty and his five riders still in clear sight riding for the horizon, he sent Sec and his *mesteñeros* down to the ford to cover Sego from that side while we got off the island. May and me saddled the horses, slung on the gold and the gun-belts. They took the water as though they knew it was the end of the trail, snorting and eager as two short yearlings. We hung on to our saddle fenders down to the crossing and until their feet struck bottom. Then we grabbed our horns, slid aboard and rode out on the north bank. There was no sight nor sound of Sego the whole pin-still way.

I felt like kissing old Sec when he shouted, *"Ole! Ole!"* and spurred Mozo forward to pick us up. But the time wasn't just yet for hugging old friends. Like Sheriff Blackburn, I first had a score to settle with somebody else.

We went on up the crossing trail to the prairie above. Everybody was as glad to see me as I was them. Yet past a tight smile from the sheriff, an awkward, hesitating wave from Billie Joe Heston and a noncommittal nod from Tobe Edwards, you would never have known it. We were all thinking too much about the same thing—where we were and who we had cornered up in those bluff rocks.

The sheriff moved quick. The storm was almost due over us now. There was maybe ten minutes of shooting light left.

He spit Sec's six *mesteñeros* three-and-three, putting half to guard the east flank of the bluff, half the west. When they were in position, he ordered Sec and Billie Joe to stay where we were, with May and the gold, watching the north front of the rise. Then he got down off his old gray, gave his gunbelt a hitch, jerked his Winchester from its saddle sling and nodded up to Tobe Edwards.

Tobe swung down, breeching his shotgun to check the chambers. When he clicked it shut, both him and the sheriff looked up at me.

My stomach pulled in and got small.

It was going to be a walk-up.

Three seconds ticked away.

"Well, Button?" said the sheriff.

Another three seconds crawled off into the stillness and died.

"I'm empty," I said, gesturing headhung and helpless toward the waterlogged .38-40 under my leg.

He looked at me. So did the others. Nobody said anything. He took two slow steps toward me, nodded, tossed up his Winchester. I caught it.

"Comin'," I mumbled, and slid off the *grullo*.

We started up the rise. Sheriff Blackburn first, Tobe to his left, me to his right.

It seemed to me we walked forever. And that in the fifty yards we actually climbed before the sheriff stopped to peer up into the bluff rocks, I rode back over every mile I had covered from my little lean-to under the six cottonwoods of the homeplace, to Mason and Dallas and back—right down to where we now stood on Ten Mile Bend of the Llano waiting through that last endless minute while Sheriff Ewell Blackburn decided his move.

I lived again those three terrible moments which had brought me here: Dad's peaceful face looking into its last Brazos sunset from the old cane-bottom rocker on the *galería* of the main house; the brutal crush and bounce of the rocks sealing Doak off from the *javelinas* in the San Saba sandstone crevice; the slack twist of Brack's body falling past the stagecoach window into the dust of the Lampasas road.

I saw again, too, Doak's crinkly smile, Brack's fierce scowl, the last proud look Dad gave me when he ordered me off with old Sec to hunt down the mustang stud.

Then the trail miles between fled past.

Of the five men who had ridden up from Mason to kill Dad, Billie Joe Heston had come in and turned state's evidence, Morgan Counts was dead, Cheyenne Carson was dead, Beatty Grimes was gone and would never be back. Only Sego Lockhart was left.

Sego, the great ugly-faced frog who walked like a man. Who limped bad in his left leg. Who had already killed two Starbucks and headed the bunch that had cut down a third. Who was waiting now, up in those silent rocks, for the fourth—for me.

Sego, alone, deserted, run down to his last mile. His horse shot dead and sprawled on the slope below him. Ringed in and trapped, three sides against the river, by ten rifles and a sawed-off shotgun. Cornered, boxed, helpless.

And still as deadly as a strike-coiled diamondback.

The sheriff was done with his peering. He broke his gaze from the rocks, came around on Tobe and me.

"You two wait here," was all he said.

"Hold on," I gulped. "I'm goin' with you, Sheriff. I got a right."

"Me too, Ewell," shrugged Tobe. "I got a badge."

He stared at the both of us a minute.

"You got a future," he said to me. "You got a wife and two kids," he said to Tobe Edwards.

We looked back at him.

"And what have you got, Sheriff?" asked Tobe softly.

"I've got a warrant—" he said. He reached inside his vest, bringing it out. It was linted and pocket-worn with the long years he had carried it there. He held it up for us to see, his own eyes not looking at it but fastened, instead, on the rocks where Sego waited. "—from Bexar County, Texas, for the murder of Ewell Blackburn, Jr."

In the quiet that followed and just as he was turning to go, I remembered something.

"Wait up, Sheriff!" I called hoarsely. "Sego, he's got somethin' too!"

He held up, coming around.

"A shotgun," I told him. "He was goin' to use it on me, come dark tonight."

"Thank you, boy," he nodded expressionlessly. He unbuckled his gunbelt, handing it to Tobe. "Gimme the Parker," he said.

"Damn it to hell, Ewell, I won't do it! You cain't jest—"

"Gimme thet Parker, Tobe."

The little deputy squinted up at him through the whip and drive of the wind. He saw the look on that old man's face there in the twilight dark of the storm. He handed him the shotgun.

He took it, turned back to the rocks, cupped his left hand against the rolling growl of the thunder.

"Sego, you hear me up there?"

There was no answer save the screech and whistle of the wind.

"Well, listen and listen good. Fifteen years ago you killed a boy down in Bexar County. He came into the law after a stage stick-up, and you killed him for it. I was that law, Sego. Thet boy was my son.

"Fifteen years, Sego. You hear me? It's a long time to trail a man with murder in your heart and a tin star on your chest to keep you from committin' it. I still got thet star, Sego, and you still got a chance."

He pulled out the warrant, holding it up into the sting and spatter of the first raindrops.

"It's a warrant, Sego. Due and legal and swore out by me, for the murder of my boy. You come down from them rocks with your hands above your hat and you kin surrender to it. You don't come down, I'm comin' up. You know me, Sego, and you know your legal chances in Bexar County. You got ten seconds."

There was no answer from above. Only the splash and rustle of the rain sifting through the dusty sage.

Sego Lockhart knew his legal chances in Bexar County.

"All right," said Sheriff Ewell Blackburn to us. "Keep him pinned where he is. I'm goin' up."

He crouched and slid forward into the heavy brush basing the bluff rocks. We saw him once or twice, working his way up to Sego's outcrop, then nothing for five long minutes.

From where we were, we could see and cover the shoulder-high pile of rock Sego was pinned back of. There was only one way for the sheriff to get up to him close enough for shotgun work. That was another outcrop flanking Sego's, about ten yards down the slope. From it, a man could step out and have him covered at so short a range as to make his Colts useless and force him to his shotgun. But that man would *have to* step out. And he would be stepping out on Sego Lockhart.

Yet, at the end of those five minutes, we saw the old sheriff top out his climb and scuttle up behind that second outcrop.

He said something to Sego. We couldn't hear what it was, but saw him cup his hand again and knew it was something, for sure. Then he straightened and stepped clear of his rocks.

As he did, we saw Sego dive and roll clear of his cover, shotgun in hand. In the same flash, we saw he had shucked his heavy holsters to lighten him-

self for his jump and rollout. Apparently, he had
figured the old man would come out shooting,
and would miss him with both barrels in the surprise of the roll-out, giving him, Sego, all the time
in the world to get back up and cut him down.

But it didn't work that way.

The old man didn't fire and Sego had to. On the
roll and scramble. From the ground and off balance.

We saw the rockdust fly right and left *behind* the
sheriff, and knew Sego had only brackcted him
with a brace of clean misses. The next second he
was back on his feet, leaping away and clawing
instinctively for the Colts that weren't there. And
old Ewell Blackburn was stepping in and giving
him both barrels from fifteen feet away.

I will never forget how small and huddled and
helpless Sego Lockhart looked, laying up there in
those Llano River rocks. He didn't look big anymore. Nor ugly, nor mean, nor dangerous. He just
looked dead.

Of a sudden, it wasn't in me to hate him like I
thought I had. But only to feel sorry for him and
for all the poor men like him, who lived so hunted
brief and lay so long uneasy dead by the lonely
law of the bullet that was always waiting.

You couldn't look down on Sego in that last
minute—with his empty eyes staring wide and
frightened and sightless into nowhere—without
lifting your own eyes up to the storm above and
thanking God that it wasn't you had done that to
him.

We left him there, back of the outcrop, a few

loose rocks piled over him to keep off the buzzards and coyotes. Nobody said any words for him, nor offered to. Only the *mesteñeros* crossed themselves. We went back down the slope and got our horses and rode quick away from that place. The full rain squalled in behind us. At the stage road we turned left for Mason City and Rance Buchanan's Lazy RB Ranch. Looking back, I could see nothing. Ten Mile Bend and the low bluffs of the Llano were already gone. There was only the cry of the wind and the slash of the rain, back there.

I rode with May, behind the others, Poquito and Little Hawk frisking to the prairie-sweet smell of the rain. Ahead, far over on the misty yellow of the *llano's* last curve, the sun was breaking through. We watched it sink into Hueco Pass, still riding quiet, each thinking his own thoughts and looking long ahead past that May 6 sunset.

Beyond it; for me, lay tomorrow and the certain delivery of Dad's contract herd from a beaten Rance Buchanan. And beyond that delivery lay all the other things that hinged on it. The things which Dad, in his strange, far-seeing way, had only talked about when we were alone those times watching the sunset clouds out past the Pecos. The things he had always predicted would one day be mine alone. The ranch. The cattle. The broodmare band. The lonely wild beauty of the Palo Pinto prairies and all the wonderful secret places along the Brazos that only him and me had understood and shared.

Yet, seeing those rich things and knowing they were waiting for me over there beyond the breaking clouds, there remained one other thing I

wanted more than any of them. One thing for
which I would happily have traded them all, and
counted myself the richer beyond compare through
all the years of my life, though I had not a penny,
nor a cow, nor a single good horse to my name.

"May," I asked at last, "what about you and me?
After tomorrow, I mean. What are you goin' to
do?"

It was like her not to dodge around it. She put
those smoky gray eyes of hers on me and said it
soft and quick.

"What do you *want* me to do, Button?"

It was the first time I had ever heard her say my
name, yet it sounded like she'd been calling me by
it since I could remember. I felt the thrill of that,
and the thrill of her looking at me like she was
and asking it so honest and straight out.

When I started talking, it was like pulling the
gate-log on a stockpond spillway.

"I want you to go with *me!*" I blurted. "Back to
the Brazos, May. We'll take María and old Jesús
with us and we'll build a ranch up there like nothing ever before in North Texas. We'll have Billie
Joe to run our cattle, Sec and Jesús to manage our
broodmares, María to grind our corn and pat out
our tortillas and be your *dueña* just like always.

"Will you do it, May?" I pleaded. "Will you go
home to the Brazos with me and Sec, and be our
best girl to love and look after and do for and be
good to, for ever so long as you'll stay and let us?"

She shook her head and kept it down and
wouldn't look up at me, or say anything. I saw the
shine of the tears going down her dark cheek and
had to turn away and set my jaw quick. I thought I

had lost her, that she wanted to say no, and just couldn't bring herself to hurt me by saying it.

I was every bit as blind wrong as usual.

The next minute her slim hand was in mine and she was smiling up at me in her husky whisper.

"Sure, Button, if you'll have me—"

I didn't answer her back and didn't need to. I just sat up sudden tall and straight in that old $5 saddle on that little $15 pony and took me another last grateful look past the thin sliver of the sun's rim still showing yonder in Hueco Pass.

After that, there wasn't anything to do save nod me up a final silent inside thank-you to the good Lord above. Which I did and which was no more than fitting I should, considering what I owed him.

I was likely the richest one man in all the quarter-million square miles of the Lone Star state of Texas.

And for certain and forever sure, the happiest.

Henry Wilson Allen wrote under both the **Clay Fisher** and **Will Henry** bylines and was a five-time winner of the Golden Spur Award from the Western Writers of America. Under both bylines he is well known for the historical aspects of his Western fiction. He was born in Kansas City, Missouri. His early work was in short subject departments with various Hollywood studios and he was working at MGM when his first Western novel, *No Survivors* (1950), was published. While numerous Western authors before Allen provided sympathetic and intelligent portraits of Indian characters, Allen from the start set out to characterize Indians in such a way as to make their viewpoints an integral part of his stories. *Red Blizzard* (1951) was his first Western novel under the Clay Fisher byline and remains one of his best. Some of Allen's images of Indians are of the romantic variety, to be sure, but his theme often is the failure of the American frontier experience and the romance is used to treat his tragic themes with sympathy and humanity. On the whole, the Will Henry novels tend to be based more deeply in actual historical events, whereas in the Clay Fisher titles he was more intent on a story filled with action that moves rapidly. However, this dichotomy can be misleading, since *MacKenna's Gold* (1963), a Will Henry Western about gold seekers, reads much as one of the finest Clay Fisher titles, *The Tall Men* (1954). Both of these novels also served as the basis for memorable Western motion pictures. Allen was always experimental and *The Day Fort Larking Fell* (1968) is an excellent example of a comedic Western, a tradition as old as Mark Twain and as recent as some of the novels by P.A. Bechko. At his best, he was a gripping teller of stories peopled with interesting characters true to the time and to the land.

□ **YES!**

Sign me up for the Leisure Western Book Club and send my FREE BOOKS! If I choose to stay in the club, I will pay only $14.00* each month, a savings of $9.96!

NAME: _____

ADDRESS: _____

TELEPHONE: _____

EMAIL: _____

□ I want to pay by credit card.

□ **VISA**   □ **MasterCard**   □ **DISCOVER**

ACCOUNT #: _____

EXPIRATION DATE: _____

SIGNATURE: _____

Mail this page along with $2.00 shipping and handling to:
Leisure Western Book Club
PO Box 6640
Wayne, PA 19087
Or fax (must include credit card information) to:
610-995-9274
You can also sign up online at **www.dorchesterpub.com**.
*Plus $2.00 for shipping. Offer open to residents of the U.S. and Canada only.
Canadian residents please call 1-800-481-9191 for pricing information.
If under 18, a parent or guardian must sign. Terms, prices and conditions subject to change. Subscription subject to acceptance. Dorchester Publishing reserves the right to reject any order or cancel any subscription.